ELIPSIONS

Gregory Morrison

Printed in the United States of America.

ISBN: 978-1-4269-9351-0 (sc)
ISBN: 978-1-4269-9350-3 (hc)

Library of Congress Control Number: 2011915658

Trafford rev. 10/07/2011

 www.trafford.com

North America & international
toll-free: 1 888 232 4444 (USA & Canada)
phone: 250 383 6864 ♦ fax: 812 355 4082

CHAPTER

Caleb's awakening

"Caleb, do you have a clean fan brush?" my father asked me, pulling me back from my daydream. I was staring blankly at the vast meadow filled with a huge variety of wildflowers and a few old fallen tree trunks. The meadow was outlined by the edge of the woods.

"Yeah," I responded, reaching down into my collection of paintbrushes to retrieve my best fan brush and then handing it to my father.

I turned back to the blank canvas resting on my easel before bringing the field that lay behind it back into focus. A small sound came from the baby monitor on the chair between us, and I looked to it quickly, hearing movement. My father stopped painting but stayed motionless, still looking at his canvas.

We sat in that position for a moment before my father resumed painting, and I simply looked at the canvas between ours. A beautifully crafted mosaic painting sat on her easel. The chair in front of it was unoccupied, its purpose now being to hold the monitor between Dad and me. She was so gifted at everything, and painting was one of her special talents.

Father and I were good, but I would say that we honestly just hoped that her inspiration would rub off on us so that we might create something as enlightened, meaningful, and beautiful as her ... as hers.

I shifted to look behind me toward our house; I focused on my parents' bedroom window, with the curtains pulled back so the bright sunshine would show through. That was just how she liked it.

She was asleep now, so I looked back to my blank canvas and wished that she were here with us instead, as she had been hundreds of times before, as she had been just four weeks ago. That was before she began throwing up without warning, too sudden for her hide quickly and do it in private. She had hidden the headaches from us, but the involuntary regurgitation had come on so suddenly that she couldn't conceal it.

We immediately expressed our concern and found out that she had had two seizures and had started going for drives alone whenever she felt mood swings coming on. These signs wouldn't be anything really alarming if we hadn't witnessed the same symptoms play out firsthand with Grandma and my aunt Becky. They had never tried to hide their signs from anyone, unlike my mother.

Grandma's episode progressed very fast, but her mental and physical decline—the speech, hearing, and vision losses—were still in my mother's dreams. Dreams that she confessed were so real—so real.

Aunt Becky went through it all, but it was more prolonged because she had a treatment plan. However, it ultimately just ended up breaking my mother's heart in a completely different way, draining her hope for a cure.

"I'm going to … going to check on Mom," I said, getting up and heading toward the house. It was about a hundred yards to the ground-level glass sliding door, which was on the other side of the swing set, just ten yards from the house. The swing set that she and I had played on ever since I could remember. Me and my best friend, the best teacher of life, because in the back of her mind she always knew life was far too short. She spent her life living every moment and teaching us how to breathe life in with our eyes, hands, feet, and souls. I looked down at my bare feet while walking through the cool, soft grass, feeling the blades tickle me between my toes.

I stopped at the swing set, which had always served as the great thinking spot where Mom and I would have many conversations. Girls, sports, morality, God, the cost of popularity—a cost that I was never inclined to pay because I felt at the end of the day it really meant nothing. She never tried to sway me into thinking her way; we just talked—and many times she was able to teach me without saying a word, and we would just swing or rock our swings next to each other. Here, like always before, but never again.

I stood there motionless in front of the swing set, angry at it for not being able to talk to me. For not holding me and for it not keeping us as safe as it had made us feel so many times before. I felt like hitting it, like tearing it down to the ground, wanting to make it feel as dead as I felt now. I shoved my hands into my pockets and quickly brushed past it, grazing one of the swings as I passed. I looked back out of the corner of my eye as its slight rocking movement stopped, leaving it motionless, dead. I then opened the door and proceeded up to my parents' room.

I stared at her, lying there like an angel. I realized that regardless of the amount of weight she lost or whatever worse happened each day, I still saw her as she always was and would forever be in my mind. I walked to the end table where all of her medications were and reached down to pick up a pamphlet titled "Coping with Primary Brain Tumors." I had already read all the booklets. Glioblastoma multiforme. It was also called a "high-grade" tumor. Leave it to my mom to be the best of the best with whatever she did. I smirked to myself impishly, trying to fight back the tears, but one managed to well over and trickle down my cheek. I wiped it away quickly in case she happened to wake; she wanted us to be strong for her, even though I wasn't completely sure what exactly she meant.

I looked at her beautiful face, which so many of my friends had fallen in love with over the last eighteen years, a face never marred by time. I imagined her eyes open, though I saw them every time I looked in the mirror because hers were identical to mine. No, mine were actually identical to hers.

I hadn't been able to look in the mirror for a little while now, and I wondered if my look had changed over the last two weeks. I imagined looking into the mirror for the first time, exactly how long from now that would be, and standing there in my reflection would be a completely different person. Maybe I would have changed colors or something, which would completely freak me out, and I would forget about the pain (at least for a moment).

I began fingering through the different pamphlets that my mother had taken from hospitals and ordered online for Father and me to read, to prepare us for what was happening. I'd read through all of them by now, but I found myself avoiding the one titled "Dealing with Grade IV Astrocytomas and Providing Comfort of Care." She had always had a knack for dealing with issues directly. I looked down at her once-vibrant hands, which now looked old and frail, the bones and tendons so prevalent from her thinness.

I reached down to hold the hand in a gesture of comfort and was taken back by how cold it was, how still it was, so I let my face fall to it, hoping to warm it with the warmth of my breath. But it only chilled my lips. I breathed a mouthful of warm air onto her hand and began rubbing the warmth into it, but it just got cool again.

I resisted looking up for as long as I could, and my silent tears continued to cover my mother's hand, seeping onto my lips as I kissed and spoke to her hand, pleading for it to warm. The salty taste of my tears somehow set my head in motion upward to my mother's face.

I was unable to catch my breath, crying uncontrollably, and I saw that her eyes were open, looking down directly at me. Her beautiful, ocean-blue eyes, with a hint of pale green that captured so many people's attention over the years. Those beautiful puppy dog eyes that would melt the heart of anyone in front of her, but not this time—this time they were without the bright light that usually illuminated them from inside.

I was not aware of how loud or frantic I was being, but moments later my father raced into the room, screaming, "What's wrong, Caleb? What's—?"

He fell to his knees at the foot of the bed, and we sobbed uncontrollably for hours, eventually ending up on the bed at both sides of her, each of us with one arm beneath her and one arm around each other while we cried and whispered our good-byes into her ears as night fell and morning came again.

The next few days were abstract at best for me; I muddled through life completely unattached. Routine tasks were mindlessly accomplished, seeming to be completed as soon as I had begun them or never done at all, as I would realize that I was still standing to do the chore several hours after I had started it. All time was without reference for me during those days. I could be sitting in a chair for what seemed like three minutes but was actually three hours, and I conceded to the clock in the same manner that I had done with the mirror.

It truly seemed like Father and I had just finished our long good-bye embrace with her five minutes ago and walked out of the bedroom door into the wake. I knew that wasn't true because I recalled admiring my father for being able to sit with the relatives and pastors who had to pull responses out of him regarding the funeral arrangements while I stayed completely hidden away from interaction with anyone. I wondered if he knew the amount of comfort that the distant sound of his voice in the house gave me. His voice on the phone or speaking with someone in the living room was the only reference of time that I actually had over those few days, but when it was silent I would be swallowed up by the trepidation of the dark for what seemed like forever.

Now I sat here at the wake, unsure of when the people actually got here or when Uncle Sebastian began playing on the piano. His real name is Seth, but before he became a very successful pianist he had conferred with each family member for their opinion on being publically known as Sebastian. He especially made time to sit with my mother because their bond was strongest—he had composed a piece for each member of his immediate family, but none were as extraordinary as the one he'd composed for my mother and entitled with her name, "Christine."

The melody was soft with an underscore of strength and the slightest tempo increases that relied almost solely on the pianist's finger impressions to exhibit the true unity of the tones. Very few ever tried to duplicate it, but the song was and always would remain an American classic.

I recognized it before he released his finger from on the first note, and I looked up past the crowd of people to meet Seth's eyes. I didn't know how long he had been staring at me. My strength depleted when I saw his hereditary puppy dog eyes filled with tears that ran down his cheeks and an unmistakable concern as he watched me intently. He gave me a small smile and turned his head down to the keys, and I knew it would have been impossible for him to continue this song while looking into my eyes. Not today, not while the pain of our loss gaped so deeply.

I attempted to dry my eyes and scan the room for my father and noticed that several sets of people—relatives, neighbors, acquaintances, and more—were all around us, many of them glancing in my direction and giving me small encouraging smiles when our eyes would meet.

The room had gone completely silent of chatter, not a sound other than Seth's incredible piano. Everyone knew the piece, and today everyone felt every subtle tone. When the song was finished the only sounds that could be heard were the respectfully quieted sobs throughout. It had to be more than five minutes before I heard the sounds of hired serving crew resuming their preparations to serve our guests.

Unable to actually muster the strength of speech, I retreated back to my room on the other side of the house, where people weren't. I lay on my bed and studied the many pictures of my mother in my head until the sleepless nights and emotional drain caught up to me. I closed my eyes to rest, but when I reopened them I found myself in the same clothes that I had worn to the wake, laying on the ground of a dimly lit forest.

All I could see were tall trees with such a dense canopy I could barely catch glimpses of a different darkness, which I assumed was the night sky. I could see that the winds were creating a particularly rhythmic sway of the trees, but I couldn't hear any sounds. Not just that, but if the trees were swaying from the wind, then why couldn't I feel the wind blowing against me?

I patted my body with my hands, but my entire body and hands were numb to my touch. Cliché, I know, but I pinched myself, half hoping to wake from this dream, but I couldn't feel that, either, even though it left a mark on my forearm, and I wondered just how hard I had actually pinched myself.

I focused on trying to hear when it became apparent that the sounds of the wind and the trees were faintly there. I kicked the leaves and branches at my feet, and the sound produced was even more subdued than the wind and trees. "Hello?" I shouted, but I simply got the same muted result with my voice.

I couldn't recall ever having a dream like this. I began to move slowly away from the small clearing that I'd arrived in, and I hoped I could find my way out or that I'd wake soon. After walking less than three feet into the woods, my motion stopped, and I looked down to see that I had walked into a broken branch, which had torn through my pants and into my leg until it tugged me to a stop.

I quickly hobbled backward but found myself stumbling after tripping over a smaller branch behind me. I fell back into the small clearing; I immediately examined the injury to my leg which seems to have entered the front, right side of my shin and proceeded to tare back towards my outer calf for about an inch on my right leg. After seeing the damage I had done, I felt relieved not to have the sense of feel. I grabbed the area to apply pressure; the blood streamed over my hands and had begun soaking into my socks and onto my shoes.

This dream was starting to piss me off! I jumped to my feet and ran to the offending branch, grabbed it tightly, and tugged it out with my blood-covered hands then commenced to beat it against the ground and surrounding trees for a few minutes before I calmed down. I thought of how quickly I had resorted to handling issues with anger and spite, which was the opposite of how I had learned from my parents to handle issues— from my mother. I looked down at the tattered, blood-covered branch and felt a rush of guilt hit me. I fell to the ground exhausted and wishing I could see my mother again, talk to her again. I wondered if maybe I could see her here in this dream—after all, it was a dream.

I looked deep inside myself and decided that very moment that just because she was gone now didn't mean that I had to become someone different, but instead I'd become someone better in honor of her ... be even more than the person she had hoped I'd grow-up to be! I rose to my feet, flipped the stick back behind me, and walked forward into the thick brush once again, but this time carefully surveying each move before I made it.

Regardless of how careful I was, new rips from branches and thorns appeared in my white dress shirt, circled by small amounts of blood coming from the scratches to my skin. After a while I thought that a few hours had passed, and I wasn't sure if I had actually gotten anywhere or if I had been just walking in a huge circle, because everything looked the same. I amused myself with the thought that if I passed by a place I had already been then I would see the trail of broken stems and blood-covered leaves.

Just then I heard the muffled sound of someone calling my name. I stood very still and listened. Yes, I heard the faint sound of my name being called, and it was rapidly growing louder. Now the voice was screaming but I couldn't tell what direction it was coming from.

The voice shrieking my name escalated until it had become so loud that it was hurting my eardrums. I squatted, covered my ears, and closed my eyes tightly until the ear-piercing voice started to fade. I struggled to open my eyes again, and when I finally got them opened I was looking into my Uncle Seth's face.

I pulled my head back against the pillow I lay on instinctively because of the shock from Uncle Seth's face being so close to mine.

"I'm sorry, I didn't mean to scare you," Seth whispered.

I knowingly pulled the blankets up to my neck like I were hiding my injuries from him, but I instantly felt foolish for thinking for a moment that I was physically harmed, it was just a dream for God sake.

"Were you just screaming my name?" I asked while noticing that I could feel the blanket in my hands which gave me comfort that I had my senses back outside of that insane dream, Seth gave me a curious look

"No, I've been whispering in your ear because I didn't want anyone to know I was in here," he said while putting his fingers to his lips as a shushing gesture. I had begun to feel little tingling feelings on my arms and body. I tried to hide any alarming expression on my face as he continued to speak.

"Your dad doesn't want anyone to bother you, but I had to see you to know you're okay." He paused for a moment and then continued. "I wanted to make sure you're managing—" he said as the little tingles I was feeling had crossed over into full fledge pains streaming down awakening my sense of feel until

"What the... Ahhh, shit!" I said low through my clinched jaws as I sprung up in the bed clasping my right shin. Seth instantly jumped back from the bed speechless as he stared at my shirt. I looked down to see all of the rips and blood stains that I had gotten from the fore... The forest in my dream, but that's impossible. I must have been sleep walking or something in the woods behind our house, but how...

"What did you do?" my uncle demanded in a low, concerned yet accusing tone.

Now I was the speechless one as he helped me out of the bed and into the bathroom. He sat me on the toilet seat and looked down at my right leg through the gaping hole in my blood soaked pants. He lifted the pant leg up to reveal the gash there, but it wasn't as severe as I had believed it to be during the dream. Dumbstruck, I wondered how a dream could possibly cause these injuries in real life and as before I came to the conclusion that it couldn't, I must have been in the woods.

"Did I leave this room?" I asked anxiously.

"No Caleb, you've been in here for the past couple of hours, it's after six, people are starting to leave, but forget about that Caleb" Seth squared up to me speaking firmly

"Tell me why you're doing this, Caleb; you know this would break your mother's heart!"

For a brief moment I was confused about what he meant. "Wha ...? You think I did this to myself?" I snapped, hoping that he couldn't tell that I was completely traumatized at the realization of what he was asking.

He narrowed his eyes while looking directly into mine. "You have a more reasonable explanation?" he asked me with a hint of parental agitation.

"I ..." I could never recall being this stuck about anything. Seth had never known me to lie or be anything but ethical, had addressed me as an adult and respected my opinions ever since I was ten years old. How could I tell him that this happened to me in a dream?

Mom would have believed me, and it would have been so easy to talk this through with her. She was the only person that I'd ever told about the ghostly people in blue who had haunted me since I was born. She said that she could feel the energies change when they were around. But I didn't have her with me anymore, now I had Dad and apparently Seth trying to portray himself as my mother and doing a rather poor job at it.

"Here's the deal, Uncle Seth," I said.

"Wait," he broke in quickly. "You haven't called me that since, well, I can't remember the last time you did." He took my hands in his. "We are far closer than that 'uncle' shit, nephew! We're right here together, you and I, and I'll be damned if you're going to start slipping away from me now! Sorry if I seemed harsh just then … it's been a hard day for everyone," he said while casting his look to the side, and he began blinking rapidly to avoid weeping as he thought about the loss of his sister, the loss of my mother.

He tried to shrug it off, but his struggle was unmistakable to me. We had all shed so many tears this week, and now right in front of me, Seth, one of the three people closest to my mother, represented the very first attempt of someone being strong enough to actually move past the pain and continue living. I wasn't even certain if he'd canceled his concert in New York tomorrow.

"I'm not your mother; believe me, I know those shoes can never be filled," he continued. "But 'Seth' is right here, Caleb; I can be a confidante as she was to both of us. I swear to you that I will try to listen with her extraordinary sense of impartiality and compassion, her infinite wisdom and pure grace of being." He said it so eloquently, it was almost as if my mother were speaking.

It was that very moment that I realized just how much he had lost too. We wanted to embrace one another and release every pain-filled tear, but I was certain that this is what she'd meant when she said we needed to be strong for her, strong enough to continue moving forward.

I focused only on his eyes and began speaking as if it were to my mother. "I was in a dark forest and my only sense that was working correctly were my eyes; my sense of touch was not there. Hearing, taste, smell—everything was gone, but it was still as real as you and I here now, but very surreal because of my senses not being there." I looked down and touched the bandage that he had just applied to my leg wound. "I knew when this happened, but I felt no pain until now."

Seth had a sudden look of relief on his face. "So this happened in the woods here?"

I almost felt guilty for having to burst his bubble of thinking it could've been that easy. Like I actually could've left this room undetected with so many guests around and he said it himself that I hadn't left the room.

"No, not *these* woods. I have no idea what forest I was in; there was nothing that I recognized," I said solemnly while shaking my head.

We looked at one another blankly until the silence began to feel uncomfortable, so I continued to talk. "I wanted to be strong for Mom, so I continued walking through the thick brush, and that's where all of these scratches came from." I lowered my head in defeat. "But I don't know if I got anywhere, or even if there was somewhere to get to." I let my head fall into my hands, frustrated and exhausted from everything.

He rubbed my shoulders encouragingly and motioned for me to go back into my room. "I'll give you some privacy as you put on some different clothes, minus the blood, and I'll use your bathroom. Then you're going to go out and thank everyone individually for coming and extending their condolences." He closed the bathroom door behind me, and I hurried to put on a different dress shirt and pants, but this time I didn't bother with a tie.

I surprised myself as I handled the roomful of people almost as well as my mother would have, touching and talking to everyone, and with my new resolve to handle my mothers' passing on courageously I quickly found that I was the one soothing others' grief, which somehow strengthened me more after each person that I would console.

As my father said his good-byes to the final few guests, Seth escorted me into the kitchen to speak privately. "You know we will be talking to your father about this as soon as the last person's gone." I knew that wasn't a question, and I felt no dread at the idea of it; as a matter of fact, I was feeling no dread for anything, as if I had been enlightened by everything. I thanked God for Seth teaching me how to be strong even though he didn't know he had.

"Seth, has my father looked you in the eye? I mean have you had any eye contact with him at all?"

Seth sighed deeply. "No he hasn't, Caleb," Seth said while grasping my shoulders, then he spoke very deliberately. "Remember always, Caleb, that we have lost someone who was very instrumental in us being who we are; we were blessed beyond belief to have had her in our lives. But your father has not just lost that, he's also lost his wife, his soul mate." For the first time I began to think of my father's loss, too, but in a different light. Seth continued, "Many people never recover from that, not when that person was their entire life. I would bet that your father has never had a moment without her on his mind since the day that they met. I can attest to the fact that your mother never had a moment without your father on her mind."

As he spoke I felt an unexpected tear race down my cheek, but this one was not for me or my mother; this one felt dressed in the honor for my father's strength to still be standing after such devastation. I felt that this tear would absorb back into my body and accompany me always until the day I died. My single absorbed tear would clarify the true love between my parents—all of their hopes and dreams—no matter what the cost.

"It will take time for him," Seth said.

"I don't care if it takes forever; I don't care if he never looks into my eyes again. I just want him to feel better," I said firmly, and Seth shook his fingers through the top of my hair, totally messing it up, I thought.

"You're a good kid, Caleb," he said. I ran my fingers through my hair to restore some order to it, but it really didn't matter since I still hadn't mustered the courage to look in a mirror—though I thought Seth was helping in that category, too. I raised my chin and looked down my nose at him silently. He bowed graciously. "I meant, a good young man," he corrected himself swiftly, and I gave him a nod of approval.

The door slowly pushed open and my father walked in, steady, but he didn't seem to notice us on the other side of the center island. His head was down as he walked directly to the refrigerator. He paused after touching the door handle and then turned slowly in our direction to see us watching him quietly. I could virtually feel the atmosphere shift into a delicately somber mood that surrounded my entire body and lingered like a cold mist.

He stood there motionless, looking in our direction, and I noticed for the first time that he must have lost fifteen pounds over the course of the past week because his tailored suit hung from his tall, slender frame. He had worn that same suit when he took Mother to their anniversary dinner last month and it fit him like a glove, accentuating his broad shoulders, muscular chest, and slim, toned waist. Now it hung off of him like a judge's robe with a thin man inside. His cheeks looked sunken in, transforming his strong, chiseled jawline and high cheekbones into the look of an older, underfed person you might see in a nursing home.

Almost instantly admiration outlined by such deep sorrow for him coursed through my veins, both hot and cold, which once again produced that single tear of true love descending, and again I did not wipe it away but left it to absorb back into me to be savored forever.

"Are you okay, Dad?" I asked gently, and his startled reaction told me that maybe he wasn't completely aware that we were actually here.

"Yeah," he responded—worryingly, because I was pretty sure I could count on one hand the amount of times he'd ever given a one-word response to any question. Could I get used to him not constantly speaking to me as the warm father always looking for a lesson to be taught behind every subject we addressed?

No matter, because I would accept him and encourage him for as long as it took to make him feel better, because right now he appeared to be waiting for the utter darkness that no doubt surrounded him to finish the job as soon as possible.

"Everything was beautiful, Patrick," Seth said lightly, and Father managed to turn up the corners of his mouth slightly for a brief moment in response. "And your catering service was fantastic all of the way through, especially cleanup," Seth continued in a little lighter tone. He then retrieved my father from the front of the refrigerator and brought him over to one of our richly crafted stools at the center island. "Here, Patrick, have a seat for a moment; there's something that we'd like to discuss with you."

After a moment's delay, Father looked in Seth's direction inquisitively then began slowly looking back and forth between me and Seth, but not making eye contact, instead seeming to be looking at our chins or mouths and no higher.

Seth leaned closer to Dad and was about to begin talking when I cut him off with a sudden gesture and began to speak instead. "Dad, we were wondering if you would be willing to take a sleeping pill tonight, because you look so tired and you need sleep," I said because it was so late and he looked in no shape to be dealing with my issues right now. He painfully forced himself to raise his eyes to meet mine. His face remained blank, motionless, and tears immediately started to fall from his eyes. His mouth started moving slowly, inaudibly, and at that moment I couldn't imagine seeing anything more painfully sad.

I fought with all of my might not to break down into tears of my own. In my peripheral vision I could see that Seth had lost that battle, and he rose from his stool and embraced my dad, both of them weeping.

I rose from my stool and touched my dad's shoulder as I passed by on my way up to get a sleeping pill. As I passed I noticed that his eyes were still fixed on where my eyes were when I was sitting on the stool. When I returned with the pill, they were in the same position. Seth and I were able to get him to take the pill without any resistance, and I wondered how much of this time period my dad would remember.

After putting Dad to bed, Seth went to the kitchen and got me a glass of water and then joined me in my room with an inexpressible amount of different emotions coursing through us. It must have been an hour before Seth broke the silence. "You were right not to tell your father about this," he said, and then he gave me a nod as he continued, "We can handle this." I was pretty exhausted now and not sure if my responding look was slightly encouraging or completely despondent.

"You have a concert tomorrow, another one three days later, and two more next week. You can't do this," I said.

"I canceled tomorrow's concert, which will cost me enormously with all of the ticket prices, advertising, preparation … basically anyone with a hand in it will have their hand out, and those that feel slighted in the least will file with the courts, so I can start adding up attorney fees," Seth said, and I could hear the concern in his voice. "You're doing all of that for a stupid dream?" I asked.

Seth looked into my eyes and spoke. "Not for the dream, Caleb. I do it for you and your father."

The amount of money he was talking about was far too much to sacrifice; I bet he could arrange a flight tonight or in the morning so that he could still make the concert. "Call the airport and get to New York, Seth; I can handle whatever this is," I said demandingly.

"You have finals this week, Caleb, and as your mom told me," he paused for quick a moment before continuing, "she says that your finals will make the difference of whether you go to Harvard or Stanford. And you know her wish was that you go to Harvard." Then he shifted to a much lighter tone. "It's just the one concert that I'll miss and I already informed them of that, so it's already set in motion." He tried to sound casual about it, but I could hear the shakiness in his voice.

"It all just seems pretty expensive is all I'm saying," I responded.

"I saw it, Caleb—at least I think I did. I didn't really think of it until we both left your room earlier today, but I witnessed a couple scratches on your cheek actually appear, and it didn't register in my head until later," Seth said very seriously. "I believe there is something to it and I want to get to the bottom of it before I leave."

I felt my cheeks for scratches and quickly found the ones he was talking about. It was clear to me now why his voice had become shaky. "Now get some sleep; I'll be right here." I looked at my glass of water that I had been drinking and then back to Seth suspiciously. He was nodding with a big grin on his face. I knew he had put something to make me sleep in my drink, but before I could accuse him of it, I was out.

I opened my eyes to see towering trees above that eclipsed night sky. I sat up quickly and I could feel the stems and pine needles through my pajamas that I had worn to bed, but I instantly kicked myself for not wearing shoes. I got to my feet, brushed off any that remained on my butt, realized that I could feel my touch, the warm breeze blowing through the trees, and the thorny foliage beneath my feet. I listened to the air swaying the trees; I could smell the leaves and other vegetation, mosses and lumbers, but something was missing still—what was it? I looked around and froze when I saw the bloody stick that I had beaten the trees with just earlier that afternoon.

It couldn't be that same stick, right? I walked to it and picked it up; the blood was still wet, so I walked to the point of the forest where I had been walking before and found stems and leaves broken and bloody. I continued to follow the trail that I had already made, finding the brush to be much less resistant this time. I thought of how nice it was when I couldn't feel these sticks and pine needles on the bottoms of my feet. I began to feel a sense of urgency, so I picked up my pace to a slow jog while pushing the branches and stems aside so they wouldn't hit my body as I ran past. I was keeping a good pace—that is, until I suddenly crashed to the ground and immediately felt a surge of pain shooting up from my right shin. Again with the right leg - really? I thought as I rolled around on the ground for a moment in a fetal position, squeezing against my shin with both hands until the pain began to ebb. Feeling no blood or laceration on my shin, I straightened my leg out and looked down to assess the damage.

I saw bruised skin and a contusion that had already swollen to the size of a golf ball, but the leg was not broken from what I could tell. I stood on it to confirm this and then gingerly walked back in the direction I had come from to see what had caused me such pain.

As time passed I saw that the forest had gotten a little lighter from the morning sun above, definitely light enough that I should have seen this three-foot-thick fallen tree that was clearly lying right across the path in the direction I was headed! I should have if I weren't so damn confused and frustrated. I looked around and started screaming as if some person would step out from behind some hidden curtain to claim his victory and reveal the secrets to this elaborate hoax.

"I give up! I surrender! You win! Please just stop all of this; it's a dream that's not a dream, I get it! You're a genius; now please allow me to wake up! Please let this all be done … no more of these dreams! Just let me know what you want from me so that I can do it and these dreams will stop so I can get on with my life, please?"

I looked down at the fallen tree I had tripped over, and it dawned on me what was missing. There were no bugs anywhere, and I heard no sounds of birds or rodents scurrying around on the all-too-quiet forest floor—there was nothing but the sound of the wind blowing through the trees. I started to become a bit nervous about the eerily howling wind against the trees in the absence of any other sound. I sat on the fallen tree to rest from my long run and my aching shin, and after sulking for a few moments I sensed I wasn't alone.

I looked up to see my mother standing directly to my right. She was so beautiful that I almost lost my breath. She looked younger, and so radiant, but even more shocking still was that she had the same bluish hue around her as the people that had always haunted me. She was casting no shadows; it was as if she were standing under a big blue light and her image was being projected here. Her image had a lot of static, and I couldn't hear a thing she tried to say, but she was here.

She had one of those dangling cords coming from behind her elbow and leading into a unit around her forearm, like all of the blue-hued people I had seen in the past, and she also had their iridescent outline around her eyeballs, which in her just added to the magnificent of her eyes.

"Mom!" I shouted, and I ran up to hug her, but I just phased through her. I turned around to see her and she was already facing me. She gracefully pointed with her delicate hands to her right, and I looked to see what was there, but I saw nothing but more trees.

I knew she would never steer me wrong so I began walking that way, even though it wasn't the direction I had been heading. We continued in that direction for a little while, and I knew I should be focused on where she was leading me, but I only could think about how much I wanted her to be able to speak so we could talk, and a new kind of sadness fell over me.

We traveled a couple hundred more yards before she stopped and gave me a very concerned look, with tears falling from her eyes. The wind ceased to blow, and everything was absolutely still—not a single leaf moved, and I felt as if I were in the middle of a still photo. The lump in my throat grew to the size of a small frog and my heart rate quickened. I looked to Mother nervously, and we stood there staring at one another for a long while when out of the blue I felt wind blowing again—but this time from every direction. The wind was colder now, and I shivered while looking into my mother's crying eyes.

An unexpected sound of leaves being moved caused me to jump back from the direction of the sound. I had no idea what was coming for me, and I was petrified of what it could be.

After a long moment I realized that there was nothing there except a line of leaves gently shuddering, as if they were beckoning me to come their way. I can't imagine my expression could have been any more sheepish than at that very moment. Mom had not moved an inch, and the look on her face told me that she couldn't take me any farther.

I decided that I would have to face whatever it was eventually, and no better time than the present. I looked to my mother as she stood so still, so beautiful as I passed by her. "I will be strong for you," I mouthed slowly to her as I continued forward to follow my new invisible leader. I shifted my gaze between the obvious signals that I was now following and back at my mother until I could no longer see her.

I continued to follow the mindless variation of signs for a few hundred yards or so and then started to feel anxious. I saw a shimmer of brilliant light coming through some leaves ahead, and I slowed my pace, hoping that it could be my way out of this forest.

Once again it was like something was urging me in that direction, but the light had disappeared as quickly as it had come. I didn't know if it was real, anyway; hell I was beginning to wonder if anything in my life was real, here or awake. Maybe this was my real life and the other was just some dream. I fell to my knees, my head drooping down to the ground. "Please, Jesus," I prayed out loud, exhausted. Instantly I saw light on my hands and on the ground in front of me. I looked up to see growing scattered prisms of light that were introduced to me by a strong gust of warm wind.

I imagined the wind was talking directly to me as to say, *Your journey through the forest is now complete, and a greater unknown awaits you beyond this point.*

I had never been in many situations where bravery was called for, but as I prepared to step through the forest's darkened veil of vegetation, I was petrified.

I stepped through the incredibly dense edge of the forest and was instantly blinded by a light so bright that my hands rose up instinctively to shield my eyes even as I tripped over something and fell to the ground. The ground felt like sand on the back of my hands as I huddled there on the ground, squeezing my eyes shut. I opened them just enough to see that the ground was actually sand with blades of shallowly rooted grass which looked as if they had grown in the sand over many years. I looked up a little more and noticed that the light was dancing all around me, like sunlight reflected off of water.

I continued to look farther up until I saw the sun reflecting off of a lake with a brilliance I'd never seen before. It was painful to look into yet impossible to look away from. That's when I noticed her. She stood grandly in the center of the lake on a sandbar or something like that. Her dark hair flowed with the rhythm of the water, and the sun's reflections from the water seemed to be majestically drawn to her, creating a natural spotlight as if she were center stage. Her face was captivating and her skin looked so soft, but she held an edgy expression that led me to believe she had experienced many things in life and that she was more mature than her apparent age, about nineteen, I guessed.

I started walking toward her and looked down to see how with every step I took my feet would push aside the blades of grass to reveal the sand beneath. I got a nervous feeling, looked up again at the center of the lake, and saw that she was still there. I decided then to keep my eyes on her as I walked.

I entered the water. It felt warm, with a sandy floor, and it reminded me of our family trips to Hawaii, except this water was murky, not ocean blue. It was not until the water reached knee level that I looked down to see my dripping-wet, bloody feet resting at the foot of my bed.

I turned to see Seth standing at the side of my bed. I looked back down at my feet, and my attention was drawn toward the golf-ball-sized contusion on my right shin. I thought that I have to start hurting the left leg to balance things out. I turned to Seth curiously "Have you been standing there all night?" I asked.

He chuckled nervously. "No, you started to wrestle around in your sleep about five minutes ago, so here I stand, and there hasn't been an all-night because it's only 3am right now" he replied.

"Ok, then you're not creepy- good" I razzed him.

"That one came just before you woke up," Seth said while gesturing to the knot on my right shin just beneath my pajamas. "Doesn't it hurt?"

"Not anymore; I've already felt the pain from it," I said with a salty tone in my voice.

"So you can feel in the dream now too?" Seth asked.

"Yeah. Taste, hear, and smell too," I responded with a little less salt in my tone. Then I bounced to my feet with excitement. "I saw Mom; she was so young and even more beautiful than ever. I think she's happy where she is now," I rattled off, but Seth looked confused.

"You mean in your dreams?"

"No, not in my dreams... She's ..." I thought about where she was, and I really had no clue, but I was more inclined to believe that the people in blue were angels like my mom had speculated, rather than just the ghostly, menacing people that I used to believe them to be.

"When I was younger," I continued as Seth looked on like an excited, eager-to-learn schoolboy, "I used to see people sort of often. People who had a blue cast on them from a blue light that wasn't there." I sat back down on the bed, and he sat down beside me. I hoped that it would be easier to explain if I wasn't looking at him.

"Mom thought they were angels, and she said that she could feel when they were near, but I think she was just saying that to comfort me. But they each have a cord coming from above the back side of their elbows and into something on their forearm. Like some kind of biomechanical modification." I looked at Seth, and his curious expression had shifted into a look of confusion. "I don't know what they are, but I know they can't be bad because Mom is one of them now," I said defensively. "And Mom had the iridescent glow around her eyeballs, so that told me that she could see me, because only the ones with that would look directly at me."

Seth looked to the floor, and I could see the disappointment shrouding him because it wasn't the answer of halos and wings that he had hoped to hear—or maybe it was just that he was starting to believe I was crazy. "I only see them like once a year—well, until recently, that is," I quickly pointed out to him, hoping it would make me appear less crazy than when I was younger.

"Okay, tell me everything that took place in your dream, and don't leave out a single detail," Seth demanded.

After describing everything to him I found myself standing in front of the oversized window in my room that overlooked the backyard and woods where we all used to paint, I couldn't see anything through the dark but I knew the chairs and easels were still there. I felt the sorrow creeping in, and to make matters worse the light from my room illuminated the swing set, which I stared at, lost in thoughts of our talks over all the years.

I abruptly swung around to Seth, still sitting on the bed, racking his brain to figure out what everything meant.

"I'm going back in right now!" I said to him defiantly. He looked at me firmly, and I wondered what his argument would be and if he knew how futile it would be to fight me about this. It was if he ran through the entire debate in his head, and shortly after that the reluctant look on his face softened into a look of defeat. I nodded in confirmation and went directly into my parents' bathroom to retrieve more sleeping pills.

Dad was still sleeping, and my guess was that he wouldn't be getting out of that bed today or maybe even tomorrow. I returned to my room after taking a couple of pills, and Seth was standing by the window looking out into the dark. "What about your finals today?" he asked.

"Not a problem, the number is in Mom's phone book in the drawer to the right of the refrigerator. Just call and tell them I couldn't make it today and they will reschedule the ones I missed for another day. Besides, I've already taken the pills, because I knew you'd come up with a reason that I shouldn't go back to sleep," I said while watching Seth's subtle disapproving body language. Deep inside he too knew this was the most logical way of figuring this thing out, but I knew his concern because it was mine too – We had no idea what was next and these are clearly not just dreams.

I hit the pillow, and before I knew it I opened my eyes and sat up to see that I was on the beach again. I was disappointed that I wasn't at the beginning again so I might see Mother, so I could take much more time to attempt to communicate with her—to be with her. I looked at the funny tracks I had made in the grassy sand previously.

I looked to the water, where miraculously the beautiful young woman still stood, as beautiful as before. I proceeded cautiously, afraid to wake again when the water hit my knees. I was pretty happy seeing that the water was now above my waist and I had not been ejected from my dream. However, being more than fifty yards out with another seventy to go until I reached her was concerning, because the water continued to get deeper. The bottom felt as if had changed from sandy to muddy; I continued to plod through, but when the lake got to my chest's level I decided to swim the rest of the way.

As I started to try to swim, the mucky floor of the lake seemed to clutch my ankles and feet. I submerged so I could get a good grip on my legs for assistance breaking free of the mud that was now holding them tightly. I tugged on each leg individually, but no matter how hard I pulled the mud wouldn't release, and I had to come back up for air. I went back down and kneeled to get a close look at what was wrong, and I hoped to dig my feet out, but when I got close enough to see, I noticed small green vines twisting around my legs. I gawked in shock at what I saw, expelling all of the air from my lungs, which forced me to lift my head out once again for more air. I immediately noticed that the water had now risen to just below my chin.

I looked to the girl, and she was the same distance away as I remembered her being just a second ago, so the water wasn't rising. I took a breath of air and went back down to see that I was now up to my calves in this unforgiving muck that was trying to keep me under with it, to be buried in these cold, dark waters. Without a doubt in my mind, if I drowned here, I wouldn't be waking back up from this dream! I rose to the surface again, but this time I had to raise my chin to keep my mouth out of the water.

"Hey! Could you ... I ... the mud won't let ... help! Can you ... help?" I called to the woman in gasps, because every time I opened my mouth water would splash in, causing me to choke. I wondered what the hell she was standing on.

I could feel the vines and mud pulling me deeper, holding me tighter. I tried to take in one last gasp of air through my nose before being pulled under, but it was too late, and water rushed through my nasal passages straight down my trachea and began filling my lungs.

An even higher level of panic set in immediately as my body's reaction was to cough the water from my lungs and inhale air, which only resulted in the complete infiltration of water. My struggle waned. The sound of my racing heart slowing to a stop was emotionally deafening—the feeling of dying, although a foreign feeling to me, but it was an unmistakable one. The murky water started to fade to black.

I looked up to see a light glowing from above me in the shape of a hand reaching down, and it touched the tip of a finger on my free-floating hand. *Mom!* was my first thought. My mother would aid me now and I would be with her again, in the blue place.

My body began to rise up and out of the water as if I were weightless. Once completely out of the water, my body fell limp, and I could feel the water splashing against me from the surface, but I couldn't feel it supporting me. I felt weightless, floating on top of the water, but separate, as if on an invisible space lay just on top of the water. I began coughing up what felt like gallons of water, which poured back into the lake below me, straight through the invisible space on top of the water on which I hovered.

I looked up to see the girl from the center of the lake, and I wasn't quite sure what my emotions were at that moment, but nevertheless there we both were, standing on water—well, not both. I climbed to my knees, hunched over wheezing for air, life slowly sifting back into my body as I coughed out the darkened death.

I looked at her beautifully delicate feet and saw the most incredibly detailed tattoo on top of her left foot. The tattoo was the top side of a flying dove with wings flowing off at both sides of her foot, the dove's head designed on top of her big toe and the one next to it.

I tried to speak but could only hunch over and cough some more before hearing her say, "Find me."

Clear images of signs appeared in my head: "Welcome to North Dakota," followed by, "Welcome to Devils Lake," and then a building that looked like it could be a high school, maybe, and finally an image of a building that could be a church, but with a neon sign above the entrance door that he read "The Dojo."

I shook my head clear and looked up at her emotionless face, staring down at me. She bore a fascinating resemblance to what a teenage Angelina Jolie might look like. I managed to clear my throat enough to speak, "Who—?"

Swoosh, instantly I was sinking below the water again, but this time the vines were much faster and more of them were reaching up and grabbing my arms, legs, and neck, pulling tightly and strangling. Two vines shot quickly up into my nostrils, and three of thicker ones went into my mouth and down my throat. They started branching off and burrowing themselves between each individual tooth and into my gums, as if they were trying to coil around the tooth roots. I was thinking, unsure if they were beginning to rip the teeth from my mouth or just occupying space, when the little oxygen I had left had been depleted. Everything went black once again.

"Breathe, Caleb, breathe!"

I heard Seth's muzzled voice, but it sound so small and distant. I felt light taps and a tiny thump followed by feathery pushes that rapidly felt more like pressure against my chest, then a big thud and the faint sound of my heartbeat starting up. My body instantly lurched, and I heaved up an enormous amount of murky water that had made its way around whatever was still lodged in my throat.

I rolled to my stomach with Seth's help and lay there face down on my bed, coughing out the remainder of the water in disbelief that I had just been dead twice in less than five minutes. Seth fell back into the chair beside my bed, exhausted from his efforts to revive me.

After regaining what little breath that I could, it became painfully apparent that the three thick vines that had slithered into my mouth and partially down my throat needed to be removed before I could breathe properly. I grabbed the small amount of vine protruding from my mouth and cringed immediately upon discovering that they felt much more like warm, slimy flesh than any plant I'd ever felt. The thought alone of this grotesque intubation definitely assisted my extraction process, as I began puking and pulling simultaneously.

I let go of the mass as soon as it cleared my lips to fall into my throw up, where it flipped and slithered around for a moment before lying completely still. I looked at Seth's mortified face as he stared at it, then he looked at me without changing his expression until he suddenly lurched forward, puking himself.

I reached for the two in my nose and yanked them out with a piercing scream, because they felt as if they were barbed. The warmth of my blood trickling from my nostrils felt good against my icy cold skin.

A feeling of dread fell over me when I concluded that the reality was, I would never live through another dream like that, and it hit me how incredibly small an issue getting into Harvard or anything else outside of my next sleep had just become. I could feel a tear beginning to well up in my eye as I turned to look at Seth's disbelieving face.

"What the fuck? I just gave you CPR and you're pulling living organisms out of you!" he said incredulously, and I was lost for words.

I felt some of the vines still moving in my gums. I half-ran to the bathroom, my movement quite labored—understandable considering my whole body was frozen and exhausted, but I needed to tweeze them out of my gums and brush my teeth. I could imagine that I must look like some scummy, maimed maniac staggering around!

"I have no idea what the fuck this is! Do you? How can I fall asleep and wake up dead?" I shouted back to him while throwing the toothbrush into the sink, shaking too much and too frustrated to actually get the toothpaste onto the brush.

Seth hurried over and hugged me. "I'm sorry, Caleb, calm down. I'm sorry I attacked you; I just didn't expect something like that," he said, but then he took a quick step back and put his hands on my shoulders. "Did you find out what this is all about?" he asked.

I just shook my head sadly, and he attempted to comfort me with another embrace. "I don't know what this is, I don't know." My voice sounded small. I didn't know if it was because one ear was covered by his cheek and the other by his shoulder as I buried my head into him, wanting to disappear forever, or maybe it was because of some strange organism roaming through my eardrum. All I knew was that at that very moment I felt safer than I had felt in over a month, and I feared that I would never feel this safe ever again. Ever!

We released our embrace, and I looked into my room focusing on the morning light that had just begun to creep into it and I wondered if I would ever see another. I looked at the championship metals, trophies, and certificates on my academics awards shelf, and across from that more stood on my athletic accomplishments shelf. I began grimacing, but not from the thought of losing everything that I had worked so hard for. Rather, from the lingering pains of the dreams and I could feel the nervousness in my stomach grow as I surmised just how little control I had over my own life at the very moment.

"I can't kid myself any longer. Regardless how fucked up and impossible this seems, it's very real!" I pointed toward the bed. "Right?" I asked as if I could get some sort of reprieve and Seth would tell me this was all a hallucination. He slowly reached to the side of my mouth and pulled on a strand of the formerly green flesh-like substance that was now brown and lifeless. He looked it over thoroughly.

"It's very real, Caleb, but that still doesn't tell us what it is."

"Maybe not what it is, but it did tell me *where* it is. I was shown a place in North Dakota called Devils Lake." Somehow the words seemed surreal as I spoke them. "There's a girl there—at least I think there's a girl there who told me to find her, but she didn't say why or how."

I focused on the floor, slowly shaking my head. "All I know is that I'm not going to sleep again until I find her, because I won't live through another dream like that. I'll be dead if I sleep again! She has to fix this, and I can't just stand here watching time tick by!" I declared. I held his shoulders and looked straight into his eyes. "I can handle this Seth," I said with a semblance of confidence.

At that very moment I felt a shift in our relationship, and I could see that acknowledgment on his face. Not a look of defeat, but there beneath the fear and uncertainty of this situation I could feel the growth of pride for a man walking out into the world who had accepted his circumstances and now went forward to change his fate.

He gave me his platinum credit card and insisted that I use it whenever I needed anything and that he would keep it funded; he also insisted that I drive his rental car, a Toyota Camry that I could use for as long as I needed it and I could leave behind if I needed to fly home instead if driving.

He lectured me on calling him and keeping him updated as we raced throughout the house, packing, unsure if we were packing me for a couple of days or a week, or—actually, I was just trying to calculate how long a person could survive without sleep, because that was as far out as I would allow myself to think. I planned my route from here in St. Louis, Missouri, to Devils Lake, North Dakota, while all along hoping that the name was more coincidental than indicative. I would make only two stops: one in Waterloo, Iowa, and the other in Minneapolis, Minnesota, which meant I should arrive in Devils Lake that night around 9pm.

CHAPTER

Elise's Escape

Life, *Time*, *National Geographic*, and *Sports Illustrated*—did they really think these were the only magazines that people preferred in waiting rooms? I would think in a shrink's office they would have a bit more insight into their customers and add more specific ones, like *Parenting*, *People*, and nudie magazines. I bet they had those types of magazines in California waiting rooms. I couldn't wait to get there, I'd come this far playing their psychoanalytical, pill-popping game, and I was only a month away now. Graduation in less than a month, and then I could escape from this hellhole, escape from Mother. I still couldn't believe it! I'd stood up to her; I'd called her out on her backstabbing, money-grubbing existence.

She'd slapped me! I had confided—no—I'd turned to her, and she'd slapped me. I believed that I was finally right—beyond his words that coaxed me to say nothing, beyond his threats to destroy everything—I finally fought through it and laid my soul out to her, and she'd slapped me. But she did divorce him, she did listen to the lawyers when they said in this divorce you could have the biggest house on the highest hill and on that hill you could live your life with anybody and everybody you wished, but your daughter could never tell anyone what happened! So we'd lived on the top of that hill, the most of everything and always entertaining was she without me. On top of the hill, hidden away in plain sight, was my life.

I still couldn't believe it ... just three weeks ago we'd screamed at each other so loudly that I imagined the neighbors might hear, and I didn't care. I stood my ground and I screamed and I said I would tell and I would not stop screaming the truth until everyone knew, and then I would leave and not stop until my skin felt the warmth of the California sun. Now we hadn't talked to each other for three weeks, and I thought I missed her—was that sick or what?

I reached for a magazine and felt a twinge of pain on the inside of my upper-right arm. I guessed I'd gone a little too deep last night. I reached under my left bicep and felt the same kind of bandages as under my right and whispered to myself, "Too deep."

But it had done the job. It had stopped the images of Chester in my mind. It may have taken twenty minutes to stop the bleeding, but that's a minor trade. I should have been concerned about having to go that deep—but it was the only way to get his face out of my mind ... his filthy, hot breath, his clammy hands, which felt like some grotesque creature. His touch to my skin sent my pores reeling closed, as if my skin was actually crawling away from its presence.

I quickly crossed my arms, fingers on the top sides, and then plunged my thumbs up into the bandages under my arms that covered the patches of serrated skin. It sent a searing pain through me, completely capturing my conscious mind and seizing its process, then for good measure I squeezed against the wounds again really hard to let myself know that I meant business and to change my thoughts, blacken out that face, smell nothing, feel nothing except for the pain of this very moment. The pain was so intense that it caused an involuntary tear to fall from the corner of my eye, and I sat there, rocking the pain away as a nurturing mother would rock her child to sleep.

Just then the therapist's door opened, and out came a homely looking little man, just skin and bones with dark rings around his sunken-in eyes. He was so pale that I could see every blue vein beneath the surface of his skin, and I found myself thinking that he would be a great subject for a biology class: the transparent man, who they'd inject with an ounce of black food coloring and watch it flow through his entire vascular system. I caught myself and looked away as I chuckled and then caught myself once again, thinking, *Why the hell shouldn't I laugh?* I'd been taught by the best that all we are is this persona, this outer layer, and what we do with it. No matter how much they smile or make you laugh, when the deed is done, all you have left is a good-bye.

But that's life, and in less than thirty days I would be out of here, so for now: manners. I stood quickly and brushed away the creases from my parochial school student uniform that had tried to make their impressions from sitting for so long in this waiting room.

"I look forward to seeing you next week, William," the therapist called out in a staunch voice with a hint of a German accent that sounded a little fake to me. The frail man nodded and proceeded to scurry out the front door.

Then Dr. Vogel shifted his attention toward me. Peering over his small, round spectacles that rested down toward the tip of his pointy nose, he raised his blond, bushy eyebrows and barked out, "Your turn, Miss Sullivan-Magaskawee."

I wondered if he had been in the military, and then I began clearing my throat to dissuade my laughter as I flirted with the thought that he had been an escaped Nazi paper-pusher who was hiding out here in Devils Lake, North Dakota, under the guise of a prick Sigmund Freud wannabe psychotherapist. There might be something there; I'd keep it in mind for Google material later if he pissed me off in any way, because I was sure he had plenty of skeletons in his closet. He escorted me into his office and gestured for me to take a seat. I could see that he was eyeing the colorful bruising on my cheek that I got from fighting last night.

"Before we begin, Miss Sullivan-Magaskawee, may I inquire as to where that mark on your cheek came from?" he asked me in a particularly monotone voice, which I hoped was to mask his alarm, or this was going to be a long orientation-like session maybe lasting a full, agonizing sixty minutes.

"MMA."

The look on his face was puzzled and disapproving. I continued.

"Mixed martial arts. It should be in my file as what I do if I am not in school or at a therapy session."

I wondered if that sounded as bitchy to him as it had to me. I mean really, I was trying to be good here, but after so many different shrinks, all asking the same questions and prefacing the questions with, "I know you might have been asked this question before, but I'm curious ..." as if he would be more in tune than the last one and he would find some issue that was previously overlooked by the others.

Around my third year of therapy I started changing my answers slightly to see if it would change the response of *my* subjects; I wondered if they knew how utterly predictable they were. I felt like the physician, able to prescribe whatever med I desired depending on the different answers I gave to the same old questions. At one time that began to be an issue, until I learned that selling the pills was more lucrative than vegetating from them, and there was always someone at the gym trying to escape from some sort of pain or another—actually, I thought I was the only one at the gym that sought pain.

"Is that what you would like to do? Talk about your file?"

"Why not?" I responded flippantly.

"Well, quite frankly I thought you may want to aid your case with any recent enlightenment." His tone seemed patronizing; maybe he really was from another country.

"Case? What case?"

"In the file you say that your mother slapped you when you told her that your stepfather, Mr. Thomas Magaskawee, had allegedly molested you. Is that correct?"

What? This guy was not from another country, he was from another planet! How did he know that my mother had slapped me, or anything about the rape, for that matter? Never had rape been a topic of conversation in all of my years of therapy. There was nothing in that file saying anything about me ever being raped, because if it had been shared with a therapist, then by law they would have brought it to attention of the authorities because I am a minor, and Mother's nest egg would disappear. My eyes narrowed and my jaw set for a quick moment and I began to wonder again why I had had to switch doctors so quickly. Why did I have to start coming all the way across town to this new guy? My mother only told me last night, via Post-it note, that I was to see this new doctor starting today and that he specialized in cases like mine—not sure exactly what that meant.

I guess it meant that she wanted me to talk about *it*, but what about the legal issues that would come from this? When my mother married Chester it was under the condition that we would all live in town on top of the hill and not on the Indian reservation. Chester was the head of his family and the chief of the tribe; he was the most instrumental part in getting the casino built here in Devils Lake, and if this got out it would destroy billions of dollars for all involved; because this hadn't happened on the reservation he would go to jail and the casino deal would fall through. What about her way of living? Maybe this was for the best; maybe it was the one chance for my mother and me to have a real relationship again, like it was before this whole nightmare began. If she was willing to give up her way of living for me, then I had to be strong and do this for her ... I would try this, but this guy better change his attitude and tone fast if he wanted me to keep talking!

"Yes she did slap me, but there was no *alleged* molestation. Chester raped me not just once, but time and time again for several years!" My voice sounded funny to me, as if it had trailed off, kind of distant and hollow.

"And by Chester you are referring to Mr. Thomas Magaskawee, your stepfather ... sorry, my error, your adoptive father. Is that correct?"

I wasn't not sure how, but he managed to sound indignant now as he spoke, as if I were being judged. He sat very still while he analyzed my movements and responses. I glared directly into his eyes of stone and emphasized both syllables.

"Ches-ter!"

"Your mother didn't believe you, did she? How did that make you feel?"

I felt a slight tapping on my legs and looked down to see it was the fingers on my trembling hands, so I quickly meshed them together, intertwined, then squeezed the tips down hard against my knuckles so tightly that they began to ache, which released my anger but once again betrayed by myself. The anger had shifted me into an emotional mess, with a million thoughts racing through my head. The confusion of why! Why did it have to happen? I'd loved him as my father! I could have fought harder; I could have bitten his hand that covered my mouth and nose so tightly that I could barely breathe, and death would have been a welcome guest compared to the worst part of it all. The worst of it all was to have my body betray me ... I quickly folded my arms, fingers on top again, and dug my thumbs into the undersides of my arms as hard as I could.

I imagine that I must have looked absolutely crazy to this prick sitting so quietly, watching me as I rocked back and forth, shaking like some insane, mute!

"It hurt." I willingly confessed to release the weight I was feeling.

He tilted his head and leaned forward slightly.

"Describe that pain, Elise."

I felt totally helpless ...

"Abandoned."

I could hear myself speaking but I couldn't feel myself talking, and the words just echoed over and over, louder and louder in my head.

"I feel ... felt alone."

"Elise, do you think that will ever change?"

"I don't know ..."

Why was I telling him all of this? Who is he? I began to look around the room for something, anything to help me regain control of myself. A diploma, University of Northern Iowa, ask him something, anything.

"What, uh … what city?"

I motioned toward his diploma on the wall and he shifted his gaze to it and then glared back at me out of the corner of his eye, motionless and silent. I pressed my thumbs up into my wounds once again as a plea for my old faithful friend pain to once again help me regain control of myself. Pain was the only friend I could always count on, even more than I could count on myself. I took a deep, reorienting breath, leaned forward, and spoke with a semblance of self-assurance.

"What city is the University of Northern Iowa in?"

My tone must have irritated him, because he snapped his whole gaze back to me and then looked me up and down slowly. What sort of response was this for a therapist? He seemed angry to have lost his upper hand as if it were some kind of game. He definitely warranted Googling!

"Cedar Falls," he said crisply.

Why did I know that?

"Elise, this session is not about me. I would appreciate it if you were able to keep focus!" he said while bringing both of his hands down in a stiff karate-chop fashion, both hands now tipped directly at me while pressed against the edges of my file, which rested open in the middle of his desk. I wondered if he had practiced that move. Without breaking eye contact, he flipped to the next page in my file, then he looked down to it and read in silence for a moment before looking back up at me with an "I got you now" look on his face.

"You say that this molestation took place over the course of five years, correct? From age seven until the age of twelve?"

I nodded in response, and I could feel the anger in me begin to rise in anticipation of his next line of questioning—and a questioning was exactly what this was. No kind of therapy session that I had ever attended was like this! This was like I was on trial.

"Why did you allow it to go on for so long?"

Are you kidding me? I thought. This bastard was blaming me for what happened! Accusing me for allowing it to happen! I could feel the anger erupting so I shifted my focus to a pitcher of water on top of his desk. I immediately noticed that the water inside of it was swaying forcefully though the desk and therapist Ludwig Vogel were completely still. This was nothing new to me, since I had long since been able to do little "parlor tricks" involving water. But I usually had to concentrate very hard for long periods of time to make something happen, yet this was all happening without me even thinking about it.

I shifted my look back at the therapist to see that he was so intently focused on my reactions and body language that he didn't even see the water in the pitcher moving.

"Miss Sullivan, I asked you a question. Why did it take you so long to report this to your mother, and why have you never reported this to the authorities?"

I could feel the confusion creeping back into my mind from the dark corners.

'"I don't know why!" I found myself at the edge of my seat screaming at him with my hands clinging tightly to the undercarriage of the chair, as if I were trying to hold myself down in my seat. Didn't he know that I asked myself that question a million times? Chester was not a small person; He played college ... he played college football ... in college ... he was a panther ... UNI Panthers. University of Northern Iowa ...

My hands flung up to cover my face so I wouldn't reveal anything, and simultaneously the pitcher toppled over from the violent swashing around of the water, which had increase more and more as my anger had increased.

He jumped up from his chair, brushing away the water that had landed in his lap and cursing—at least I think he was cursing—in German. *"Hure, du ruiniert der datei! Hure!"*

He continued to scream *"Hure!"* at the top of his lungs while slamming his fist into his other hand and stomping toward the window. But then he seemed to see something outside that instantly stopped his ranting. He stood completely erect and then turned to me slowly, adjusted his tie while looking down toward me in my chair, and spoke in an accomplished manner.

"Did you know that self-mutilation like cutting oneself can legally be construed as a potential danger to oneself and others?"

He walked past me and straight to the office door; he turned the knob and opened it. Then he turned to me and spoke before leaving the room.

"I have to grab some towels to clean this mess up."

So much for indiscreet dialogue, but I felt compelled to see what, outside that window, could have caused such a transformation. I rose from my seat to look out of the window. To my lack of surprise I saw a state mental hospital vehicle in front of the building and two attendants getting out and walking toward the entrance.

Okay, so that's how it is! I'd been pretending all this time, trying to hold on to something that probably was never there. If I was going to be alone then it would start now. I quickly left the office and looked around corners, listening for any sounds that resembled doors busting open and large men intending to attack me with a straitjacket, as I navigated my way through the building. Escaping seemed to be as easy as evading any areas with worn carpets, because those are the areas that people use and to keep going down the stairwells. I came to the exit at the back of the complex unseen by anyone, which would have been impressive if it weren't after six and basically everyone being out of the business district by now.

As I quietly slid out of the door and made my way to the corner of the building I thought that I might be acting a little too dramatic—until I saw one of the orderlies who had obviously gone up to get me from the doctor's office running back to the "short bus" flailing his arms and screaming into a walkie-talkie. Unfortunately his vehicle, parked at the front of the building, stood between me and my car in the front lot. The man then walked to my car and continued to talk into his walkie-talkie as he knelt behind it, no doubt verifying the license plates.

I quickly ducked behind the cars parked in the back while looking up at the building from the rear to confirm no had one spotted me from the windows. After clearing the building's view I did my best GI Joe impersonation, which surprisingly was pretty impressive—no, scratch that, extremely impressive, as I used absolutely every shadow to my advantage. In a town as small as this every face is almost a neighbor, so avoiding being seen by anyone was quite a challenge.

I'd always been withdrawn but attracted to the shady areas of life as a comfort in which to hide, and it had always been somewhat difficult to be obscure in a town this size when you lived on top of the hill and absolutely everyone that saw you commented how much you looked like Angelina Jolie, but the wounded badger act can be pretty repelling—even more so if it's not an act. Just be yourself, isn't that what they say?

As the sun eased my task by lengthening the shadows until they had completely engulfed all light, except that cast by the street lamps just starting to come on, I found myself looking down while walking and noticing the brightening of the concrete with every step. I raised my head to recognize the isolated, eager brilliance of the neon sign that signaled the place I almost called home—my gym. I spoke its name aloud. "The Dojo."

Its sign was flickering, not quite dead but dying. It was about time for Jed to change those bulbs. Jed. His face flashed and then faded along with brief recollections of an encounter that he and I had. But before I could recall any details worth remembering, I saw a set of headlights pulling up to the curb about a block ahead, and I swiftly dashed to the shadowy edges of the walls. I hugged the shadows and nimbly made my way toward the door beneath the ominous Dojo lighting. I slipped in through the door and breathed a sigh of relief to be inside.

The Dojo used to be a large warehouse that was gutted out many years ago by a very successful evangelistic church, replacing more than half of the exterior walls with massive stained glass murals of biblical scenes. Six months later they proceeded to have a third of the ceiling removed and replaced with an enormous stained glass ceiling mural of Jesus with open arms beckoning to all from above. At night the image of Jesus was a ghostly presence against the dark backdrop, even somewhat ominous during nights with lightning and thunderstorms; however, nothing did it justice like the backlighting of a sunny day, as it cast its myriad Technicolor shadings throughout the entire building.

Directly below the image, in a very sharp contrast, stood the octagon cage that stretched thirty feet across from corner to corner. The once-light-colored padded floor was now so badly bloodstained that you would think its color was intended to be charcoal gray with a hint of crimson.

Owner Jed often pointed out this irony and called it "The Cage of Calvary." He was constantly screaming out things like, "Say hello to Jesus!" when a fighter got laid out on his, or in my case last night, her, back.

I had to get to my locker on the opposite side of warehouse from here, which meant I had to walk past the cage and everyone. I always kept a couple of extra sets of clothing in my locker for particularly bloody days of sparring; I felt a surge of pride along with my dubious grin about that most times it was not my blood. I suddenly felt anxious as the door slammed closed behind me and some nearby heads turned to me. Jed was on his hands and knees the middle of the cage, screaming at Frank to lock out an arm bar that he was trying to get William to tap out with. Jed was so sadistic that if he was not the one fighting then he had to be as close as possible to others fighting and coaching them on how to break their opponents' wills, or bones, whichever came first.

Jed looked up and winked at his girlfriend, Jill, who was sitting with some huge person beside her who I'd never seen before. I thought it was a girl because of the pig tails and pink ribbons, but I couldn't tell because I couldn't see the face. Jed followed Jill's line of vision, which led straight to me coming through the door. His face tightened up instantly, and he leaped to his feet and headed out of the cage.

This could have been my sign to run, considering Jed was the brother of our town sheriff. I slowed my pace down and prepared to reverse direction back out of the door but waited for just a moment to determine what he was doing. He swiftly ducked around a person that was working out on the heavy bag just outside of the cage and headed straight for me. After having witnessed his fighting style for so long I could see that he was not bearing down on me offensively, and his facial expression was beckoning me as if he had something important to tell me. I took a step back toward the door and angled my body to quickly grab the knob and exit if he were to suddenly lunge for me.

"Elise, don't run!" he hissed out to me so no one else could hear.

"What?" I said apprehensively with my hand back on the doorknob; I couldn't tell if his expression had changed because my eyes were too busy darting all around the room like some caged animal expecting anything and everything to suddenly pounce on it.

"Settle down and act normal, damn it!" he whispered harshly. "He called me and said to let him know if you came here. He said they're waiting at your house. What's going on?"

His eyes were sincere and I relaxed slightly but kept a watch out on the room, particularly his little tenth-grade girlfriend, who was definitely too young for Jed, going on twenty-seven years old, but nepotism carried a lot of weight in this town.

"He told me that you had gone off the deep end and attacked someone and that you're dangerous." I could hear the skepticism in his voice, which trailed off into a low chuckle.

Should I tell him? What if I told and they found out, which could very easily happen. What if this was all just a bluff to scare me into keeping quiet and if I said something now the shit would really hit the fan? Who am I kidding? The development of that casino meant billions to this town, and they weren't going to allow me to jeopardize that! Why was I so stupid? Why did I make that stupid threat?

"It's just a big misunderstanding." I tried to sound convincing and remorseful, just in case this conversation did get back to the powers that be.

Jed's face became very serious and his eyes were borderline sorrowful, as if he were a doctor informing a patient that she was terminal and had no time left. "Elise, I know my brother. This is nothing close to a misunderstanding, and it's not going to just blow over. What happened?"

I felt like an elephant was sitting on my chest and my breathing became shallow. *What am I doing? Hyperventilating? Am I ...?* I quickly opened the door, shoved my head out into the cool night air, and took several deep breaths, which seemed to open up my airways. I composed myself and began to think about how strange this conversation must be looking to anyone watching, and I calmly turned back to Jed.

"What's going on, Elise? You can trust me; you know I don't kiss and tell."

I gave an incredulous look to him and then to his tenth grader and back to him, which caused me to bring up the memory of the one night that I had made the mistake of being with him. *Mental note to self: never again wrestle with anyone that I am even slightly attracted to without adult supervision!*

"Okay, bad choice of words—besides, that was a totally different situation."

"Jed, I just came to get a change of clothes and then I am out of here, okay?"

"He said they have your car, and he figures if you don't stop here then you'll just be walking straight home. So there's no major rush to leave, 'cause he trusts me to call him if you show. Otherwise he says he'll just be waiting there for you at home ... so don't go home!"

Just then we were both startled by Jill and her Amazon friend, whose curiosity had gotten the best of them. Now that she was close enough, I could see that she was a girl from the overuse-of-makeup-as-an-obvious-compensation school of thought, but I couldn't imagine anyone choosing to make fun of her to face, because at about six feet tall and being built like a farmhand I didn't think she would have to take it. "Elise, this is Gretchen," chirped Jill's tiny, arrogant voice, which was befitting of her five-foot-tall, ninety-pound frame. She was always a very sheepish girl, so I wondered what she knew. I nodded suspiciously and waited for her to continue, since she seemed eager to say something. "She's a senior, too, just moved here." She gave a devious glance to the girl while curling up her upper lip and then slyly looking back at me.

"Uh, yeah," Jed reluctantly added in as if he had more bad news. "Her father's the new town shrink." Gretchen gave Jed the evil eye and cleared her throat. "I mean, psychologist."

Gretchen lurched forward with her fist clinched, and inadvertently spitting in Jed's face, she shouted, "Psychiatrist!" with a husky voice.

Jed flinched and then the two stood toe to toe in a brief staredown. I began to second-guess my ruling of it being a girl; I wouldn't rule out the possibility of her being in drag or on horse steroids just yet.

Jed brushed it off, and I wondered if this wasn't the first time that these two had gotten into it about this subject. He shifted his attention back to me and rolled his eyes while gesturing the cuckoo sign about Gretchen. "I guess crazy is getting really catchy when Devils Lake needs our own Psy-chi-a-trist," he mocked in Gretchen's direction, clearly pronouncing every syllable.

What an intense feeling—realizing that I had already met her father earlier today and he'd tried to have me committed. Mr. Second-in-command of the witch hunt for me. I glared at her, and she instantly snapped her attention in my direction as if she had felt my look. It must have been pretty obvious because Jill took a step back and Jed eagerly leaned into me almost whispering "Gretchen here claims to have an MMA championship belt in Iowa." Jed said

I spoke quickly without breaking our stare. "I'll just need to change my clothes."

Jed shifted his weight to shield our conversation from anyone's hearing.

"You should know she says that she took Carlisle in forty-five seconds—and she gave some pretty specific details about Carlisle!"

Natalie Carlisle, my one and only public bout—and it had gone to the last round before she forced me to tap out with an arm bar …

"That's the only fight you've—"

"I know! Center ring, Jed; I need to change!"

I could hear the level of excitement rising as I made my way to the locker room, and I could see Jill in the reflection of the mirrored wall as she bounced from person to person, promoting the big clash. As I passed by the water fountain on my way to the locker room, the water began to run as if someone were drinking from it, and I noticed two boys on their way to get a drink from it suddenly stop and begin to investigate it. I yanked the locker room door open, and the usually resistive door swung and crashed into the wall so hard that it must have put a hole into the Sheetrock.

I had no idea why I was so hyped-up but for the past several hours I'd been feeling different—tight muscles, limber agility, kind of like when I was walking on my way here and hiding in the shadows I moved, as if I were some kind of feline. It must be the adrenaline of the whole situation, even before this thing with gargantuan Gretchen came up. Even as I changed my clothes it was as if I could feel the fibers of every muscle in my body twitching with the anticipation of releasing their built-up energies, ready to explode.

I took the extra set of clothes and shoved them into my duffle bag along with an extra set of sneakers and a light jacket that I had left in my locker previously. I made my way back to the gym and headed straight into the cage. As I passed by the boys still fiddling with the water fountain, the water began to shoot up higher and with much more force. I entered the cage with my bag in hand, Jed walked up to me, and Gretchen followed directly behind him. I angled my head to the left to see around him and stare directly into her eyes, and all I felt was the boiling of my blood as I thought of her father blaming me for what had happened, plotting to lock me away forever.

"I'll take that," Jed said as he reached down to my bag, I thought; I couldn't tell. I just stared coldly into the girl's eyes—I couldn't feel anything but anger. The sounds in the gym faded into a faint background white noise of tiny voices and water spattering on the floor. Then it all surprisingly melted into calm, even, deep heartbeat filling my eardrums. I was not sure how long our stare down lasted before Jed's face popped into my vision, causing me to lean back slightly from the surprise. His lips were moving as if he were trying to tell me something, and he was gesturing down. I looked down to see he was tugging at my bag, but my grip was so tight that he couldn't get the bag out of my hands. It was like I had to tell my hand to unclinch, so Jed could take the bag.

He had a very curious look on his face as I watched him take my bag and exit the octagon cage leaving just Gretchen and I in the blood stained, fenced in battle zone. A quiver of doubt shuttered through me as the click of the cage door closing was all I heard as I stared at it.

I looked back up at Gretchen just in time to see the knuckles of her huge fist crashing down into the side of my face. The force of the blow caused me to stagger back about two steps, but amazingly I was still on my feet. I stood, looking into her eyes, waiting for the pain that didn't come. Her eyes were full of surprise to see that I was still standing, and she quickly jumped into the air with one balled fist raised high, which she sent crashing down on my head with the weight of her entire body behind it.

The blow knocked me back against the cage, which sprang me back toward Gretchen, but right before crashing into her I leaped so high and fast into the air it was like I was bounding off of a trampoline. I cranked my knee up with all of my force to meet her jaw. I could feel and hear her teeth and bones giving way from the impact of my knee. Her body completely arched backward, and she crashed to the canvas, flat on her back. I continued to soar beyond her, landing on my feet. I turned back around to look down at her and saw her attempt to open her mouth to scream out in pain, but her lower jaw slid lifelessly down and to the side, clearly dislocated, and blood ran out of her mouth and landed on the canvas in splatters. She crawled to her knees with her mouth gaping and her jaw twisted to the left, blood pouring off of her chin and onto her sweatshirt image of a muscle-bound SpongeBob SquarePants, which was now almost entirely covered with her blood.

I walked to her and grabbed the hair at the back of her head and I could not help but to think of how her eyes looked like those of a frightened deer that had just been run over by a car and was gasping for its last breaths. I bent over to whisper in her ear, "Give this message to your dad for me!" and I brought my fist down into her temple, sending her unconscious body crashing to the floor, where she lay bleeding.

I reached down and rolled her onto her side so she wouldn't choke to death on her blood. I looked up to a roomful of mortified faces. A couple of people were jumping to their feet and into the ring to help Gretchen, and a couple had already begun calling out on their cell phones. At the corner of the cage were three boys comparing videos that they had shot of the fight on their cell phones, and another boy that was even still recording.

They're coming; I have to get out of here! I jumped over Gretchen and the couple of boys who were kneeling there trying to revive her. I headed straight for the cage exit, the several people jamming up the doorway with horrified looks on their faces quickly spreading apart to let me through, as if I were royalty or a leper. Jed rushed up to me with my bag in his hand, shoving it to me while whispering in my ear and rushing me toward the exit.

"You have to hurry and get the hell out of here—out of this town, Elise; they will be here any second and they'll know you're close! Run, fast, and don't go home!"

I grabbed my bag from him and ran as fast as I could for the door, which for some reason had been lodged open. I'd stay off the sidewalks, hit backyards and dark alleys until I got out of town—hell, for that matter, until I was out of the next few towns. Where the hell was I going to go? I wished I had my car, but then I would have been an easy target.

I could feel the emotions in me starting to well up into tears as I darted through the doorway and turned left. I had already taken two more strides before my brain registered that I was on a collision course with a person who was coming into the gym. I quickly shifted my weight to the right to avoid him, but it was too late. The left side of my body bumped into him which in combination with my forward momentum sent me spinning through the air towards a parked car until I heard the short, hollow sound—that metallic thud a car makes when a ball or a human body bangs into it. I saw a flash of blinding, white light and I felt a sharp pain on the back of my skull.

CHAPTER

Uncertainty

Opening my eyes, I saw three young men floating sideways. As I squinted the figures slowly shifted to become one person. I quickly realized that he wasn't floating sideways but that I was lying on my side. I brought my free hand up to the back of my head to feel if it was bleeding and to ease the pain as I tried to sit up. The young man helped me up into a sitting position with my back against the parked car I had just crashed into. I sunk into a deep dent in the car that I assumed I had just made.

"Are you okay?" he asked with a cracking voice.

I wondered if it was because of the bump on my head, or was there something strange about this guy's eyes? Was he a cop? No, he looks 17 or 18 years old, too young to be a cop, and besides, I knew both of them in this town. What was it about his eyes?

"Uh … yeah, I think I am," I managed to say, but I still felt light-headed. What was it about his eyes?—basset hound! That was it. They looked like a basset hound's eyes, but rather than brown they were ocean-blue with a hint of pale green mixed in. They looked innocent, kind. His jaw line so clean and strong, like a model but not cold or pretentious but warm and real, not striking a pose, but like every move he made could captured and deemed flawless.

"Are you sure? You hit this car pretty hard." His eyes shifted from me to the dent several times, back and forth. "Yes I'm sure … just give me a minute." What was I thinking? I didn't have a minute; I had to get out of here now. I tried to look as composed as I could while staggering to my feet with his assistance. "Yes, I'm okay, I have to go!"

He swayed back with a curious look on his face in response to my aggression but still held my arm so I could maintain my balance. "You can't drive in this condition," he insisted.

"I'm not driving, now let me go!"

He released my arm and I staggered sideways two feet before my left foot slid off of the curb and I bumped back into poor victimized parked car again—much lighter than last time, but I still hoped I hadn't done even more damage to it. I shifted square against the car with my backside and bent over with my hands on my knees, looking down at the sidewalk to try and focus on one spot with the hope that I could restore my equilibrium, but knowing it was hopeless with the little time I had to spare.

"Please let me give you a ride," he said intently as he picked up my bag. I tried to figure out what time it was but with so many distractions I had a hard time calculating. I would think early evening because of the amount of teens in the Dojo, but with only the last 2 days of school before summer I can't go by that indication. I was at the doctor's office for a while and it was dark already before I got here, but now I can't even… What's it matter? I have to get out of here now, and I don't give a shit if it's eleven or midnight!

I focused on some spots of Gretchen's spattered blood that had landed on my shoes, and it gave me a sudden rush of confidence at the fact that if he were to try anything I would add his blood to my shoe's collection. He held out his arm for me to grab and then led me to his car, which was four cars behind the one I had been abusing. We got into a new or newer Toyota Camry which is definitely conservative. He helped me into the passenger side, then raced around to the driver's side and bounced in, started the car, and pulled away from the Dojo. He seemed to be a little too pleased with himself about this whole situation; I decided I better watch him very closely.

I had regained my focus, but the tradeoff seemed to be a headache starting to form from the area where I had hit my head. I slouched down in my seat so no one could see me from outside of the car and noticed the young man giving me a strange look out of the corner of his eye.

"Are you okay?"

"Yes," I snapped.

"Where would you like me to take you?"

I wasn't thrilled with his choice of words, but he sounded innocent enough for me to chalk it up to my current heightened sense of paranoia. "California," I scoffed.

He looked down at me with a boyish grin, and a sparkle of excitement gleamed in his puppy dog eyes. "Okay," he replied eagerly. "I'll have to stop and get my bags first, though."

I frowned at him disbelievingly. "I was kidding." His face dropped, and he turned his attention back to the road. I added, "A bus stop a town or two away would be fine."

He creased his eyes toward me, and to my amazement they still retained their droopy Baskerville shape, making me think to myself that this guy couldn't look angry or intimidating to save his life.

"Is it just me, or do you seem like you are trying to run away from something?" he asked.

"You could say that, but enough about me. So why haven't I seen you around here before?"

He shifted uncomfortably in his seat and sat quiet for a moment, as if he were debating with himself about what to say next. He looked at me with an agonizing expression on his face and then quickly shifted his attention back to the road. "Because I'm not from around here," he confessed.

"It's not that big of a town; I already knew you weren't from around here. I guess I'm asking why you're here. It is a school night, after all. You do go to school, right?"

He looked completely uncomfortable with the subject but then slumped, exhaling as if he were just defeated, and he gave me a sincere look that, blended with those eyes, sort of made him look exceptionally pathetic. "Well, I came to see you, Elise."

How did he know my name, and what did that mean—he came to see me? I pivoted in my seat to brace my back against the passenger door and brought my feet up onto the seat facing him so I could meet his head with the heel of my shoe if he tried to lunge at me or something stupid like that—which I highly doubted he would do, traveling at sixty miles per hour, unless he was suicidal. I wasn't sure that this night could get any worse, but it clearly was, and I wasn't going down without a fight!

"Really, and how do you know me?" I said defensively. My voice cracked, though I was fighting hard to not appear nervous or scared. I very keenly watched his every little movement as he attempted to answer my question. He sighed deeply before speaking.

"Well ... I had some dreams and you were in them." He nervously glanced over at me and then back to the road. His hands were so tightly gripping the steering wheel that his knuckles were ghostly white. I held the headrest of my seat firmly with my left hand, and my right hand was braced against the dash for extra leverage for a possible kick.

"I know this sounds crazy, and I hardly expect you to believe it, but my dream said that I would find you here in Devils Lake. There was water in the dream, and you stood on top of it, and I sank." His voice was shaky.

I didn't know how I had missed it before, but there seemed to be desperation in his face and mannerisms. His eyes seemed worn down, tired, and I wondered if I had been distracted by his puppy dog eyes too much to see his desperation. He seemed to be telling the truth—or at least what he believed was the truth—and that what he was trying to describe to me had a serious impact on him. It was that, or he was a hell of a liar.

"My uncle revived me in my bed." He looked over into my wide, confused eyes with deep sincerity. "I spit up lake water and ... some type of weedy, living, moving creature onto my bed. And I don't know why it wanted me to find you, but I haven't dared sleep since then, and that was more than two days ago." He looked forward, and I could see the relief of finally completing his mission in his body language. His grip on the steering wheel was now relaxed.

I felt sorry for him, but just because he seemed to believe what he was saying didn't mean that I did too—and besides, according to what he said he'd done his job, because he'd found me.

"It sounds like it was your fate to get me to the bus station." I tried to be convincing, but I think it came out a little sarcastic

With an inquisitive expression followed by a sigh of relief, he spoke as if my statement were his epiphany. "You're right, it was my fate. And now I will be able to sleep and get back before finals."

I nodded in agreement, but I wasn't quite sure if he was asking me or making a statement when he said that, and I wasn't sure if he knew either. Suddenly he stiffened up, wide-eyed with surprise while looking at the road, and I snapped my attention to the road and saw a familiar turquoise glow in the black night sky just beyond the light of the headlights. I glanced over to him, and he was definitely looking at the same turquoise glow. I scanned my memory trying to recall when I had seen this particular color before, and I began to feel panic as I remembered. I looked, disbelieving, back to it, and our headlights caught up to it; it was only about fifty feet in front of us. My jaw dropped as it got larger by the second.

Then I could make out a man in a skintight jumpsuit with cords dangling from his elbows to a device in his hand. He seemed completely oblivious to our oncoming headlights as he aimed the device in several different directions, discharging spiraling white lights from it that seemed to go so fast that I could barely discern them with the naked eye. The turquoise was a hue that came from him; he appeared to be glowing like some sort of celestial, being because there was no source from which that light was cast, and its glow never dimmed as our headlights approached. As a matter of fact, our headlights shined right through him, not reflecting off of him or causing a shadow to be cast behind him. I felt the car slow as the young man removed his foot from the gas but to my surprise he wasn't applying the brakes or even swerving to avoid the man standing in the middle of the road.

I covered my face for the split second that would have been the impact of his body, but I felt nothing—no one's body being pulverized by our car, no feeling like the car had just gone over a speed bump at sixty miles per hour, no smashing of the windshield or squealing of our brakes. I felt the car picking up speed again as I quickly turned in my seat to look out of the back window, aghast at how the man with the strange turquoise lighting was still standing there in the same position firing his weapon in several different directions.

I looked at my driver, and he was ghostly pale, eyes wide with disbelief, and his grip on the steering wheel was tighter than ever before. I stiffly adjusted in my seat to look forward into the night as tiny sprinkles of rain began to fall against the windshield.

I remembered seeing people like the one in the road before, when I was young, so many years ago that I had basically written them off as dreams—somewhat bad dreams, actually. I recalled that no one else could ever see them, and my mother had said I was imagining them and she would insist that I stop watching scary movies. Funny thing is that she never knew what I was watching, because she never took the time to check on me wherever I was in the house-not her-that was Chester's assumed duty. My hands began to rise to the shredded skin under my bandages as a voice broke through.

"Why did you look out the back window?" His expression was scared and pleading, as if I was supposed to step out on a ledge to save him or something. He might have been into letting complete strangers see his skeletons, but I'd already done that once today, and look where that got me. He must have seen it too or he wouldn't have reacted the way that he did. "Why did you slow down and why do you look like you saw a ghost? Did you see something, maybe on the road?" He slammed on the brakes, and I quickly shot my attention to the passenger-side mirror to see if anyone was going to crash into us, but I saw no headlights behind our car. The drizzling rain that had fallen on the road caused the car to slide and I could just imagine us spinning and flying off of the road, but thankfully we only drifted slightly to the left. After the car had stopped, he released his foot from the brake and slowly drove onto the gravel shoulder of the road. As he threw the car into park, I repositioned myself with my back against the door, feet up on the seat and ready to thrust-kick into his face. He was just sitting there staring forward with a blank look on his face. What is it with this day?

He pivoted toward me quickly, and I realized that his eyes *could* appear angry—no, not angry ... frustrated and desperate. I began feeling around with my right hand for the handle without taking my eyes off of him.

"Three days ago I was nothing like this!" His tone was defensive. "I had that damn dream, and now nothing's the same." Just then I found the door handle. "If I were you I would run because nothing I've told you makes any sense, and to add to that, yes! Yes I did see something in the road—someone—but I've seen people like that before, and the only reason I'm saying this is because I got the feeling that you did too. Elise, please just say if you did or not."

To my surprise I hadn't opened the door and run yet, but what he was saying was impossible. How could he know what I'd seen so many years ago? I hardly remembered it myself. I wanted to know, needed to know more.

"Strange lighting around them that seems to come from nowhere?" I asked him sheepishly.

After what sounded like a sigh of relief and a pause so long that I began to think he had fallen asleep, he began to cough for a moment and then labored out words. "Do you still believe I'm here to give you a ride to the bus stop?" he asked between coughs.

"I really wasn't sold on that from the beginning, so what happens now?" I responded.

He appeared very serious as he adjusted himself and looked to me. "I've missed finals by now, and honestly, I'm afraid to have you get on a bus if we're wrong. If it's okay with you I would rather take you where you're going and figure this thing out along the way."

I thought to myself, *He seems safe enough, and no crazier than I am outside of the whole dreams thing.* I said, "Okay, as long as you promise you're not a rapist or murderer."

He chuckled at me and put up some sort of Boy Scout sign, saying, "I swear to God that I have never done anything like that, and I never swear to God." I felt comfort in the sincerity of his words and tone.

"Since we're going to be driving together for a while I should get your name."

Realization dawned on him that he hadn't introduced himself to me, and a shade of embarrassment rolled over his face. "Sorry, Elise, I'm Caleb."

For some unknown reason things suddenly felt awkward, and I turned forward to face the road. "Can we go?" I could tell he felt the same awkward rush as he fumbled with the gearshift and then away we went to California.

"I have to go back to my hotel and get my bags first, okay?"

Great, we had to go back to Devils Lake. Well, after one small detour, we'd be headed to California, I slouched down in my seat, hopefully enough for it to appear as if there was only one person in the car ... I couldn't believe it, California. Not exactly the situation I thought I would be in when I finally got the chance to go—zero support or family, completely alone. Well, not alone, since he was here. But he'd be gone in a few days. I felt a tear welling up and dropped my head into my hands. *What am I doing, what am I going to do?* I felt the car U-turn and head back toward town.

"It'll just be a quick stop; I'll run in and right back out, I promise," he said, his voice quavering slightly.

Realizing he was reacting to my agonizing over my own bleak future, I quickly responded to let him know I was not that much of a bitch, but I kept my face in my hands to hide the tears. "No, it's not that, take your time," I said

After a short coughing fit he managed to speak, but quietly, gently. "Elise, can I ask what you're running from?"

Great, it wasn't bad enough that I had to face it in my head, but now I had to hear myself talking about it? I didn't answer for a moment, hoping that he would get the hint and change the subject, but he just patiently waited.

Finally I said, "Soulless, gold-digging, vindictive mother, who's plotting with a soulless pedophile—adoptive stepfather—I call him Chester." I was speaking so fast that I could barely make out what I was saying and hoped that he was missing it all. "And his college classmate who happens to be a psychologist and is trying to have me committed for life because I threatened to speak out and have Chester put in jail!" I peeked to see his reaction, but I couldn't make out anything as he sat there expressionless, driving. I looked directly at him but still saw no response. "Did I mention that if they succeed, they get like a billion dollars?" I barked out with a haughty tone.

A small grin touched the corners of his mouth, and he turned his tired eyes to me and spoke in a shaky but at the same time somehow confident voice. "Is that it?"

I turned to face forward in a huff and crossed my arms. Yes, that's it—that's enough to turn my world upside down. What more did he want? Masochist! I calmed my voice before speaking.

"Yes, that's it. Why? Not enough disaster for you?"

He scoffed. "No, that's not what I'm saying; that is plenty, believe me. I just meant from the sounds of it now that you're out of town they'll probably just go on with their lives and leave you to yours."

I frowned and tried not to sound as hopeless as I felt. "I have nothing, Caleb! No one to help me through any of this—and I'm not saying I need someone, because I can take care of myself. I'm just saying."

"Please don't get upset, Elise; I'm just trying to figure this all out. I can tell you're a very capable person; I don't doubt that." His voice suddenly became very shaky, "It's just that recently I was drowned more than once and probably have pneumonia from it. I am afraid to go to sleep because I may not wake up alive. I'm not trying to out-disaster you; I just wanted to know if there was anything physically trying to hurt you. You know, in a supernatural way."

What was with this guy? Why couldn't I manage to stay pissed at him for more than a minute?

The ride back to town was pretty quiet, but I did notice that we were both glancing around nonchalantly in search of glowing people, and I strangely found myself wishing he'd say something, not just to distract me from my bad situation but to hear his voice with that calm, rhythmical, light pitch with just enough bass to alert you that he was a man. Not abrasive, not aggressive, but still a man. I futilely tried to divert my attention to the off-and-on-again speckles of rain hitting the windshield, but they were too erratic to keep my attention, and then he finally spoke.

"Can you drive for a little while?"

"Sure," I said quickly, and I immediately wanted to slap my forehead for acting so damn female.

"We're here now; you can drive after I grab my stuff, okay?" He chuckled as the tire rolled over the curb from turning too sharply into the parking lot, and a flash of lightning streaked across the night sky. "I think that'd be best for both of us."

I slouched as low as I could get in my seat and peeked out of the passenger window to see Charlie Harrison behind the front desk of the hotel lobby wearing the same North Dakota State University cap that he always wore, and I wondered to myself if I had ducked in time for him not to see me and I also wondered if he actually slept in that hat, too, as rumor had it.

The hotel was one of those rambler-type hotels with outside room access, the kind that mainly housed truckers and unfortunate travelers who were getting too tired to continue driving and saw it from the highway. It was pretty run-down, and I really doubted that Charlie was very diligent about changing the sheets since he obviously couldn't even justify changing his hat once. As luck would have it, Caleb's room was the room closest to the office, and I wondered if I would be able to stay low enough the whole time so Charlie wouldn't see me. I was certain that the word had already spread throughout town that the police were searching for me.

Caleb had slowly dragged himself out of the car to go into his room, and I followed because it looked like Charlie had begun to get up and come outside to see who had just parked and I could just imagine sitting there when he came up to the car window. We got to the door before Caleb sluggishly removed his keys from his pocket and entered the room, at which time Caleb and I exchanged an odd look when we smelled a putrid odor that wasn't there a moment ago, but no time for accusations. I looked over my shoulder at the office to see Charlie watching us as he was opening the office door. I slipped inside the room and closed the wooden door quickly behind me, and to my relief that nasty smell wasn't inside the room.

"Hurry, I think he's coming!" I whispered urgently to Caleb.

Even as I said it I was stunned by that odor again; it was seeping in from outside. I knew there was something strange about the way the smell was traveling, but I brushed it off and sped to help Caleb gather his things together, hopefully fast enough for us to escape before Charlie got to the door. As we threw items into Caleb's luggage, the smell only increased in intensity. I looked to Caleb, and it was clear that he smelled the rotten stench too.

The aroma had struck us like an invisible wave, and we both backed away from it as if it were a presence, a smell so horrible that it evoked nausea and so rich that you could almost taste it. But that wasn't all; it smelled burnt—no, burning like decay, toxic and burning, a malevolent odor carried through the air in the form of smoke. It was just then that I realized that there was actually smoke creeping in from around the door.

As if that weren't bad enough we began to hear a sound so faint, yet so distinct, and slowly growing closer. I turned to Caleb with fear in my eyes. "Wha …?"

His face was contorted in pain from the smell, and he was straining to make out what the sound was. Screams: hundreds—no, thousands of cries in the distance, muffled or matted together as if from a single source then it would trail off into the even higher-pitched hysterical scream of an infant, gasping, hacking, straining to breathe against its own relentless wailing.

What could make such a horrifying noise? A noise that had grown so loud and was coming from all directions; it was everywhere! Suddenly I could feel vibrations of something pounding on something, and I looked around frantically until I found the source, as I saw the door shaking so violently that it felt as if the earth was moving. The pounding suddenly stopped and was followed by what looked like four enormous bear claws ripping downward through the wooden door, but instead of sawing with blades the wood was being cut by the flaming heat of the claws, leaving smoke and tiny ignitions of fire in the trails of the gashes.

I began to see bright lightning flashes through the torn openings in the door. One flash was so bright that it seemed to strike us directly with a fury, so loud that it felt as if it had caused my eardrums to burst—and then as sudden as it all had started, it faded to a complete stop, leaving the room clouded in a thick, rancid smoke from the burning wood that lingered along with the ringing in my ears.

I could barely see anything and realized that my back had been pressing against the wall behind me with so much pressure that my legs were starting to feel the strain. I felt a brush against my hand and jumped away, unexpectedly releasing my first scream. I knew I had tried to scream before now, but I had been too horrified to even find my voice.

"It's me, Caleb … Elise, it's me!" I heard in the background of the ringing that still remained in my ears but had begun to fade. I felt his hand find mine again and then pause as he was feeling around for something else.

"Take this," I faintly heard him say, followed by a sensation of a small thud against my chest. I jerked backward by instinct and then realized that he was handing me something. I felt for his hand and took the handle of what I assumed was a bag. Then he was tugging me in the direction of the small flickering flames on the door.

He slowly cracked the door open, and when the lighting flashed I saw fractions of his silhouette as he peeked out of the door. The rain was coming down so hard that it seemed like someone was pouring buckets of water from the sky, and for some odd reason I felt comfort from that.

Caleb quickly pushed the door closed again and lunged slightly to his right while still holding my hand, but now stiffly pushing me back. I heard through the now-faded ringing the unmistakable sound of vomit hitting the floor as he squeezed my hand tightly with his left one, still keeping his arm stiff against me as if to say, "You're not watching this." I didn't fight against it one bit but squeezed his hand back, hoping that it comforted him. All I could think was, *please just let this be a nightmare.*

He reached for the doorknob, swung the door open, and pulled me through in one fluid motion, tugging me toward the car so fast that I almost didn't acknowledge that the ground under my shoes was shifting and squishing as we ran. I looked back when he stopped to open the passenger-side door and shove me in. That was when I saw the hat, sliced in half and still smoldering, soaked in blood and brain matter, which as a sight was nothing compared to the rest of Charlie's body, mangled and torn into tiny pieces barely recognizable as human, thrown and splattered against every nearby surface, including the car, and once again I was thankful for the rain.

We drove out of Devils Lake so fast that I half expected the car's motor to explode or cough and just die.

"Do you think the rain made whatever that thing was go away?" Caleb asked with voice and hands alike trembling as he drove. My face has been in my hands for a few minutes now trying to go through in my head what had just happened.

I shook my head, uncertain of anything, and my voice cracked as I spoke. "I don't know ... That would make sense, I guess."

He adjusted himself in his seat before speaking again, but instead of speaking, he bent over and wretched a couple of times as if he was going to puke again, I was glad that he had already drained his stomach of everything back at the hotel.

After a long pause he mustered up the courage to speak about it again, but this time extremely fast and brief. "I have no idea of what that was or if it's following us or what it even looked like!" he said, but I had nothing to add to his rant; I just sat in shock, listening to the tires against the road as we drove.

After a while of silence Caleb's head began to fall back slowly and then jerk forward quickly. He did this about four or five times before I realized that we were no safer in this car than we were at the hotel, with Caleb's driving while so tired.

"I think I'm okay to drive now, Caleb," I said softly.

"You think you are?" he said after sensing the reluctance in my voice.

"It's just that I hate driving in the rain, but faced with what we're dealing with now I think I can get over it. You need rest, and I couldn't do any worse than you're doing right now, I assure you that."

He quickly pulled the car over to the side of the road and placed it in park as he said, "Works for me." It was clear that neither of us wanted to go outside in the sheets of rain coming down and God knows whatever else was out there, so we just looked at each other shyly.

"I can go under," he said, gesturing to a path under me and to the passenger seat.

He swung his right leg over the center console and began to slide over it as I went over with my right leg and placed my right hand against the driver's headrest for balance. When I turned to see his next move so I could go opposite and avoid getting all tangled up, our faces met just a half an inch apart.

I paused for a moment, looking into his eyes, and I could feel his nervous energy radiating from his body, so I knew he could definitely feel mine. I thought about the hotel room and wondered why I couldn't smell any repulsive odor coming from his mouth and I tried to recall if he had brushed his teeth or chewed gum since then. My head began to tilt slowly, starting to close the empty space between my lips and his. I wondered if this was such a good idea while simultaneously thinking how warm his full and perfect lips would feel. I closed my eyes, and my mouth was prepared for the kiss, but instead of feeling a kiss I felt his firm touch against my shoulders pressing me back. Then he caressed the left side of my face so gently with the tips of his warm fingers. He lightly framed the side of my face with his incredibly calm right hand, which sent chills through my body because of the tenderness of his touch. He looked deeply into my eyes, but there was sorrow—or was it fatigue in his eyes? I really couldn't tell.

"You're so beautiful," he said, and I could smell the sweet warmth of his breath as it fell upon my face like a warm towel soaked in lovely fragrances, how could that be? He stared at me for a moment longer but then he continued sliding into the passenger seat. I gave a tiny shake of my head when he wasn't looking as I attempted to clear it and focus on driving. I adjusted myself into the driver's seat and reached down in front of it to search for a seat adjuster.

"It's on the side," he said calmly.

"Thanks," I responded in a somewhat hurt and definitely puzzled voice. I don't understand why he refused my kiss, am I not attractive to him? Can he see inside my shredded heart and crippled emotions? Am I going too fast or did I already miss my chance by not being flirtatious, which is honestly something I have no clue of how to do. Why does it have to be so damn confusing!

I tried to divert my line of thought with a quick visit of my thumbs under my arms which reminded me that some fresh cuts were desperately needed. After adjusting my seat I checked to see if there was an even higher speed for the windshield wipers, because fastest was not near fast enough for the amount of rain that was falling, but when I put the car in drive the rain parted like the Red Sea opening up. It was like when driving in snow when the flakes come directly at you and then blow to the side right before they hit your windshield, except the rain was parting far ahead of the car, near where the headlight beams ended.

It was pretty neat; any direction I would look, the rain would part away so I could see clearly. I could even allow it closer so I could create figures and faces out of the rain by imagining them in my mind, so as I drove it was like detailed plays or scenes from a movie were taking place in front of me to keep me entertained. I looked over to Caleb to see he was constantly rubbing his eyes, trying to be sure of what he was seeing.

"Pretty cool, huh?" I said to him with a bit of excitement in my voice.

"Absolutely ... cool," he said in a very groggy voice.

I created an image of me in the rain with a detailed rose in my hand and let it go. It slowly came to the windshield while rotating, which was not as easy as it might sound, because I had to work with the speed of the car to make the rain hover. Then I let it gently smash into the windshield and disappear like a cup of water had been splashed against the window.

Feeling pretty talented, I looked at Caleb, and I don't know why but I was half expecting to see that he was reaching for the flower. But to my surprise, he was already sleeping, and I felt like kicking myself for having had those stupid schoolgirl thoughts running through my mind for the first time in my life.

I scraped at the wounds beneath my bandages once again and then focused on how my empty thoughts brought me great images and scenes in the rain outside of the windshield and they were only disturbed twice by Chester's face popping up in the middle of them, I noticed that every time he would pop up I accelerated until his image crashed violently into the windshield. I thought this could be considered therapeutic but at the same time increasingly dangerous for Chester if I ever saw him walking on the street.

Things were good, it was 3am and we were just minutes from going through Williston ND, so we were making great time especially in the rain, when suddenly Caleb's chest lurched forward, his back arching so severely that the top of his face buried itself into the backrest of his passenger seat. He held his right arm at the elbow tightly, and his right hand was frozen in such a tense position that I could see the bones of his knuckles pressing the color from his skin just before it began shivering from the pain he was obviously feeling in his hand or arm. I immediately swerved to the shoulder of the road, wondering if this was a nightly ritual for this guy or if it was a whole new kind of monster that I had to face tonight. Should I run screaming or begin to kick? I slammed the car into park and paused for a brief moment as I contemplated the consequences of waking up a sleepwalker ... sleep screamer, as he let out a howl—and that sort of painful scream could not be faked.

"Caleb, Caleb, wake up, you're dreaming!" I screamed at him, but he continued to howl in pain with his eyes shut tightly; was that because of the pain or because he was still asleep?

I grabbed his shoulders and had just begun shaking him when his eyes sprang open wider than I had seen eyes open before, and he stared in fear at his arm while still moaning in pain. I looked to his arm and saw the deliberate changing of his skin from pale white to a subtle red and then finally a bright red. His entire forearm and hand were swelling before my very eyes, and then they began to blacken and blister while sending out the smell of flesh and hair burning.

The skin had begun to crack, and it was like watching volcanic lava solidifying as the top layer hardened and turned black when it hit the cool air but then cracked from the shifting surface to reveal that below it was still a raging inferno. Small fires began to ignite on his hand and forearm, and I instinctively swatted at them to put them out, which turned Caleb's moans back into screams at an even higher level as the blackened skin peeled away at the touch of my hand.

I quickly grabbed my bag from the backseat and opened the driver's side door. I opened my bag, snagged a large sweatshirt, and held it out in the rain. When I focused on the sweatshirt it was as if the rain attacked it in dousing waves of water so heavy that I could hardly hold it. I swung to Caleb with it and in one swift move wrapped it around his affected hand and arm.

His screams seemed to ebb slightly, so I reached over him and flipped his door open while holding his arm up. I helped him lean out of his door so the rain could fall on the sweatshirt around his tortured arm. Once the rain hit it I willed the water to get colder and continue pouring directly on the sweatshirt. It must have caused him relief, because his screaming soon stopped completely, and he simply sat there moaning and shivering.

"We've got to get you to the hospital right now!" I insisted.

He turned to me, but I wasn't sure if he'd heard a thing that I said, and then his eyes began rolling up into his head as he passed out from the pain. I reached over him, closed the door, and headed straight to Williston to find the nearest hospital.

CHAPTER

Derrick's war

I had attended two schools every day for several years now, public school and a school that could be considered a college-by-night, but it was no normal college at all. No credits toward any accredited facility or anything like that, but the same courses. The night school had four college professors brought into LA who taught our group seven subjects per semester, and my group would be the first graduating class ever; from "prodigies" to "savants." All of this and much more were parts of madman Markus's "New World Order."

While walking to my car from day school—or should I say, regular public school—I began to think about how this whole thing had started in Markus's life. He hadn't chosen to watch his twin brother be mutilated in front of him by the police and National Guard one night during the riots. He hadn't wanted to be restrained and forced to watch his brother's life stomped out of him, and he certainly hadn't chosen to see it reenacted in his dreams nightly.

I hopped in the car and revved the meaty engine a couple of times. I wondered what it would be like to have a twin brother, one who finished my thoughts as I did his. To be so in tune with someone would be … would be like you were never alone in this fucked-up world, I guess. Never lonely. I can't imagine how it would feel to have that connection for thirteen years of your life and then to have it brutally destroyed in front of you. What God would do that? Create such a bond and then to have it shredded to pieces right in front of you? Maybe something was up there, but what the hell for? Everything I had gotten in life was gotten by me.

I'd almost bought into their sheepish ways of following God until Markus showed me the real.

I laughed to myself, thinking of how my moms used to drag me to the church till I was nine—all that talk about sacrificing yourself for yo fellow man and even your enemy? I looked hard to see that shit, and I never ever saw one person step in front of a bullet or push another person out the way of a bus that hit them instead. But I had seen people push others in the way of a bus. Hell, I'd seen gangstas grab innocent people and use them as human shields. If God was real than he needed to show me some real sacrifices, and then maybe we could talk. I laughed to myself at the thought of it all.

I wouldn't dog all of it 'cause for as bad as LA was, I always thought it was coo' how that block where the churches were was probably the safest place in the whole damn city, but still that shit never took to my ass. Like Markus said, "That's just people writing books to try and keep their sheep in line. Simply look at Jesus's color to understand that one." A mad-ass genius is still a genius, right?

It was all great; he provided us homes, vehicles, and educations that put us far above most high school students, in exchange for our services in an almost failure-proof way of selling his drugs. The drug-selling part had always been cloaked so deeply that even I didn't know to this day if any or all of the other nineteen students were selling for Markus in their high schools.

He looked like a hero in the community's eyes and like a lord on the streets, as he had united large gang sets of Bloods and Crips together as his silent partners out there. He put more money in their pockets than they'd ever had, and he had the ability to control gang-related diversions throughout most of California as needed to fit his objectives.

The good of it all confused me a lot, mainly because he was an atheist, but it all was unmasked two years ago when he informed us that he would be filing paperwork and funding the remaining costs of our college educations. All of us would leave his movement highly educated with career paths mapped out, all for the simple price of starting an epidemic.

Ever since then all I had really wanted was out, but subsequently punishment for errors from that day forward had changed from slaps on the wrist, to second chances and expulsion, to merciless disembodiments performed by the most unlikely of henchmen. The price of attempted desertion would be unimaginable and would most likely include your family as well.

Curtis and I had decided to ride together to this, our graduation day, and there he was waiting on the sidewalk outside of his house for me as I pulled up to the curb. Curtis hopped in and we took off for the Hive. "MIT, huh? You're going to have to wear that face even in your sleep, my man," I teased.

We called it "our face" when relating to Markus's New World Order; perfect English was the only way that Markus would have it. I had never appreciated Markus's criticism of slang because it was all we really knew up to the age of nine, and quite frankly, the only way you could survive in LA.

That was an argument I wouldn't have with Curtis. I mean, he was coo' and all, but the first two things Markus taught us was to trust no one, and that there was no place in the jungle that softness survived because a soft mutha fucka is a dead mutha fucka out here! I was always trying to teach Curtis the how to intimidate peeps but it was just not inside him, so I watched his back when I could.

"What can I say, it suits me. After all, MIT only admits less than 13 percent of applicants per year, and it's where Markus attended college," he said smugly.

"Well you're not Markus," I responded.

"Not yet," he said sincerely, and for some reason the thought chilled me. I thought about how he was the closest out of all of us to being exactly like Markus, following in his same footsteps.

I had always wanted to ask Curtis a few questions that would have gotten me killed if they ever got back to Markus, and even though we were graduating today by no means were we finished. I ran the question through my head to make sure I could back out of it if I needed to.

"Does it bother you that some of these people might be coo', or how you might feel after doing this?" I asked, but a little too sheepishly for how I'd wanted to deliver the question.

"Is that a joke? They never cared when they enslaved us and then made sure that we didn't learn how to read or write because they knew we would find the laws against their rules that allowed them to sanction us to be worthless pieces of property," he said quickly—too quickly and passionately to be just reciting from books.

"Come on, man, you know that none of those people are still around; they were these people's ancestors," I said.

"It's a moot point, Derrick. Essentially their ancestors couldn't give a shit about me, and from what I've seen in my life these people could care less about me, too, so now I'll mean something to this country's history whether they know it or not!" he said defiantly.

If I was going to continue this conversation it was going to have to be delicate, I was thinking, when he unexpectedly turned the tables on me, shifting his full attention to me and speaking very fast and defensively. "He orchestrated this inquisition, didn't he, Derrick? He doesn't believe that I'm ready and he instructed you to be my judge." Curtis leaned closer and I felt his focus shift to my steering wheel. I immediately glanced to the speedometer and instantly resented my heavy foot, as I was just clipping above seventy. I eased my foot from the accelerator even as I felt him coming closer still.

"If you find me to be inadequate, Derrick, are you going to be the one assigned to chop me into pieces? Does he see you as my best friend and subsequent wielder of the blade, Derrick?" my friend asked me in a sinister tone.

I knew I had to act now, because the whole conspiracy theory he was conceiving was gonna be my certain death should he run to Markus, and if he grabbed the steering wheel at this speed in this highway traffic our future was no brighter.

"What are you talking about, Curtis? No one instructed me to ask you anything you fucking spliff," I said with a jolly pitch. "Dude, you're the man in the eyes of Markus. To say that you, his damn doppelganger, are not ready would be like him saying he's not ready," I added, hoping that he would ease up because of the compliments.

"Oh … I just … I anticipated this night to be the greatest one of my life, and I'm having difficulty believing that it's actually transpiring. Just waiting for the proverbial wrench, you know what I mean? So when you asked those questions I naturally assumed …" he said apologetically, which made me feel pretty good about getting out of this alive—until he continued to speak. "Ironically, Derrick, the only logical explanation that I can come up with as to why you might ask me those questions would be because you, yourself are having second thoughts."

"Me? Are you serious?" I said with laughter. "Hell no, I'm good to go!" I said confidently as Curtis eased comfortably back into the passenger seat. The next few minutes were spent in an awkward silence while I ran through all of the possible thoughts Curtis might have in his mind right now.

"After all, he did try going through the legal systems for years to resolve the murder of his brother," Curtis said, and I was relieved that his mind was off of the questions I had asked.

"Man, I have to ask you, were you thinking about grabbing the wheel when you thought Markus sent me to question you?" I asked. He looked around, uneasy, as we were entering the parking lot to the Hive.

"Dude, don't beat a dead horse; I already said I feel like I'm going crazy over here. Besides, I have already divulged my regret earlier, so chill," he said absently.

Just then I spotted the source of his distraction, following his silent glare to see the group of foot soldiers; the Bloods and the Crips were hanging around the front of the complex that we called the Hive. He was staring at one in particular who went by the name of GutTer, spelled with the second *t* capitalized so people knew its true meaning. I was positive someone much smarter than him helped him with that name, because *stupid* is a huge step up for that cat.

GutTer hated Curtis with a vengeance even more fierce than he had for white people. GutTer elbowed a couple of his boys and pointed at us then huddled together closely so we couldn't see what they were doing with their hands. I parked my car next to Markus's red and black Viper, which was about the safest car in the hood, so I always parked by it whenever I got the chance. We went on with our daily walk from the parking lot to the front door, which most times was pretty uneventful, but you never knew what was going to go down when you were with the person known as the whitest brutha in the hood.

Nora's convertible VW bug swung into the parking spot that Curtis and I were just walking past, which made Curtis leap about three feet backward while dropping his books. He bent over with his hands on his knees, catching his breath from the scare, and Nora was laughing too hard to breathe. She cut her engine and hopped out.

"Are you ready for the big day, boys?" she asked with that alluring voice of hers while picking up Curtis's last book from the ground. She tilted her head sideways and spoke directly to Curtis. "You shouldn't be so jumpy; you know they sense fear." Her beautiful caramel-colored eyes twinkled; as if she weren't cute enough, "the powers that be" apparently felt they needed to also give her the most beautiful eyes imaginable. "Besides," she said seductively while looking Curtis up and down. "They're just jealous, boo." I imagined that she must practice this stuff night and day to be so damn good at it!

She had always been beautiful, but over the last year or two ... "Wow," I accidently said, and they both looked at me.

Curtis's look was of disbelief that I would ever let a response like that slip out of me, because I was definitely not the type of guy who overtly responded to a female's call for attention. Nora, well she just had a little accomplished smirk on her face as she slinked between Curtis and me, embracing both of our arms and leading us to the entrance. It was then that I noticed she didn't have any books with her. "Do you know something we don't?" I asked her knowingly.

"What up wit' my bitches?" GutTer barked out when we got close enough to hear him. Curtis began to slow down but Nora pulled him along so that we kept a united front. I suddenly looked at her in a new light, obviously willing to stand strong and against anything for this cause; I could see it in the way she walked now.

It didn't hurt that everyone assumed that she hung with Markus on a personal level, which for that matter would bring on a new brand of savage punishment for someone who hurt a hair on her head.

"Chill out, GutTer, no one's fucking with you!" Nora championed while letting our arms go and stepping ahead until she was between the two parties. I could tell that she hoped it would all stop there and we could go into the building, but GutTer's boys were already starting to circle us, which meant he intended for this to go much further. "Bitch, shut it 'fore I GutTer that pretty face of yours!" GutTer shouted while shoving her aside and heading straight for Curtis. She stumbled from the push and I quickly stepped forward and caught her before she fell.

After she had regained her balance I shifted my position and rushed to stand between GutTer and Curtis. GutTer and I glared into one another's eyes, neither of us willing to balk an inch. We were the exact same height at 6'2" but he was quite a bit larger than me in the muscles category; however, I could hold my own. Without hesitation he stepped forward until he and I were nose to nose.

"Aiight then, I'ma douse yo little fuckin' flame, nigga," he said as his eyes began to widen, which made him look even a little crazier than he usually did, which was hard to do. I actually saw his eyes starting to lose focus on mine without his moving in the slightest. Then his eyeballs began shaking so slightly that I wouldn't have noticed from a foot away, but up close and personal like this, well, I saw nothing else. My adrenaline began to rise quickly because those crazy eyes were for real and this shit was about to go down right now.

"Whatever it takes to teach yo ass not to touch a lady like that again, nigga. What the fuck you waitin' for bitch?" I shouted while looking into his eyes without an ounce of doubt that I wanted to rip his fucking head off. I tried to quiver my eyes slightly by looking back and forth between his eyeballs quickly, but I knew it couldn't get close to being as threatening as his mentally unstable eyes flickering between consciousness and some fucking crazy place he went in his mind to release the GutTer—and I eagerly awaited his arrival.

His boy Andre, who'd obviously seen this dude in action, knew we were just a blink away from ripping into each other old school when he shouted out, "GutTer, the trick ... make that bitch do the trick for us!"

GutTer's eyes slowed their quivering and he slowly began to focus on my eyes again. I could tell that he was easing down from his crazy place, but then suddenly he shifted his weight and threw his hand into his coat pocket. I started to lean forward to fight for the gun as it was coming out; my hand clutched his wrist as it came forward quickly, but then I released his wrist as quickly as I had snatched it when I saw his hand had nothing in it.

It was clear that he had done it on purpose and that his boys thought it was funny by their laughter, but GutTer didn't laugh, his eyes still intent on my face. "Give me somethin'!" he called out to his boys while backing away from me. I watched Andre reach into his pocket and pull out a box of stick matches.

I knew exactly where this was going now. Really ... this mutha fucka took crazy-ass behavior to a new level. Andre tossed the box to GutTer and I'd swear he didn't even glance in that direction; he simply shot his hand into the air and snagged the matches without even seeing them coming.

He pulled out a single match, flicked it at me. It bounced off of my shoulder and onto the ground. I looked down at it and then back up to him with a "fuck you" expression on my face. I couldn't believe that this shit was turning into a display of this little stupid parlor trick I could do. I looked around to each of his boys—five against essentially one and with only one outcome, which would be me, dead. So parlor trick it is.

"Aiight then. Bitch, here, you pick one," he said while tossing me the box of matches, which I caught. I rolled my eyes at him then picked out a single wooden match. I held it at the bottom of the stick between my thumb and forefinger. I pointed it directly at him, and with a flash the whole match ignited into a flame.

They all stepped back, shocked that the rumor was true, and I was somewhat shocked too because usually only after about fifteen seconds of concentration I could ignite just the red tip of the match whenever I'd done this odd little trick before. This was much quicker and the whole match … I was a little confused, but it obviously had to do with my current adrenaline level.

I was still pretty angry, and I could feel the source of another heat surge inside of me rising. It was strangely easier to identify now as it formulated in my gut like an invisible piece of *fiery will* expelled from me to wherever I directed it. I flicked the whole box back at GutTer with a tiny piece of my fiery will traveling right behind it.

Just as he caught the box of matches in his hand my will had caught up to it, and the whole box ignited into a flame, charring his hand. Without hesitation or thought, GutTer was coming at me—he came so quickly that I didn't even have time to drop down into a defensive stance.

Just before he crashed into me his boy Andre slammed into him, and they soared off to my left, both hitting the ground hard. I assumed he did that to protect his crew from the wrath of Markus.

"Go!" Andre screamed to us as GutTer was rolling on top of Andre and striking down with his fist to Andre's jaw. The others in his crew rushed and grabbed GutTer's arm as it was bringing another punch down to Andre's face. They hauled him off of Andre as Nora grabbed our arms and dragged us into the building.

I looked back at GutTer before the door closed; he was calming down but still stared at me with one of those looks of "I'm going to kill you if it's the last thing I do." I did my best to return the exact same look, but all I could think about was that I couldn't wait to get the hell out of this place; eighteen years of this shit was enough to last a lifetime. Fucks like that were everywhere here, and they could give a shit if they lived or died, so how much could someone else's life be worth to them?

Inside the entrance stood our whole class with concerned expressions on their faces—all but Sean, who was nearest to the door with his arms crossed and a smug look on his face.

"What's going on out there?" Sean asked while safely trying to peek out of the door before it swung shut. "Sound like fight to me," he said, slyly looking back in Nora's direction.

"If that's what it sound like to you, why didn't come out to help us?" Nora snapped back at him.

Sean shifted an uncomfortable glance around at our classmates in the entryway; most of the guys looked at the floor quickly. One of the two girls began to speak up as if she had tried telling them the same thing when Sean cut her off quickly.

"We figured wasn't none of our business!" he said defensively. The three of us looked at each other and began to walk toward our classroom. Sean lightly took hold of Nora's arm as we walked off, and she pulled away from him with a disgusted look on her face.

"So what up, what was it all about?" Sean asked, trying to sound concerned. Nora threw her hands onto her hips and strutted out her words while moving her neck in rhythm. "As you said, mutha fucka, ain't none of yo damn business." And then she turned to walk off with us. When he reached for her arm again he received the same response of her pulling away, but this time she spoke with anger in her voice. "What now?"

He held his hands up as if he were surrendering and then leaned in toward her and spoke with a lower voice, but by no means modestly. "I was just thinking since our colleges will be really close, you would want to get together sometimes—I mean maybe you can drop some old thing and try a fresh young buck like me." He flashed a few looks around the place with a big smile on his face, like he was in a groove or something.

Nora took a small step backward and crossed her arms while looking him up and down slowly. "You maybe on to something," she said in a very sultry voice. Curtis and I shot confused looks at one another, and Sean's face was momentarily surprised, but then he played it off by nodding with a big smile on his face.

"Really ... I mean, I knew you would come round."

Nora looked around with a confused look on her face, and everyone was looking at her strangely. Then she threw her hands over her mouth with an "Oh ..." followed by a giggle that rapidly changed into laughter. She tried to contain herself. "Oh, I'm sorry ... you thought I meant about you and me?" Her laughter was mocking. "No, Sean, I meant that you actually ... had a thought ... you might be on to something there?" She was holding her side now while continuing to laugh. "No, Sean, don't you worry your little ..." she sized him up and down once again with her eyes while still laughing, "your little head about me in that category." And then she somehow was able to take taunting laughter into a sensual tone. "I am more than fulfilled in that area, and believe me when I say that you couldn't get close to filling his shoes."

With that she abruptly spun, linked her arms with Curtis's and mine, then we walked off to the classroom under a loud chorus of laughter and chatter as the students firmly grasped Sean's public humiliation and were not about to let him live it down.

Nora tugged on my arm so I would lower my head for her to whisper, "You're going to have to let me in on how you do that fire trick, you know." I felt a little relief that we reached the classroom and that was the end of that discussion, but still I was wondering myself about why my fiery will was so much stronger now.

As we all piled into the room the chatter faded when we all saw Marcus sitting silently, looking down at his hands, rolling them slowly together. I'd seen him do this many times before, but only when he was thinking of how to properly phrase his thoughts. He usually spent short moments rolling his hands together when talking to the foot soldiers.

There was an uneasy feeling about the scene; most of us were looking around the room at one another inquisitively. He was clearly emotional and twisted in thought. Was it because we were the first graduating class that would be implementing his plan nationally, America's introduction to the second phase, which he'd been plotting for years?

"I heard a man speaking on the radio today about the racial conflicts in the '60s. This man trivialized our entire history as unfortunate. He was confused about why black people would lash out in the '60s when everything had changed for us," Markus said. As he spoke I looked around the room and noticed that most of the students were hanging on his every word.

"This man asked why we would complain about the neighborhoods that they allowed us to buy homes in, which basically was an experiment in segregation where they allowed black families to buy homes in small portions of large cities. They would overpopulate these areas with families— and here's the kicker."

Markus walked around to the right side of his desk and tried to run his fingers over the smooth surface of one of his many crystal sculptures, which were rumored to have cost $2,000 just for the designer to draft each of them and anywhere from $25,000 to $100,000 cash (like most of his transactions, no paper records, no worries) to have each one custom sculpted in New York. I saw Markus's hands begin to shake from his anger, and after just a moment he decided to just pick one of the sculptures up, maybe to cover up the trembling so we wouldn't notice. It was one of the most detailed pieces of his collection, a cargo airplane, and if you looked close enough you could see the New World Order's crest on the crates in the airplane and on the crates parachuting to the ground.

Markus looked at us as his entire body was starting to tremble with emotion. He turned his back to us and then carefully placed the crystal piece back on his desk, and I heard a collective sigh of relief, including my own. He turned back to us after composing himself and continued to speak.

"As I was saying, the kicker of it was that these overpopulated areas of each city were guarded from the outside by the police whose directive was to keep us in, like prison guards keeping the prisoners from escaping— granted, there were no fences locking us in, but cross that invisible line and you would find yourself in a hospital, prison, or missing indefinitely. Cops were rewarded by how sanitized they kept the neighboring white communities of black people. Real estate agents would receive 100 percent declines on applications by black people outside of that overpopulated area."

Nora's hand went up immediately but it was met with one quick motion of Markus's hands and a piercing glance. With an incredulous expression on her face, she pulled her hand back down even faster than it had gone up. This took the entire room by surprise and produced a loud, inappropriate snort from Sean. Markus glared at him even more fiercely.

"The man I heard on the radio today said that every black person was at fault because we didn't side with the oppressive, corrupt police force and the government-sanctioned National Guard, but especially in Watts during that five-day-long bloodbath of white man and his guns, versus blacks with only bricks and rocks to lob in retaliation … bricks which came from the abandoned, decrepit buildings that were never removed or rebuilt by our great city."

Markus sent his left hand slamming into the heavy lead-crystal sculpture, the impact of his blow snapping it into three large pieces that flew through the air and smashed into the wall behind the desk, shattering them into tiny crystal fragments that slid on the floor in every direction. One thick piece of crystal pierced deeply into the wall and left a six-inch jagged shard sticking out from the wall.

The room was categorically silent; not even Sean was dumb enough to interrupt Markus at this level of rage. I looked around the room at the terrified faces, wondering what would happen next—all of the faces frozen except for Sean's and Nora's. Nora looked like she wanted to run up to the stage and embrace Markus, and Sean's face simply looked bored and covetous.

Once again Markus composed himself enough to speak. "It is that very egotism that they've exacted by destroying countless black people's lives that will be their demise!" He moved so effortlessly to the front of the stage that the sounds of his wingtip shoes barely made a discernable sound against the polished hardwood stage amid a room of captivated students so quiet that you could literally hear a pin drop on a carpet. He stretched his arms out to us and spoke.

"What you, the 'inaugural nineteen' graduates mean to New World Order is momentous; what you mean to anyone of color is immeasurable and will heal centuries of injustices," Markus said eloquently, and it was immediately followed by an outburst from Sean.

"Yo dog, you mean twenty, right?"

I could immediately see the remorse on Sean's face for using slang. Markus slightly shook his head while looking at Sean intensely. "English, for fuck's sake! Have I taught you children nothing in all of these years?" he snapped out quickly.

"I'm just saying that there are twenty of us, sir, and you just said nineteen," Sean said while rolling his eyes, sounding like an angry child that was just scolded.

"Nineteen," was all that Markus said to respond to that, and then he continued to address the class. "This information is a bit dated because I believe they stopped doing studies like this after reading these results. Drug usage data in virtually all areas of America show that white people consume more than 60 percent of the drugs, yet more than 90 percent of people incarcerated for drugs are black, and the numbers for those given life sentences because of drug activity are even greater. This is their American justice system, which lost all of its credibility in 1989—does anyone know what happened in 1989?" he asked as he virtually glided down the stairs to address us directly.

After a pause: "In 1989 the first wrongfully convicted man was released from prison because DNA evidence proved beyond the shadow of a doubt that he was innocent of the crime that he was convicted of! That first case proved *one* undisputable fact ... their justice system is based on prejudices of race, religion, creed, income, location, and absolutely any other excuse that they can conjure to let us know that this is their country and that their foot still remains upon our throats!" Markus shouted out to us.

It seemed like he was heading back up that excitement ladder again, but this time his words were met with cheers from the students, as if a preacher had just made a strong point for God during church.

"Since that day there have been more than 250 convicted innocent men that spent more than ten years of their lives in prison then were released due to DNA," he said as disgusted sounds murmured throughout the classroom.

"The question I ask is, why were they convicted in the first place? Since DNA, there have been tens of thousands that were prime suspects in cases that were released later because DNA proved they were wrongfully accused of the crime. False accusation that served the sole purpose of breaking up our family units! And then they complain that our black children's problems stem from not having two parents in the home!" he said triumphantly. "Why the hell do you think that is, white America? We were all family units when we bought homes in those tiny sections of the cities you allowed us to live in!" he concluded, almost breathless.

The supportive jeers in the room were significantly louder now and some of the students were even out of their seats cheering him on. Even I found myself standing in support of what he was saying.

"Their sins have come to roost! We shall take their futures from them, as they have always taken ours from us!"

We all chanted in unison, "Let it burn! Let it burn!" The adrenaline fumed through the room so strong that you could feel it connecting us all as one, like a magnetic bond, and I found myself wishing, if only it could be done another way. Everyone settled down as Markus continued to speak

"This may come as a surprise for most of you, but each of you were selling in your respective schools, and everyone was above any suspicion whatsoever—that is, all of you but one," Markus continued on a new subject, looking at Sean, who was now beginning to realize that he might be the one not graduating today.

"You were using the exact same process you will be using in your colleges, but the one difference is that you will be using white distributors to move the product and white dealers to sell these drugs to their white friends because, as the stats show, they're the ones using it and not being arrested. They will make more money than they can imagine, and because this drug has been manufactured to be ten times more addictive than any drug previously known to America—and yes, that includes crack—this means they will be as loyal as dogs to you."

I looked around the room to see the students whispering to one another with rather congenial expressions. We were clearly good at what we did in order not to have had a single person using or distributing the drugs for us mentioning our name—and that was with regular drugs. At the same time, I shivered at the thought of how this one mad genius could literally change this country drastically, and I couldn't get the image of Hitler out of my mind.

I really couldn't believe it, but after all of the signs given to Sean so far, he had his hand up once again. Markus was very irritated when he called on Sean this time.

"May I ask who's not going to graduate and if there is a chance that that person can do it next year?"

"It's you, Sean, and no—oh, and to address your next question, it's because you, Sean, are quite predictable," Markus accused. "Do you recall our combat training that was brought into the boxing ring? You believed Derrick and Kenneth were too afraid to take on their opponents when it was quite the opposite. Brains' over brawn scores points in virtually all of our teachings and in absolutely all of life's tests.

"Don't get me wrong—you were entertaining, even motivational to anyone watching it. But ultimately all of the fights that day were in one of three categories." Markus looked around the room. "Who can tell Sean one of Sun Tzu's most basic rules when going into a battle?" Markus asked, and nineteen hands went up. "Perry," Markus chose confidently.

Perry adjusted himself in his chair so he was sitting up high before he answered. "The first of three basic rules when heading into battle is that if you have assessed your opponent is weaker than your armies, then bait them in, feign disorder, lack of leadership, lack of loyalty. Make them feel overconfident, lure them in, and then decimate them!"

Markus turned his attention back to Sean. "Those in that category did so and all won decisively. Can someone tell Sean the next basic rule?" Everyone's hand went up again. "Nora, enlighten us," Markus said, and she instantly perked up when she began to speak in her fantastically seductive voice, which sounded more like a sex line operator rather than an eighteen-year-old high school student.

Damned if I knew how she was able to take her seductive voice rhythmically up and down so smoothly, nearly imperceptibly changing pitches within the very same tone and at the most perfect times of her delivery. It made you feel like her voice had a motion, starting slower and then increasing its pace, mixed with subtle pitch adjustments, and in the end leaving you feeling emotionally, physically, and in some way consciously bonded with her.

"If evenly matched or, as Sun Tzu so eloquently puts it … if he is secure at all points, be prepared for him. Essentially meaning to fight, but … do your very best; it may in the end rely solely on which side is most in accordance with you—I mean, their ruler—so that they will follow him regardless of their own lives. The cause is much greater than any one life."

There was a long pause after she finished talking, and even the other two girls in the room stared, one of them biting her lower lip while the other just gawked. Nora's delivery was so astounding that even Sean had completely forgotten about his situation for a moment and simply stared, lost in her.

I realized that this was the first time I could remember when I wasn't caught up in her hypnotic delivery. Something she said had pulled me out. It was when she said *you*, meaning Markus, and followed that with being in accordance, as if there were no other choices in life other than fighting to the death for this cause. My stomach turned at how bleak that really sounded when one saw this movement as a deeply conceived, elaborate plot of revenge that would most likely blanket this country.

"The last rule is, when outnumbered or overmatched, retreat and live to fight another day," Markus said directly to Sean. "I want you to know that I blame myself for you, Sean, because I should have never allowed you into the program. You were a fantastic foot soldier, and against my better judgment I allowed you to sell me on the fact that you believed you could do it. Look at us now, to have four students at Wilson High School name you as a source for getting drugs. Well, Sean, that's why nineteen is the number."

Sean's face dropped instantly as it seemed to dawn on him that his future was shifting before his very eyes, and it was not a spot as a prodigy that he was fighting to keep, but the fight was now a fight for his life. Markus approached him, and Sean stood nervously from his seat, unsure of what to do. Markus put his right around the boy as if he were consoling him as they walked to the front of the room, up the stairs on the right side of the desk. I instantly focused on the shard embedded into the wall.

In an instant Markus shifted his weight to the left as fast as a cat, his right arm sliding under Sean's neck and into a chokehold. Sean's hands grabbed at Markus's forearm in a futile attempt to break his hold, which was cutting off his airflow. All nineteen of us remaining students adjusted in our seats to get a better vantage point, not believing what we were watching.

When Sean's struggles started to weaken Markus turned him to face the shard in the wall and then made one sudden move, crashing his right knee across the back of Sean's knees, sending them collapsing onto the floor so fast that Markus had to pull back on Sean to keep him from being impaled by the shard. Sean opened his eyes to see the very tip of the crystal shard less than an inch from the lens of his right one. Tears welled up in Sean's eyes, and as the first tear began to roll down his right cheek, Markus tilted his head up just slightly and leaned him in so the tip of the crystal shard pierced the falling tear and the cheek just slightly, introducing a swirl of blood that changed the clear teardrop into red.

Markus put his mouth close to Sean's ear. "But like I said … I blame myself for your situation." He then pressed Sean's face into the crystal point a half inch deep and turned Sean's head to the left, slicing his right cheek across to his ear. Blood gushed from Sean's face as Markus released his chokehold and helped Sean's trembling, weak body back to his feet.

Markus pushed a button on his desk and two foot soldiers marched into the room. I recognized both of them, but one stood out painfully obvious, since he was Sean's roomie and number-one dude, Casper. Casper looked nervous, and I couldn't help but think, was it his concern for his dude Sean or for himself?

They retrieved Sean, and as they exited the room, Markus shouted out casually, "Sean, you haven't been telling people about this movement, have you?"

The soldiers stopped with Sean as he looked back at Markus and barely coughed out his response. "N-no sir, I-I would Nev-errr …" The words trailed off as his head dropped, I presumed into unconsciousness, and I wondered if I would ever know how this one would end.

"You'll have your chance to sell me on that!" Markus said loudly, as if he were proud of himself for giving someone a second chance.

"There are those who will jeopardize our movement, and I will not stand for that—nor should any of you!" Markus said sternly. "As I said before, you nineteen will be our initial insurgence on the colleges across this country and will begin to steal *their* children's futures right from under their noses."

He laughed maniacally to himself. "And they actually thought that crack was addictive after just one hit. Wait till they get a whiff of this!"

CHAPTER

Derrick's Not-So-Hard Choice

My eyes mindlessly followed my headlights as I turned right into my driveway and pulled up to the house, but not even a full moment later I realized that I had just seen a figure standing in the shadows beside or behind the low bushes between my house and my neighbor's. Who was that? Is he still there?

I held my breath, waiting for bullets to riddle my car and me. I waited a moment before breathing a sigh of relief and reached under my seat where I always kept my two-and-a-half-foot-long heavy steel rod. I gripped it tightly, and I could feel it slipping in my grasp from the moisture of my palm.

I dried my hands on my pants to get a better grasp on my weapon. I had no idea why I ever thought that a rod could help in a situation like this. You don't bring a knife to a gun fight, I scolded myself. Why had I not at least gotten a rod with a nice handle on one end?

I leaped out of the car heading in the direction of where I thought saw the figure, but I stopped dead in my tracks the moment I saw the shadowy figure standing there, as still as a statue, just watching me.

The figure seemed too small to be GutTer, and I instantly began going through my mind to recall the sizes of the boys of his who were with him earlier. I peered around for any movement and listened for any sounds from the area. I raised the steel bar in a threatening manner.

"Is that you, GutTer? Step out let's get started, mutha fucka."

The figure crouched down quickly, taking a step back. The move allowed me to see the figure more clearly against the dim street lighting. When I made out a female figure I felt a little relaxed for a split second, but what kind of woman would be stupid enough to be out here alone at this time of night? Once again I began looking around for others with her.

"I'm not ... GutTer ..." called a shaky female voice from the bushes.

"Who's with you, where are they, where's GutTer?" I screamed.

Her hands went up in surrender, and her voice actually managed to sound even shakier than at first. "I don't—I swear I don't know anyone by the name of GutTer. Please, I'm alone; I'm just looking for someone."

I took a couple of steps toward her and could make out long, dark hair that flowed down into the shadows. Her dialect proved she was definitely not from around here because she sounded white. She seriously had no right being out at night in this neighborhood—or more importantly, every neighborhood around this one, which were ten times worse.

I could sense the anxiety as she nervously took a defensive posture. I stopped walking toward her and she raised her chin but maintained her stance.

"You're looking for someone by searching through bushes around this neighborhood? A neighborhood you shouldn't be in at all," I said.

"No, not in the bushes!" she replied. "I'm waiting in these bushes because I was told that I would find Derrick here. I was told that Derrick drives a flashy Lexus and lives at this address," she said while pointing at the Lexus Marcus had bought me on my sixteenth birthday. He did that for each prodigy. "So can I—find Derrick here?" she asked, but it sounded more like a statement than a question.

"Maybe. What do you want him for, and who are you?" I demanded.

She stepped across the cover of shadows and entered the light, and her beauty caught me completely off guard, forcing me to momentarily drop all of my defenses. She moved gracefully but aware, like a cat's sleek, defensive saunter. Her face was beautiful with lips so full and delicate that I imagined they would barely show movement as she spoke, which was saying a lot for a white woman. High cheekbones, strong jawline, and eyes so sultry that I was tempted to keep all of my defenses down.

"I'm Elise. I ... we need your help badly; I can't even begin to explain," she said, and I noticed I was right about the movement of her lips.

"My help? I don't even know you, why should I help you with anything?" I replied, feeling stupid after asking a question that had such an obvious answer as to why any man would want to help her. She looked stuck, confused about what to say next, and simply looked to the ground, dejected. I began to back up toward my car to lock it up.

"Why don't you go home to whoever 'we' is and figure that one out before you come back?" I looked around again. "How did you get here, anyway?" I asked, puzzled.

"Taxi," she answered quietly while still looking down. I felt bad for her, so I figured I would at least make sure she got back out of the hood safely.

"Can I call you a taxi?" I asked.

"Not if you have ever wanted to know who the people in blue are—you know, the ones that only you can see. Or why you have some strange control over fire," she said crisply, rendering me completely speechless.

The fire thing she could have known from many people, especially GutTer. I had just put the key into the car door to lock it but pulled it straight back out without doing so. I turned and walked directly to her. She didn't flinch or take on a defensive position at all.

There was no way she could have known anything about the blue soldiers; my moms didn't even know about that—I had never told a single soul! "Who or what are you?" I demanded.

"I'm Elise—"

I stopped her there with that tired response.

"No, Elise, who sent you here and why?" I was now standing close enough to her that her fragrance was identifiable, nothing fancy, recently bathed, and she obviously spent more money on her shampoo than on her bath soap because I caught a hint of a honey satin that caused me inhale deeply when its scent hit me.

"I honestly don't know. I mean, there's just me and Caleb—Caleb has dreams. I know that sounds a bit off but he does ... and these dreams hurt him, Derrick, these dreams leave horrible wounds, and I swear to you, Derrick ..." A tear began to roll down her cheek and she looked away, wiping the tear away at the same time. She took a deep breath, turning back to me and pleading with her eyes as she continued to speak. "I swear, Derrick, he's dead if you don't talk to him now."

"Why tonight? Why can't we do this tomorrow instead?"

Her answer was short but weighty. "Because I don't know if he has a tomorrow, Derrick."

I walked to the passenger door and opened it. I waved my steel bar in the air aggressively. "If this is anything other than what you're telling me, I swear to you that this bar will be lodged in that pretty little face of yours. Do we understand each other?"

Oddly, the tone she answered in was a relieved one. "Absolutely, no tricks, I swear," she said while running to the passenger side and hopping in. I got in and we were off.

We pulled into the Kingston Hotel parking lot off of South Atlantic Avenue and South Atlantic Drive, which was about three miles from my house. All she would say to all my questions about this Caleb guy was "you'll see when you get there" and that "he will explain." The Kingston Hotel was a single-level run-down hotel that most occupants leased out for months at a time, or by the hour. I began to wonder how long they had been here. There were people scattered around the outsides of their rooms and in cars doing transactions of various kinds.

Outside of room 23 there were three broken medication vials that had apparently fallen—just my luck, at the exact door where she stopped and inserted the key. I tried to catch a name or type of medication from the label as we entered the room but the poor lighting combined with Elise's fast pace made it impossible to read. They obviously had not been here long because those broken prescription vials would be an invitation to all junkies in the area—which this area was full of.

The sight of the broken meds made me tighten up even more if room 23's occupants were junkies, which had my hand gripping my weapon tighter. When we stepped into the room I felt the rush of warm, humidified air. The room was very clean, much cleaner than a paid maid would have done and I wondered why so tidy inside but leave the small mess outside.

The room had a separate bedroom, the door partially open, and through the crack I could see that the lights were on and that there were machines running and LED lights flickering. Elise pushed the bedroom door open and spoke softly into the room. "Caleb, Derrick is here."

A muffled but surprisingly excited voice answered from the room. "Really? That's great. Will he come in?"

My attention shifted to the large, clear plastic tent-like thing hanging over a bed, which distorted my vision of who was inside of it lying on the bed. Suddenly my mind flashed to the blue people, my special abilities with fire, and to freaky science fiction movies as the figure behind the curtain raised its arm painfully slow, gesturing for me to come closer.

"Please, Derrick, sit over here beside me," he said, and I realized his voice was being muffled by the plastic curtain. I tried to look around the curtain while meandering around the foot of the bed to a chair on the other side.

I sat in the chair and could see through the plastic a bit more clearly from this seat. He looked human, as best I could tell, but with dark arms, legs, and torso. I couldn't quite make out if he was a black person with socks, gloves, and bandages or a white person with clothes on. Were those blue shorts, or …?

"Derrick, could you help me out and unzip this thing? I would like to speak to you face-to-face if you don't mind," Caleb said.

I saw a zipper starting down by my left foot and extending up and across the top of the plastic curtain then heading back down to the foot of the bed, and I figured that this was the side he got in and out on. My heart raced, and I found myself hesitating to reach for the zipper.

"Maybe you can just tell me what all this shit's about first," I said while taking a firm grip on the steel rod in my right hand.

He paused for a moment of thought before speaking again. "Yes of course; I'm sorry for not … for assuming that you would want to see what's inside of my plastic tomb here, but I'm not contagious, I swear."

I nodded slowly while looking at the table full of pills and ointments, even some injectable meds, and best I could tell they were all forms of pain meds—no antibiotics, though, which eased that thought but still left about a million questions to be answered.

Caleb coughed for a moment, cleared his throat, and spoke with a raspy voice. "Derrick, do you have any idea who the blue people are?" he asked, and I remained quiet. "Yeah neither do we. I was hoping you could shed some light about them for us."

They're looking for answers from me, is that why I'm here? I looked up suspiciously to locate Elise, who was just then walking back into the room, and I raised my weapon to my lap to assure them that we had just run into a problem. I stared at Elise as she walked up beside my chair with a curious look on her face.

"I was told that you had the answer to that question," I said to Caleb accusingly while standing up from my seat and backing into the medicine table, sending a few of the medicine bottles to the floor. I was now at an angle to see them both, and the chair was now serving as an obstacle between Elise and me.

What stupid situation had I gotten myself into? I began to think of my training in hopes that my wits and brawn could get me out of whatever this was. How stupid could I be to have been drawn in like this?

"Derrick, please, you're safe here with us. We would never try to hurt you," Caleb said quickly, and Elise raised her hands to show no attack posture.

"I didn't say we had those answers, Derrick," she added defensively.

"The hell you didn't! I told you if this was anything other than what you said—" I raised the rod as if I was going to strike her, edging in her direction, and she backed away. I parlayed around her and backed up toward the door to get the hell out of this place.

"Elise, I said no lies; we can't lie to one another about anything in order to make it through this!" Caleb said to Elise, but I felt like he was trying to send me a message too.

"He was calling me a taxi, Caleb, he had said no! And you're not making it through the night without him! What the fuck did you want me to do, let him go into his house to sleep the night away as you lay here and *died*?" Elise screamed out in anger. I was just about to clear the door and run the fuck out of there.

Caleb beckoned, "Derrick, what she's saying is completely true, and I've accepted that. I also understand if you want to leave, but please, just one more moment, I swear!"

Elise hadn't come any closer to me since I made my way past her, and Caleb has barely moved in his "plastic tomb," as he called it, so I stopped at the door and glanced around behind me to make sure no one else had come into the front room of the hotel apartment. When I looked back at them they still hadn't moved an inch, so I felt safe enough to hear him out. "What?" I said with a frustration-soaked tone.

Caleb attempted to sit up but collapsed back down onto his pillow, breathing hard and coughing. After a moment he began to speak again. "You have a gift of fire, right?" he asked me.

"I wouldn't call it a gift—a parlor trick at best, but yeah, I can start matches without striking them, so what?" I replied, salty.

"Have you noticed any changes in that gift … in that ability recently?" Caleb asked.

I thought of the whole book of matches that I'd ignited in GutTer's hand and began thinking of how this guy could possibly know that unless he knew someone like GutTer, but a scheme like this was far too sophisticated for GutTer to have thought up, but I still don't trust them so I simply lied. "No," I answered dryly.

"Oh," Caleb replied, disappointed. "Well could you just try once before you go? And I promise you that we won't bother you again," he said sincerely.

I rolled my eyes at the two of them and called for my little source of fiery will that I would use to start matches—but I didn't have to look for it; it was already waiting for me, and it was not so little. I brought it up and directed it out of my outstretched hands, but rather than a tiny bead of fiery will flying through the air, it—no, they came out as streams of fairly continuous flames torching from my hands.

The flames were headed straight for Caleb's plastic tomb, and I quickly pulled my hands upward, directing the rolling, breathing flame to arch to the ceiling, leaving a charred trail on the ceiling from just above the tent stretching out until it was directly above me. Flames continued to hurl from my hands and began to catch the ceiling on fire. I regained my senses and clinched my hands into fists, which instantly stopped the flames coming out.

I was shocked more by what I was just able to do than by the tent melting down quickly at the foot of the bed; small flames ran downward, igniting into larger flames and sending the fumes of burning plastic throughout the room. Elise quickly raised her hands toward a pitcher of water across the room from her. The water flew out of the pitcher in a thick tubular stream straight to the plastic tomb, dousing the flames I had accidentally ignited. The water continued to soak the flames, and it was clear that more water was coming out of that pitcher than was in it to begin with. I was staring at the pitcher of water, amazed, when Elise startled me with the urgency in her voice.

"Put the oxygen mask on him, hurry!" she screamed, and I quickly looked at Caleb. His eyes were squeezed shut tight, his teeth clenched from the pain. He began gasping for air. I turned to locate the oxygen tank, flung the mask onto his head, and it automatically began to run.

Elise closed her eyes while reaching her hands out toward the pitcher of water again, but this time a mist came from the pitcher of water and created a constant stream directly to Caleb that covered his body like a blanket. The constant flow of mist poured over the edges of the bed and hovered low on the ground, which started to make the room look like a frigid, macabre scene from a horror movie. I could feel the frosty nip of the mist as it began to fill the entire room.

I realized that I had put the oxygen mask on a stark-white face. He wasn't a black man wearing gloves, socks, or bandages around his head.

What I had been seeing was his bare skin. His arms and legs had been charred, and now there was barely enough burned muscle and skin to hold his limbs together. I couldn't be sure, but it looked as if some of the blackness had been scraped away and left little exposed flesh, mostly only tendons and bone remaining.

"Shouldn't he be bandaged? Hell, shouldn't he be in a hospital?" I asked Elise, and she opened her eyes to give me an agitated look.

"The doctors told us to do that but bandages really just cause much more pain and damage when they catch on fire and have to be ripped from him as *it* is happening, since the burning seems to start inside of the bones ... Removing burning bandages can also remove the melting flesh down to his bones as well," she said to me in an irritated tone, immediately closing her eyes again to concentrate.

I looked at the pitcher and noticed that it was still full to the top with water but also that while she was talking to me the constant stream of mist had stopped. Now that she was intent again the mist resumed racing to continue covering Caleb's body.

I thought it would be best if I left her to focus on what she was doing, and being from California, I really wasn't used to cold temperatures— I left the room and closed the door behind me, walked to the couch, and began examining my hands curiously.

After about two hours Elise came out of the room to find me sending small flames from one hand to another and casting them out to dissipate into thin air. I could see the frost from her breath as she spoke with a shivering voice. "He's better now and wanted me to see if you were still here because he needs to talk to you."

I could see her relax more with every step she took toward my extremely warm area of the room, and the color was returning to her face as she approached. I gave her a nod and headed toward the other room as she sat exactly where I was sitting and reached for a blanket to wrap-up in.

"I'm sorry about that, Derrick, but you can't begin to imagine how glad I am you stayed. Thank you," Caleb said, and for the first time I was able to see him clearly. His eyes were so innocent and pulled down at their corners, making them look like those of a baby basset Hound. They were so blue that they looked like the idyllic scenes of an ocean shown on TV and in magazines.

I glanced at his wounds and almost felt like throwing up, so I turned my attention back to his unharmed face. "It's coo', but why aren't your hands, feet, or face burned?" I asked.

"I don't know; I guess they're next," he said.

I moved around in my chair, unsettled by the excessive cruelty he had obviously endured and the fact that some of his flesh even smelled of decay; I wondered, why does he continue this? "Was that what takes place—what just happened, I mean?" I asked him.

Caleb laughed unconvincingly. "No, that's nothing compared to the pain that you cause me when I can't fight my sleep anymore."

I peered at him incredulously. "Me?" I said flatly.

He attempted to sit up again, but as before, he collapsed flat, grimacing in pain for a moment before he was able to speak again. "Not you directly, but until you choose to join us this will continue." He paused for a moment to deal with the pain before continuing. "When I sleep ... I get to know about you and your life, where you are, and since three of us are in the same area I also get to know about other ... important people and situations in your life. But the cost is what you see here." His face contorted once again in reaction to the pain, and then he began coughing again, but this time a small stream of blood fell from the corners of his mouth.

"There seems to be a time clock placed on us to find you and to unite us all—with you it's fire, and until Elise joined me it was dreams of water, which meant that I got to drown more times in a night than I ever would have imagined was possible in a single lifetime," he said.

He was asking me to join them, but this was ... what was this? "Join you to do what? I assume you're going to tell me that earth and air are the last two to join this group, right?" I spouted sarcastically.

"Yes, as a matter of fact, I would expect those to be next if things work out here. But we don't know what this is all about or if there's anything that we're supposed to be doing," he said sadly. "Our powers will be greatest when we are all together," he concluded confidently.

I leaned in toward him and spoke very directly. "You've got to be joking!" The innocent, surprised expression on his face blended with sincere confusion told me he was serious about everything he was saying. "I have a life and obligations that will see me dead before seeing me walk away. I have a family to protect," I continued. "You have no idea what and who I am dealing with in my life and you want me just to pick my ass up and join you two on what could be some stranger-than-fiction wild goose chase?" I said in one breath, then I paused for a second before continuing. "Man, let's be real. What's option two? And make it a way I can keep this fire power shit, too." But even as I said all this, in the back of my mind I was starting to think that this could be a perfect way to get the fuck out of Markus's crazy world.

Caleb shook his head while looking down. He said, "First of all, Derrick, I believe these gifts are from God, so I have no idea of any way to keep them except for us all being together."

"First and last of all on this subject, Caleb, I don't believe in that God stuff, so save your breath 'cause I'm not the one!" I said first 'cause I definitely wanted that shit out the way. I was not hearing some Bible thumper trying to convert my ass!

Caleb looked hurt but continued on. "I know more than you would imagine, Derrick; I have dreams, remember? I know what Markus wants you and your classmates to do."

I was startled by his mentioning Markus's name. "And what *exactly* is it that you think you know?" I asked him directly, feeling obligated to pump him for info.

"He wants the prodigies to quietly befriend students in various colleges that each of you will be attending." Caleb paused to think for a moment. "How did he say it? Oh yeah—everyone experiments, but imagine these kids away from home for the first time, and here you are giving them the best of any drug they desire. But it doesn't stop there, does it, Derrick?"

I slowly began shaking my head while leaning closer to him so I wouldn't miss a word.

"No, that's just the beginning," he continued. "Because how many kids in that situation actually say no, especially with Markus's money allowing them to do it for free for a little while—and then you'll give them an option to sell the stuff to a few of their friends. Oh, and as if the ridiculous amount of money that they would be making isn't enough, add in the fact that they'll be addicted after a couple tries and they'll cast their morals to the wind. Basically the epidemic of the poison will be this country's pandemic overnight—does this sound about right?" he asked, concluding in a sputtering cough.

The coughing left even more blood on his lips and some running from the corners of his mouth, and I jerked backward suddenly when Elise's hands came into my vision as she leaned over to wipe the blood from Caleb's face. I looked to Elise, who was frowning at me; I turned back to Caleb to see he was looking at me, patiently waiting for my full attention.

"You're just afraid that it will work so you're trying to stop the movement, right?" I accused.

"No, Derrick, I'm certain it'll work; he's trained each of you very well to ensure it. It's the stage that follows that I think you should know more about."

Okay, he had my undivided attention now, because no one knew what that stage was except for Markus, who had only hinted to a few things dealing with legislation—new laws that truly would address black people's daily concerns over equality.

Caleb sat up, fighting through the pain that had stopped him from doing so several times before and tears welled up in his eyes but they didn't fall. "Did you know that the New World Order was almost out of money two years ago and that since then Markus has been completely funded by three terrorist cells here in the USA?" he said, and it struck deep in me because I had suspected our leader was being funded. Two years ago—funny, because that was when Markus informed us of what we were expected to do and when everything took a turn for the worse.

"He didn't turn easily, Derrick; he fought against what they wanted for a long time because he just wanted something good to come from what he was doing. They finally put his hands to the fire when they involved torture for three days straight and informed him that they had found his successor ... that his agreement was no longer needed and that they were just going to kill him. It was then that he turned into the tyrant you know now."

I was emotionally drained merely from the thought of how many unanswered questions what Caleb was telling me had resolved, and I began to feel a deep sorrow for Markus.

"They plan on using several of the white people whose lives you and your classmates have destroyed, along with innocent children, and giving them a choice to die right there or be sheltered, kept high day and night, provided with sex and many other things while at the same time training them for the day when they will walk into police stations, fire stations, and hospitals throughout this country strapped with explosives—essentially creating chaos all across America," Caleb said as his body trembled against the pain of holding himself up. "They plan to come forward to the world about how they were able to steal the lives of their children all across the country, and the day that Markus is taken to jail, the bombs will be sent."

Caleb collapsed back onto his back in great pain, and I moved aside when Elise quickly pulled out a syringe that had already been loaded and injected it into an almost completely exposed vein on his right arm. Caleb instantly began to relax, and I could see the high in him as if he were a heroin addict that had just taken a hit.

Elise gave me an accusing look and spoke in a low tone that in no way hid her anger. "He'll be dead if he has to keep talking to you, Derrick, and what I just gave him will calm him from all of this, but there is also a chance that he'll be out soon. He has successfully fought sleep on this drug before, but if he falls asleep, you'll be right here beside me watching him die, you fucking bastard!"

An overwhelming wave of guilt ran through me but I fought it back with all of my strength. I snapped my attention to Caleb and began shouting at him.

"How can you just expect me to—!"

"Derrick, he's going to name each one of you publically, and your lives will be over. They use children too, Derrick, children like Chris and …"

His speech was starting to fall off, but his eyes remained pleading and fighting to keep contact—wait, he just said Chris.

"Chris? Do you mean my little brother?" I placed my hands on Caleb's cheeks and gave him a little shake to keep him here and talking, which worked for a moment as his eyes widened. He was nodding so lightly that my hands on his cheeks barely felt the movement.

He managed to say three last words: "They … are … monsters." And with that said he slipped into unconsciousness.

I frantically looked back at Elise, who had a blank look on her face as she watched us. "I'm going to need you to stand out of the way." She pointed to the door. "Go over there by the wall. You might want to brace yourself for what's coming."

I pensively made my way to the door, watching her prepare medications, pitchers of water along with towels and ointments, and lastly placing a wooden stick on the pillow beside the charred young man's head. Caleb lay motionless on the bed, and I decided to quickly get some questions in with Elise before whatever was going to occur, did.

"Was he talking about my brother?" I asked.

She spoke to me while tidying things, much slower now, as if she were debating if she should tell me. She looked at Caleb with the most melancholy expression I had ever seen before and then shifted a glare to me. "Yes—are you actually stupid and pretending to be smart? Markus plans to medicate your brother along with many more—but your brother is tops on Markus's list."

I was flabbergasted by what I was hearing, but inside I knew it was all true. I was speechless.

"They also plan to make him known as some great mastermind plotting to destroy America alongside the terrorists. You and your classmates will face the death penalty with him!" she concluded fiercely while finishing draining the last of the liquid medicine from a small medical vial, and then she whipped the empty vial straight at my face with the speed and accuracy of a professional pitcher. I was barely able to slide my head out of its path, feeling the air move against my cheek when it passed by.

"What the hell do you care?" she barked out at me loudly. "Chris is nothing to you anyway, just another dead person in your sick, twisted plan for revenge! Revenge for things that happened before you were born, Derrick!"

I was finally able to muster a paltry defensive response. "It's not my plan, Elise ... it's not ... I didn't do this, I'm not ..." I just wished I could make her understand, but how could she?

She was shuddering as she stared at Caleb, lying there. "Why does he hang on ...? If there is a higher power up there?" Elise said, face to the ceiling. "If you're real then you know he believes in you, so why the fuck are you doing this to him? Take him, take him now, and don't make him go through this anymore!" she pleaded, and then she stared into my eyes and I could feel her fury. "Finish this tonight, Derrick! Leave now, and if there is a God, I pray that you're next to go through what Caleb has!" she shouted.

I stepped toward her, raising my voice. "I don't expect you to understand because you're not black! I don't expect you to under—"

She stepped around the bed and directly toward me. "Understand what, Derrick? Understand prejudice, hate, and discrimination? I do, Derrick, I face it every day. But unlike you, women face it no matter what color they are!"

I felt small as I took a step back, so confused. "Am I ..." I lowered my head in shame. "Am I the villain?" I asked, unsure about everything at this moment in time. "I'm just trying to survive and take care of my family ..." I explained, but Elise just looked defeated, with tears trickling down her cheeks.

"No, Derrick, you're not the villain ... you're one of his puppets," she said and then returned to face Caleb and the horror that was about to begin.

At that very moment I began to smell flesh burning, and I could see Caleb's exposed bone beginning to sizzle the muscle still attached in that area. I looked at his face, and he was just beginning to sense the pain. His soft eyes sprang wide open, expressing every ounce of the worst pain imaginable followed by a bloodcurdling scream of terror. I turned immediately and exited the room, closing the door behind me.

CHAPTER

New Life

Elise stepped out of the room and proceeded gingerly toward the couch. She took a seat beside Derrick, whose head was still lowered with his hands over his ears. She leaned her shoulder into him as a lighthearted nudge. Derrick looked to her curiously, and she returned his look with a smile. Relief washed over Derrick's face and he knew that his decision was not too late, but he still found himself deeply concerned about the severity of Caleb's injuries and wondered how he could be so concerned about a complete stranger's issues. Although really that question was easy for him to riposte with two simple facts. Fact one was that he was really starting to like both Caleb and Elise and fact two was that Caleb had shown Derrick an answer to a question that he had been asking since he was nine. Caleb had simply answered that question by being himself and by throwing himself under a hundred-ton bus because of his passion for something he believed in.

"So it stopped?" Derrick asked.

Elise nodded in confirmation. She was a little reserved and Derrick was curious as to why, but before he could complete that thought she slyly pulled a couple strands of her hair past her left ear and a small amount beautiful, dark hair followed in sequence, flowing down until it was a thin veil between her and Derrick.

"I'm sorry for the things that I said; I really wouldn't wish what he's going through on anyone … well, maybe one." Elise cast a measuring glance to Derrick and saw a puzzled look on his face. "But you don't know him," she added quickly so Derrick didn't think she was referring to him.

Derrick was instantly relieved that it wasn't him, even as he wondered who she could hate enough to wish that kind of suffering upon. It was also crystal clear to Derrick that Elise was not the kind that liked to apologize about anything.

Elise folded her arms across her chest and dug her thumbs into the shredded, self-mutilated areas under her arms to receive the painful reminder not to think of Chester, but instead of the searing pain she felt only dull tingle beneath the bandages. She pressed again and received the same small tingle and realized that she has not given herself any fresh cuts since she'd met Caleb two days ago. She strained her mind to figure out if it was because of all the pain that Caleb was going through, or …?

She looked out of the corner of her eye through her thin veil of hair and remembered that Derrick was still there beside her. He was sitting patiently, studying her, and his puzzled look had changed into a devilish grin as he began to think about how interesting she seemed: beautiful, without an ounce of conceit, but a dark side lying in the wake. He leaned forward to see her face around the curtain of hair and then motioned toward Caleb's room.

"You two are together, right?" he asked while studying her face. She looked at the door and began to relax, moving her hands down to her lap and fumbling with her fingers.

"He's a bit goody-two-shoes, but he's pretty tough to go through the shit he's going through," she replied.

"Why does he? As bad as all that, he has to know he's living on borrowed time," Derrick exacted.

"I don't know. I've asked and all he would say is that he has to 'be strong,'" she said with a blush of admiration. "But how strong can one person be?" She looked back to his door.

"I didn't figure you were the type that falls for nice," Derrick said.

"I'm not," Elise answered while still staring at Caleb's door. "Usually," she added quietly.

"Yeah, well, I still think we have our hands full trying to keep him alive. We need cultures run and antibiotics. He should be in a hospital and you know that, right?" Derrick said, and Elise glanced at him.

"No, I think we're going to be okay. Go look."

Derrick was confused but he stood and began walking toward Caleb's room, slowly. Not that he was squeamish to such mangled, torturous sights. He was building a pretty high level of respect for Caleb and was beginning to imagine that if he weren't on his deathbed, they might have become good friends. He opened the door and entered the room to find that it was very clean, no more burnt plastic or soiled linens or anything. Elise had done a fantastic cleaning job, but Derrick thought that she had been in the room with Caleb to assist him medically during those episodes, like a nurse, not like a maid.

Derrick disregarded the cleanliness of the room and focused his attention on Caleb in the middle of the bed, when Derrick's mouth fell open with astonishment. He crept toward the bed, his eyes wide with disbelief. The entire left side of Caleb's neck, chest, and shoulder had been completely healed; Derrick looked closely at Caleb's left bicep and saw billions of miniscule mites rebuilding a whole infrastructure of his bicep bit by bit.

Derrick reached down with his right pointer finger to touch the newly healed skin on Caleb's left shoulder, which had been charred to the bone just hours ago. It felt like human skin and not some synthetic replica. Derrick's curiosity led his finger down Caleb's shoulder and to the bicep muscle currently being repaired, just far enough until the tip of his finger scarcely touched the tiny mites.

He pulled his finger back as quickly as he could when he felt a tiny shock at his fingertip and he saw Caleb flinch. Derrick looked at his fingertip and saw microscopic mites working their way down it, changing his fingertip. They started thinning Derrick's actual nail and transforming his brown skin pigment into white. It felt like it was just happening on the surface of his fingertip, and Derrick was relieved when the transformation stopped after completely changing the top one-third of his pointing finger. He stood frozen, just staring at his fingertip, fearing any more damage and cursing his curiosity silently. He looked down at Caleb's bicep and saw where his pigment had gone: a perfect circle of brown skin right in the middle of Caleb's left bicep.

Disappointed about what took place but relieved it wasn't worse, Derrick gave a last look at Caleb before leaving the room and noticed that Caleb's lips were moving. Derrick moved around the bed to Caleb's right side, where the mites had not started repairing yet.

Though his mouth was moving, no words were coming out, so Derrick leaned a little closer, trying to make out what Caleb was trying to say. Mimicking the movement of Caleb's lips, Derrick began to form the words but in the back of his mind was hoping that Elise didn't walk in because it may look like he was going in for a kiss.

"Aub …" Caleb kept repeating, Derrick's lips now moving in sequence with his. "Aub … Aubrey."

Derrick felt pleased with himself to have interpreted the name Caleb was trying to say, and he wondered what it could mean or who she might be. He continued to decipher what Caleb was saying until he had gotten it all, because Caleb was just repeating the same phrase over and over again like a mantra.

"Aubrey, Aubrey, my dear Aubrey, thank you so much. You're an angel, Aubrey, my angel Aubrey."

Derrick stood up, confused but also a hair hopeful, because this could mean that there was already someone in Caleb's life—and though it might be hard for Elise to get over Caleb, Derrick could be there to help her through it, and maybe she could grow to like him that way instead. Even so, he sincerely didn't want Elise to find out that there could be another woman involved in Caleb's life this way. He stuffed a few Band-Aids into his pocket and wrapped one around his fingertip then made his way out of the room, closing the door behind him.

Derrick was taken by surprise not to find Elise asleep on the couch or at least sitting somewhere. She was nowhere in sight, but then he heard the silvery, high-pitched sound of a utensil hitting the tile floor in the bathroom.

"Elise?" Derrick called out, and there was no answer. He brought his hands up from his sides and small, bluish flames began circling up in his palms. "Elise!" he called once again, but this time in a threatening tone.

Her response was hesitant. "Uh, I'm in the bathroom."

"Are you okay?" Derrick called out, thinking to himself that ever since he'd walked into this hotel room every moment had been unbelievable, so something dangerous jumping from the bathroom wouldn't surprise him. But what did surprise him was his strong desire to protect his newfound friends. He walked toward the door slowly, listening closely to feet shuffling around in the bathroom, and he doused the flame in his left hand to reach for the knob.

Hearing Derrick's hand touch the doorknob sent Elise scurrying around in the bathroom wearing only her bra and panties. "I'm just getting in the shower," she shouted out to Derrick, and he paused for a moment with his hand on the knob, prepared to push in the door. Elise quickly turned on the shower water and slid the shower curtains open and then closed for effect. Derrick relaxed and backed away from the door, taking a seat on the couch to wait for her.

In the bathroom Elise quietly retrieved the sharp scalpel from the tile floor, placed it back into its container, and concealed it in the bag too. The blood had already stained her bra because of the interruption and was now streaming down the sides of her lean waist toward her underwear. She grabbed some tissue off of the roller and began applying pressure against the fresh cuts under both of her arms.

This was the first time that she had cut her legs, too. She felt it was a good thing though, because now she was using the pain from her fresh wounds for more than one reason: to deal with the intense situation of almost getting caught mutilating herself, and to hide her mind from all of the unbelievably gruesome images and situations that the past few days had inherited to her.

She sat motionlessly on the bathroom floor with her knees drawn up and arms wrapped around them, thumbs buried deep and twisting against her freshly serrated wounds. She was almost taken by surprise when she opened her tear-filled eyes to see drying blood that had run down from the cuts on her inner thighs had utterly ruined her underwear. The bathroom was filled with steam from the shower, and all she could manage to do was sit there on the floor, both blood and silent tears falling into puddles on the tile.

After finally taking a shower, bandaging all of her wounds, and with wiping the bathroom clear of any bloody evidence, Elise finally emerged from the bathroom. She began to lean toward Caleb's room but Derrick quickly attempted to stop her.

"Elise, I was wondering if you could hang with me today." Derrick asked while rising from the couch and heading in her direction.
It was morning and even though they had gotten no sleep, Derrick couldn't right now anyway knowing that Markus would find out very soon that he did not attend his session and that quite literally is a death sentence at this stage of their movement. Elise looked puzzled, and she recoiled slightly when she saw Derricks quick movements as he made his way to her and pivoted so he stood in her path to Caleb's room. "Since I'm doing this thing with you two, I have to make some serious arrangements before I can go," he said while casually blocking her way.

She let out a small sigh, tilted her head at him, and wondered what he was up to but she was pretty awake after her bathroom fix, and was beginning to feel a bit stir crazy from being locked up in hotel rooms. She decided that the fresh air (as fresh as LA could offer, that is) and a chance to get her mind off of everything happening could be a good thing.

She tilted her head to the other side and looked at Caleb's door with concern etched throughout her entire body. Derrick noticed her expression and gracefully stepped to the side to gesture free passage to Caleb's door. "I just checked on him and he's continuing to heal; believe me when I say that there's nothing you or I can do for him except to give him a lot of space … time to rest and heal, too. Look, I'll show you," Derrick said as he reached for the door, opened it, and allowed Elise to look in.

Caleb was steadily healing. They could see that the left bicep was healed and the mites were now working on the forearm. Elise narrowed her eyes, looking directly at the brown circle on Caleb's arm. "I don't remember that circle on his ar-" she was saying before Derrick cut her off.

"Yes, I'm sure it was there before, just harder to see little imperfections when you're looking through rose-colored glasses." He paused for just a moment, hoping that she might be second-guessing her memory right now. "See, all we can do to help is nothing," Derrick said smugly.

Elise squinted again and began to sway forward. "He's saying something, his mouth is moving. I should find out if he needs something."

Derrick reached across her, easily stopping her from entering the room, edging her back, and pulling the door shut. "I was just in there, and all he's doing is just praying … I almost interrupted him when I bumped the table; he almost stopped, which I'm guessing means that the healing would have stopped too," Derrick lied to prevent her from going back in and figuring out exactly what he was saying.

Elise thought about it for a second and then finally agreed that getting out of the hotel and seeing some normal people doing normal things would be a helpful change. "Okay, so what are all these things that you have to do, and do any of them involve destroying that monster of yours called Markus?" she said with a nasty little grin on her face.

Derrick laughed to himself and said under his breath, "Not today." Elise wasn't sure if she heard what he said but felt confident that they were both on the same page as they left the hotel room. Derrick was ready to reach down and clean up the vials but they were gone already so he and Elise just hopped into his car and drove away.

CHAPTER

Falling Fast

"How long have you lived there?" Caleb asked while entirely absorbed in every word that Aubrey spoke. He paid little attention to her healing hands, which hovered over the scorched areas of his body, but instead he found himself awestruck by the elegance of her movements. So mesmerized by her beauty that it felt like love at first sight, and if it wasn't love than at the very least it was complete devotion—or, he wondered, would it be servitude to be so enamored by someone, that no request imaginable would be out of the question? He kept his questions short and open-ended so he could listen to her speak.

It was as if her voice softly touched down in the middle of his mind like a leaf on the water, which sent ripples echoing throughout. Cosmically colorful ripples bouncing off the walls of his mind then flowing back into one another to embrace in pairs. Pairs that would swirl off like a choreographed dance, swirling into areas of his mind that he never knew existed—areas that had no barriers, no fears of loss or foolishness; areas that told his entire being that there was no need to guard or hide a single thing but to entrust even the deepest, darkest corners of his mind so she could bring her cleansing light to them.

"I was born there. Actually I was born in the living room of our house." She gave a small mocking chuckle. "Yeah, I know it's weird." She shyly glanced away, incredulous, struggling with herself to divulge such personal information for a slight moment before looking deep into Caleb's eyes and continuing. "My mother loved our home and our family so much, even though at the time it was just the two of them, but she loved it so much that she wanted to birth me there so the most important moment of their entire lives would always be there with us."

Caleb felt the warmth of her words filling his whole body; his eyes drew up pleadingly, anguished, as if he could hardly bear the onslaught of emotions. He knew instantly that it wasn't a story she shared often.

"That's possibly the most beautiful gesture that I've ever heard," he said while reaching for her hands, hovering above his left thigh as they performed the healing process. The top half of the hospital bed that Caleb had been lying on began to rise until he was sitting upright, and he pulled her closer to him. "You've been blessed; please never be ashamed of that," Caleb said with an aching sincerity.

She paused for a moment and then began to smile. "I have always been happy about it inside, but it's just so weird to talk about it. I've only told one other person about it, when I was seven, and she thought it was gross and weird so I haven't spoken of it since. But with you it's like I want to share everything." She looked down—embarrassed, Caleb could tell, from the simple fact that her flawlessly radiant, golden skin began to push forward a pink blush in her cheeks.

Leaping to his damsel's distress Caleb responded with the most heartfelt emotion that he could translate into words. "Aubrey, you're an angel, and I hope to God that you would be my angel."

The rose color in her cheeks deepened and she looked up at Caleb, smiling from ear to ear, but quickly replaced the smile with a sobering expression. She removed her hands from Caleb's and returned to healing his left thigh. His look was puzzled, and fear wanted to set in but there was none; why would there be? Nothing had ever felt so real, so pure, so promising toward every aspect of his life—till death do they part?

"Is something wrong?" Caleb asked tentatively.

"I just hate that when I wake up this will all disappear. Even though I doubt I could ever forget this feeling, so real ... but it is just a dream," Aubrey said sadly.

Caleb released a sigh of relief along with a small laugh. "This isn't just a dream, Aubrey. I know it's hard to grasp, but as soon as I'm healed I'll be coming to you," he said.

Her face showed she was not quite convinced as she looked around at the beautiful environment. "This is my dream, Caleb," she said confidently. "If this is your dream then why are we surrounded by images from my mind?" she added in a melancholy tone.

He looked around from the top of the tall hill full of wildflowers similar to the ones in the meadow behind his own home. These wildflowers cascaded to the bottom of the hill, where they faded into the sands of a beautiful white-sand beach that sprawled more than three hundred meters across and about one hundred meters from the edge of the hill. To the left side of the beach volcanic rock made its appearance, creeping out from the ocean and up onto the shore where a small cluster of the material sat, compiled by nature to nudge into the base of the tall rock shelves that stood as nature's retaining walls holding the vast outreach of a beautifully mature forest that climbed the mountainous hillsides in that direction.

The right side of the beach backed up into the grassy land lined with Hawaiian rain trees scattered about. One grew from the sandy beach and stood about twenty feet tall, its fronds stretching out from its trunk about fifteen feet, toward the ocean, as if they were trying to unite with it, like a moth drawn to a fire but suspended in animation. Surely the tree was just growing toward the sun, Caleb imagined, but the moth thought amused him more—the tree drawn to the beauty of the ocean, whose salt would be its demise.

"This place is a combination of three places that I know, so they have to be *my* memories, my dream, right?" Caleb posed his statement as a question so it wouldn't sound condescending.

Aubrey paused, looking at Caleb inquisitively, and then pointed at the left side of the beach. "Kauai," she said.

Caleb was startled by her knowing where his memory was from, but not extraordinarily; after all, Hawaii wasn't exclusive to his family alone. He pointed to the right side of the beach. "That's Honolulu. I know that because one year we picnicked at that park behind the grass over there, and I definitely remember climbing on that exact tree."

She pointed at a Y-shaped bifurcation in the tree's trunk. "I got stuck right there and my father had to get me down," she laughed at herself. "But even back then I knew it was a special place to me."

Caleb broke in, "Because the view from that tree was one of a kind, high enough that when you looked straight out you couldn't see the beach below you," Caleb said, but it was her turn to cut him off.

"Yes, it made you feel as if you were flying above the ocean, alone in the universe."

"Exactly, and without knowing, you would just keep creeping farther and farther up that tree's limb until the moment someone got your attention and you actually looked around, and you had no idea how far up the tree you had gone," Caleb said, and they both laughed nervously. They laughed at themselves for each getting in the same situation, but mostly at the fact that after all they had each seen in this world, they both had found the same place in the world to love the most.

"I've spent too many hours in that tree not to recognize it or its surroundings," Aubrey said while laughing, and to Caleb her laugh sounded like wind chimes ringing at an octave that only his ears could hear.

"And this hill we're on?" Caleb said anxiously. She shook her head in defeat at the question. "I don't know where this is, either; they look like the wildflowers in my backyard," he said as Aubrey spun in elegant circles like a ballerina.

"All I know is that wildflowers in the wilderness are among the most beautiful sights possible," she sang out. "I've never seen them on hill like this before, not so many, but I love it."

Caleb laughed at her uninhibited expression of joy and thought to himself how uncanny it seemed that they would be so alike. His thought up to now was that it was the differences of lovers that brought them together, the new experiences and exposures that they could teach one another. But he now realized that it was the similarities that had brought him and his potential soul mate together: the appreciations, approvals, and disapprovals for virtually the same reasons. New experiences and exposures could still be encountered, but together, in sync with one another—as if given a companion of support and motivation, together forging through life.

He closed his eyes and tilted his head up toward the sun, concentrating on its rays along with the unimaginable fragrances of the wildflowers blending with the ocean air, which seemed to fall upon his body like a cool mist, incredibly balanced with the warmth of the sun.

His eyes sprang open when he felt the gentle touch of Aubrey's hand on his thigh. He slowly looked down toward her, being careful not to surprise her with even the slightest of gestures that could be interpreted as disapproving or uncomfortable. There was nothing close to an uncomfortable feeling about this in his entire mind or body. He had been longing to feel her touch since he had first laid eyes on her, and now after getting to know her, he firmly grasped Albert Camus' enlightened phrase, "The warm beast that lies curled up in our loins and stretches itself with a fierce gentleness."

In response to her delicate touch Caleb's body brandished thousands of goose bumps rushing to the surface, and he wondered if that was a reaction of his mind, or was there some form of magic involved? Then he unconsciously halted all speculations, gave Aubrey a warm smile, and raised his face back up to the sun. But now completely oblivious to the relaxing beauty of the environment, he focused only on her mercifully tender touches.

"So, is the dream yours, mine, or ours?" she asked playfully.

"It's definitely ours, to be here together ..." Caleb paused for a second, thinking, hoping that she felt the same way about him as he did about her. But then he cast out any feelings of insecurity, which would pale in comparison to the rewards of baring his heart to her entirely. "To be here as one," he finished.

Aubrey gazed at him expressively before moving slowly to him as he sat back up, stopping when their faces were less than six inches from each other, and then Caleb leaned in until his lips met hers. After the long, passionate kiss they stared into each other's eyes in silence for a moment before Aubrey began to reflect.

"The funniest thing is, I could never recall having a dream ever before—and now two times in a row," she said as if thinking aloud.

Caleb looked at her inquisitively. "You don't have dreams?" he asked.

"Not that I could remember, not a single one until last night."

Caleb sat forward. "Could you tell me about it?"

She shifted around uncomfortably and then stared at him blankly, apparently trying to raise the courage to tell him about the dream, and Caleb immediately became rigid with concern while in the back of his mind he already regretted asking the question. But he knew that there had to be some relevance in her dream for her to just suddenly start remembering them happening. For the case to be otherwise would be too much of a coincidence.

"Something was chasing me, something big and foul." Her voice was shaky as she tried to hold back tears.

Caleb reached down and took her hands into his for support. "Go on," he said softly.

"It was awful ... it spewed out some kind of toxic stuff from its body, it had intestines from its stomach dragging on the ground, one eye was melted halfway down its face, and there were black, rigid teeth. Smoke came from several breathing holes around its body ... holes that opened and closed like they were slimy mouths blowing out smoke." She paused, and the first tear was released to flutter down her beautiful face. "Birds of all size, dragonflies, bees—anything that would fly into the smoke would drop lifeless to the ground."

Caleb searched his mind for details of the incident when he and Elise had been attacked by some creature, but when they had escaped he couldn't recall seeing dead birds on the ground, just the grotesque vision of hotel manager Charlie's mutilated, smoldering body, which once again made his stomach turn, but he pushed that thought aside to focus on Aubrey's dream. "Was there an unbelievably bad smell?" he asked, thinking that it could still be the same creature.

"No, no smell, but I never got that close to it, either. Every tree or bush it touched would turn brown, then black as it fell like ashes to the ground." Her voice trembled, "The ground—the grass would die instantly all around its feet." She pulled her hands from Caleb's and buried her face into them, weeping for nature and for herself. Caleb watched helplessly, anxiously rattling his brain to figure out a way, any way to ease her pain.

"Aubrey, we don't have to continue this ..."

Aubrey pulled her face up from her hands to look at Caleb and seemed to gather strength from his compassion. Caleb hadn't believed it would be possible for her to look any more beautiful than she already was, but in that very moment he discovered an additional reason besides his mother to be strong. He opened his arms and she stepped into his embrace, and they held each other with a gentle strength that seemed to comfort one another and strangely restored their intestinal fortitude. After a long moment they pulled apart, looking deeply into each other's eyes, completely rejuvenated and determined to get one another through this. "You can do this," Caleb supported.

Aubrey took a deep breath and continued describing her dream. "I ran, but no matter how fast or slow I was going it was the same distance behind me, effortlessly plodding along, killing every form of nature in its wake. I cried horribly when I ran through a field of wildflowers and glanced back to see what that thing had done to them." She shook her head slowly, recalling the next part. "I thought I could lose him by swimming across a lake so I dove in and began swimming as fast as I could, but the monster's disgustingness filtered through the water even faster than it did through the air. Fish began floating lifelessly to the surface ... I could feel their dead bodies hitting me from underneath as they died. I had to swim through them to reach the far shore and then I crawled back up onto my feet and I ..."

Aubrey paused for a long moment and Caleb reached to embrace her hands again. She took a deep breath. "There was a beautiful ghostly woman on the shore pointing me in a direction; I have never felt threatened by them—"

Aubrey stopped suddenly, as if she had mistakenly mentioned something that she hadn't wanted to talk about. The look on Caleb's face showed his confusion about her last statement. He began to ask her about who it was that she'd never felt threatened by, but then she quickly moved her fingers up to his tender lips, assuring him with her eyes that she would broach that subject soon.

She went on, "I ran in the direction she had pointed out to me. I looked back to see if the monster was the same distance from me as always, and I was astonished to see these ghostlike blue people fighting the beast back. It was now retreating very fast to get away from them. I stopped running and watched with an ounce of amusement as that filthy creature ran from my protectors."

By this time Caleb's speculation that she was talking about the people with the blue shading around them had been confirmed. The very same people that Elise, Derrick, and he himself had seen since birth. The very same people that he had feared until just days ago when he saw that his benevolent mother was now one of them. "You've seen these ... protectors all of your life, haven't you? But more frequently lately, right?" Caleb posed as a question though he already knew the answer.

"Yes, and now you are the only person on Earth that knows that. Boy I must really trust you, Caleb," she said in a heartfelt tone.

"I've told you about Elise and Derrick, and now with you we are a covenant of four strong. Each of us has seen the people in blue our whole lives; it is what it is, and it hasn't seemed to affect anyone's life negatively, but I think we have to figure out who or what they are," Caleb said.

"Crusaders," Aubrey said quietly. She recognized the confused look on Caleb's face. "I was able to speak with her." Aubrey took a firm grasp of Caleb's hand and looked squarely in his eyes. "Caleb is your mother still alive?" she said sensitively. Caleb just shook his head slightly. "Can you describe her to me?" she asked.

Caleb pulled away from her slowly, raising his hand to the sky as a tear began to well up in his eye. Aubrey looked to the sky to see the most beautifully soft image of a woman, which Caleb had willed the clouds to form from the picture of his mother in his mind. She gasped silently at her beauty and they both watched the cloud formation of his mother for a long moment before Aubrey turned to Caleb, who was still staring at his mom's image with a tear rolling down his cheek. Aubrey reached to wipe the tear from Caleb's cheek but his hand caught her wrist before she could touch the tear.

Caleb had not moved his head at all, still focused on his mother's image in the sky, and Aubrey was startled by his response. He turned slowly to Aubrey. "That's my mother's tear," he said, closing his eyes and inhaling deeply. The tear visibly absorbed into his cheek. He looked back to Aubrey. "Sorry if I startled you" he said while trying to compose himself.

"No ... I ... I knew she was beautiful... she *is* just so beautiful," Aubrey was able to correct.

"That was her guiding you last night, wasn't it?" Caleb asked with a hint of jealousy in his tone.

"Yes, and she said that her son Caleb needed my help. I guess that's why I wasn't so surprised when I walked upon you here, lying unconscious in this bed. I had no doubt in my mind that you were Caleb. I had no idea I could do healing like this, either," she said as she returned to healing Caleb's left leg once again. Now his wounds were healing quicker than before because her hands were no longer hovering above but were in direct contact with his burnt flesh.

"I'm sorry if I seemed defensive. It just all happened so quickly; she passed away about two weeks ago and ... well, it's not so easy," Caleb said apologetically before asking with excitement, "What else did she tell you?"

"Well, not that much of it makes any sense." There was a sparkle in her eyes as she continued. "Like I said before, the people in the blue hues are called Crusaders, and they protect *Elipsions*—I hope I'm pronouncing that right."

"Elipsions? What are Elipsions?" Caleb asked.

"I think she said that they're our source of life," Aubrey said without much certainty. "We're each born with ten Elipsions and they each last about ten years each."

Caleb's brow pulled together with confusion. "So why haven't I heard of Elipsions?"

"Because they aren't visible to us here on Earth, well I should say here on our plane of existence... Ok, what I mean is here on Earth, everything we see and know to be real is one layer, but there is another layer behind this. That is the layer or plane of existence where the blue hued people live. They can see our Elipsions and fight against the things that feed on our Elipsions. They could be standing here beside of us right now or even occupying the very same space but since it's a different layer, plane two that is, well we would never know it unless we could see into plane two."

Caleb tried to piece all this together in his mind while speaking aloud. "So the bluish people are here on Earth with us but on a different plane of existence-plane two. They are there to protect our Elipsions ... our source of life, which are supposed to be one hundred years for each person, right?" he asked while Aubrey nodded. "So are they guardian angels of some kind?" Caleb asked

"I don't know, Caleb; she said that there is so much more to learn about that place, nuclear technologies that will revive the world's economies, architectures, transportations and much more," Aubrey said, almost breathlessly with excitement.

Caleb remained silent as he tried to imagine all that Aubrey was saying and patiently waited for her to continue, hoping that she had more to tell.

"But yes, I think I see them as guardian angels too" Aubrey agreed.

"But if they are guardian angels then why is my mom there?" Caleb asked and then thought aloud "I'm not sure if it says in the Bible where guardian angels come from," Caleb said inquisitively.

"She seemed to speak of it as if it were a whole society of bluish people, or guardian angels," Aubrey stated. "But it seemed like her most pressing subject—other than you, was when she spoke about the increasingly severe weather. She indicated that what they call the 'Age of the Tornados' is almost here and that's just the beginning as it'll be immediately followed by immeasurable earthquakes, tsunamis, floods, and volcanoes that will finish off mankind if we don't succeed."

"Succeed at what? ... What do you mean? We're just five teenagers with abilities that can be duplicated with a flame thrower and water hoses, Band-Aids and what, maybe a blow drier? How could we ever stop something like that from happening? That would be impossible; how are we expected to make a difference like that?" Caleb said with frustration.

"Faith, I guess." Aubrey chuckled. "Like I said, doesn't make much sense," she agreed. "But why did you say five? I thought you said earlier that there were just four of us."

"The way I see it is that Elise has powers to manipulate water and Derrick can control fire. You have yours in the area of earth, and that would just leave one more," Caleb said with a hint of pride at his deductive reasoning.

"Air," she said, realizing that they represented the four elements. She tilted her head to side again and asked, "And what about you?"

"Not sure. I mean it's clear that I have been assigned by ... well, I like to believe we're all in this thing, this boon together, by manner of God ..." He studied her reaction and sensed none, positive or negative. "I believe that I'm going through this," he gestured to his wounds, "because it's God's will to bring you four together ... I don't know why but I believe that. Oh, and yes, the creatures you and I have seen are real, and I have no doubt that we will have to confront them at one point or another."

A shiver of fear rolled through Aubrey's body. "Them?" she asked with a shaky voice.

Caleb immediately wished he hadn't said it. "But together I believe there's nothing we can't do, so let's not think about that part until the time comes, okay?" he said pleasantly to curb her line of thought.

At that very second Caleb became very still. "I hear something," he said.

Aubrey looked around and listened intently.

"No, not here; I hear something in the hotel room," Caleb said as he adjusted the bed back down to lie back flat on it, his eyes wide and affixed on the sky while he was concentrating. "Someone just came into the hotel room, and I don't sense that it's Derrick or Elise," he said with fear in his voice.

Aubrey stood frozen with concern.

CHAPTER

Relocating

Derrick and Elise had just purchased two very large suitcases and were hauling them out to Derrick's car. Derrick pushed a button on the key fob to release the trunk and then began moving items around in the trunk to make space for the suitcases.

"I'm trying not to be judgmental or anything, but mass addictions and murder—how could you ever live with yourself after doing something like that?" Elise asked.

Derrick slowed as he moved the last item out of the way and turned to place the first case into the trunk. He knew that he would never be himself again after it was done, and he had always had reservations since the day he found out what they were expected to do. "We don't know that I would have done it," Derrick replied, and Elise just gave him a shrewd look.

Derrick still tried to consider what he would have done if Caleb and Elise hadn't come along. He had been engulfed with thoughts of all the good he had received from Markus before the terrorists had gotten hold of him. Things were very different back then when they were all just trying to rise above it all by making their minds superior, and the clash of being a murderous regime, haunted by the knowing that to run would be certain death for him and his family, really had left him with few options in his mind. But he nonetheless had been looking for an out and had hoped to find one before the fall semester began.

Derrick was beginning to see this escape as a reprieve on his life sentence to certain agony, imprisonment, and eventual suicide as he drew similarities between himself and German soldiers whose jobs had been to fill the buildings with Jewish people and piped-in gas through the fake shower heads. He wondered how many of those soldiers had committed suicide because of it, and he knew in his heart of hearts that regardless how he looked at it, to go through with Markus's plan meant he would be dead one way or another within two years.

"So what are we going to do about it?" Elise asked in a rather defiant tone.

After placing the first bag in the trunk Derrick turned to retrieve the next bag from her but found himself tugging against her for the case. He looked past the bag to see Elise looking stern as she waited for the answer to her question.

"He's not a bad person; this has been forced on him just as it was forced on me, and I don't see me just destroying everything without trying to save them," he said, realizing the only answer possible.

Elise lowered the bag to the ground with conflicted thoughts, but she knew that meant only one answer too. "You know this means we have to take out the cells, right?" she said as a statement more than a question, and Derrick gave her a ratifying nod while donning a devilish grin.

"We leave no man behind," he said jokingly as he saluted to her.

"Fair enough, would tomorrow be too soon to start working on this?" she asked.

"I think we need to gather some information first and there is only one person that knows it all. So we're going to need to get Markus alone," Derrick explained while picking up the second case and putting it into the trunk. "But I have to get some money together because we still need to get my family someplace safe first," he said decidedly.

"Caleb has his uncle's credit card with more money than we'll need to spend. He says it's for funding us," Elise said.

"Why that dump of a hotel then?" Derrick asked.

"Because we were racing the clock and we wanted to be as close to you as we could get."

"That makes sense, but it's a very rough area" he said, and Elise quickly crossed her arms to dig into her wounds as a defense from thinking of anything bad happening around there because things are already bad enough.

"Then we should hurry and pick your family up so we can get to a different hotel until we figure out the next move we need to make," Elise said, but Derrick hesitated for a moment but then decided to use his slight leverage to find out what was up with Elise.

"We're not going anywhere until you tell me what's going on with you," he said firmly.

"What do you mean?" Elise asked delicately.

"I know the drill, Elise; it takes more than a shower for you to emerge in a different mood, and who takes two hours to take a shower?" he stated as she dug deeper into the wounds under her arms. Derrick pointed directly to her thumbs, which were now working so hard to help her mentally escape from his interrogation.

"What kind of itch do you have there, Elise?" he asked to see if she would be honest and tell him about her suspected heroin usage.

Elise caught his drug reference and simply decided that it was time to let him know that he wasn't the only one of the group that had had a fucked up life. "It's not what you think," she said while digging a little deeper. "It's my way of escaping."

Derrick scoffed. "I've heard that before. How long have you been using, and how much a day?" he asked

"I was raped," she said quietly. "I trusted him and accepted him as my father." A tear fell from her right eye. Derrick stood still, speechless. "He was my stepfather and he's stronger than I am, and I know my mother knew," she said angrily.

Derrick felt the guilt of his being insensitive welling up inside him. "I didn't …" He moved in cautiously and put his arms around her, and her anguished tears absorbed into his warm shirt.

"They're cuts … cuts that used to just keep his image out of my head, but now with everything happening … I used to use them to know that I'm still here, still alive. But now I use them to detach from everything when the intensity of all this starts to drown me …"

Derrick's guilt began shifting to anger. "Where is he?" he asked with a strange determination.

"He's in North Dakota; that's where we have always lived," Elise answered.

Derrick looked puzzled for a moment. "Do you know the name of the jail or what city it's in?" Derrick exacted.

Elise pulled back and looked into Derrick's eyes. "He's not in jail," she said, and Derrick looked at her skeptically.

"You didn't report it to the police?" Derrick asked, though gently so as to try to withhold the sting of accusation from the question, but Elise still lowered her head in despair. They released their embrace and she moved a step back, looking at the ground.

Derrick put his arm around her and walked her to the passenger side to let her into the car. "I guess we know where our next stop will be after dealing with the New World Order, right?" he said, and to his relief she nodded with a small smile of satisfaction, knowing that Chester would finally pay for the damage he'd done. Elise climbed into the car feeling stronger, feeling that strange warmth and comfort that one feels with a loving group of family or friends—an emotion that she had not felt in many years.

They drove through the city, and Derrick slowed the car down two blocks away from his home in order to survey the area before parking in the driveway and going in to retrieve his family. Elise was in complete agreement with Derrick's plan to get his mother, brother and sister over to the hotel room with them for protection until they could all figure out a safe place to hide from Markus's wrath, which was sure to follow.

When they entered the house, Derrick's little brother and sister were running toward him to give him a big hug but stopped immediately when they saw Elise step out from behind him. Derrick knew that their eyes were huge with surprise because they had never seen a white person in their house before.

Derrick had only seen this situation from his point of view—what had to be done to protect his family—but it was now starting to take a different shape. The dread in his mind was not because the kids' reactions, but his mother's.

Derrick's mother flew into the living room from around the corner and came to a shocking halt when she saw Elise. She tried to compose herself for a moment, but then her emotions won out. "Boy, where the hell you been?" she boomed at Derrick with one hand on her hip and the other pointing at Derrick, bouncing slightly with every word she spoke. Derrick's mother, Tina, was only five-foot-four and maybe 110 pounds, so Elise was surprised when she found herself backing up and sliding in behind Derrick again.

Tina's eyes were filled with the anger and concern that any respectable mother would have when she was worried about her child possibly being in a life-or-death situation, especially around this area, where danger lurked in so many different disguises and around virtually every corner. Elise was trying to imagine how awful it would be to have to raise children in a place like this when, as if on cue, gunfire rang out.

The two children were the first to hit the floor, followed by Tina and Derrick, who dropped simultaneously. Derrick reached up and pulled Elise down to the floor. Derrick's little brother and sister were the only ones moving as the gunfire continued to ring out in rapid, unforgiving sprays of bullets that rattled throughout the neighborhood.

As terrifying as this situation seemed to Elise, it was even more frightening for her to see the children crawling toward the gunfire until they reached the front window and began scaling up to their feet in order to peek out and get a bird's eye view of what was taking place. "Chris, Lashey, get the hell back here right now!" Tina screamed out to the children. Derrick quickly shushed her while trying to gauge the distances and types of weapons used so he might determine if this was a direct attack on him.

Chris and Lashey dropped back to the floor and began crawling back to the others; Derrick was slightly at ease when he realized that the bullets were *not* shooting directly at their house; there were far too few guns, from the sound of it, and the calibers were too small to be an attack sent by Markus. Just another all-too-familiar random shooting; they had become a particularly sore spot in Derrick's life over the past few years for a variety of reasons.

This shooting rang through his head as if it was an explosion, the final straw, and he wasn't going to take any more. "We're getting the fuck out of here today!" he said in a grating tone. Now that the gunfire had stopped, everyone was returning to their feet.

"Watch your language," his mom spouted toward him. "And where the fuck we gonna go, Derrick?" she asked.

"Far away from here and this life!" Derrick retorted.

His mom looked around the room, but no one was sure if she was looking for bullet holes or being nostalgic. "We ain't leavin', Derrick! You sayin' that you 'fraid of some damn gunshots? You been hearin' 'em your whole life, boy, why you trippin' now? 'Cause your li'l skinny-ass white Polly Purebred there tellin' you it ain't safe?" Tina rattled off so fast that everyone paused for a second to catch up to what she had just said.

Derrick's look of warning to Elise expressed that she might want to be prepared to duck. Then Derrick seized the opportunity to break in during Tina's pause, which also took her attention off of Elise. "We leave now or Markus kills all of us!" he said bluntly.

"What in the hell are you talkin' 'bout? Markus would never do something like that! He gives, not takes," Tina said, although with a touch of doubt in her voice, because she had always wondered how Markus has all of the money to do what he does .

Derrick approached her, took her hand, and sat down with her on the couch. He looked into her eye, still holding her hands. "He's not the man that you think he is," Derrick said, and a sadness rumbled through his torso as he listened to his own words being spoken, his confession of deceit. "Markus supported us through school to increase his drug sales to students ... he's making sure we go to college because he wants us to spread an especially addictive drug to the students there. He plans to steal their futures from them, to steal them from their parents. But you are right, Mom; Markus had good intentions, but ..." Derrick paused for an instant, thinking about how crazy this whole cloak-and-dagger statement was sounding, but rather than question his own sanity he simply continued. "But he's being led by terrorists now, and it's gotten ugly."

His mother sat silently and Derrick guessed that she was not having a hard time believing his story, because she had always thought that Markus was too good to be true.

"You're not doin' it! I ain't raisin' drug dealers! You're too smart for that, Derrick, so you just go tell Markus that you ain't doin' it!"

Derrick looked down to his mother's hands. "They've dismembered people for far less than walking out, Mom. It's all gone wrong now, Mom, and nothing short of death is about to stop it." Derrick cringed at the thought of them trying to deliver just that to terrorists.

Elise stepped forward and piped in her support. "He's right, and they have plans to grab Chris and keep him drugged until he's ready to walk into a police department with explosives!"

Chris's eyes got wide with fright at what Elise had just said. Derrick glared up at Elise as Tina stood quickly, staring Elise down.

"Who's this white bitch, Derrick, and why she saying shit like that? How you think you know what they're gonna do, is you one of 'em?" Tina screamed at Elise while picking up an ashtray from the table.

Derrick stood up quickly and pried the ashtray from his mom's clinched hand. "She's telling the truth, Mom. It's hard to explain, but it seems like I have something pretty important to do," he said.

"What's that?" she barked out at him.

She now had him backed into a corner because he had no logical answer for what he, Elise, and Caleb were setting out to do. Suddenly they all froze, speechless, as murky water began streaming down the walls, followed by the loud ring of a window in the back of the house being smashed. The sound of the breaking glass was accompanied by the echoing crack of its steel rods—in place in the kids' room's window for protection—as they hit the floor, sounding like thunder. Knowing the weight of those bars Derrick quickly ascertained that who or whatever had the power to push those bars in had to be a serious threat.

Derrick instinctively called upon balls of blue flames, rolling them in the palms of his hands. Tina fell back onto the couch when she saw the flames as Derrick was poised to attack, ready to pounce on the first person he saw coming up the hall.

The kids' eyes sparkled with excitement when they saw Derrick's new trick, but that excitement instantly shifted to fear as the piping in the kitchen and bathrooms swelled and then exploded, which sent streams of water pushing up to the ceilings in the kitchen and bathrooms.

"Derrick, what …?" Tina was able to get out before she stopped, staring in shock at what was coming out of the kids bedroom. It stood about six-foot-tall at its shoulders-hunched over. It had a three foot long skeletal neck bone hanging down with a skeleton head that looked like an alligator with the jaws of a great white shark. It was a wonder that the relatively small neck bone could hold the four foot wide, three and a half foot long head. The creature's neck not only held the bulky head easily it also moved it agilely in virtually every direction, but it mostly left it in the hunched over position hanging about three feet from the floor.

Its eye sockets and mouth constantly expelled murky water and when the creature would show its great jaws in a thunderous chomping display its bottom jaw would crash against the floor creating a loud thud before it slammed shut, showing its razor sharp teeth combined with speed and enormous power. It would creep painfully for a split second, and then the next second it would be in fast motion for about five feet with its webbed feet and hands slapping against the floors and hallway walls, leaving deep punctures through those surfaces from its sharp talon like claws. It repeated this movement three times until it had cleared the hallway and stood about ten feet from Derrick and his family who stood by the front door now as Elise was just five feet to Derrick's left.

The creature raised its head quickly, stopping less than an inch before slamming into the ceiling, then slowly looked to its left at Derrick's family for a moment before it looked directly at Derrick for an extended amount of time. It stretched its neck out to get closer to Derrick and begun sniffing for Derrick's scent.

From that very second on the creature paid absolutely no attention to anyone in the room except for Derrick. It started to grind its teeth back and forth as if to display their serrating action then hunched back over taking an offensive stance. Derrick wasted no time launching a rolling ball of flame at it. The creature leaped back several feet while simultaneously regurgitating a large amount of dark water onto the fireball before it hit the floor. The water extinguished the flame into a large plume of opaque steam. The creature emerged from the steam confidently and now stood just six feet in front of Derrick.

Elise hugged close against the wall and starting sneaking around the back side of the creature while contemplating what she would do if it snapped out in her direction. To her surprise it never diverted an ounce of its attention, which remained totally on Derrick. It brought its hands up, and misty water from the entire room started accumulating into a growing swirl in front of it. It was easy to see the difference between the clear water from the house's broken pipes and the dark water from the creature as they mixed together.

Derrick brought up a white-hot fire shield circling an inch in front of his outstretched hands, reaching from the floor to a foot above his head. Mists from the water near the shield evaporated instantly into steam as the room's temperature instantly began to rise. Derrick looked to his terrified mother and the two children huddled in the corner by the front door.

"Go, go, get out of the hou-" he screamed to them, but just then it was as if a hundred pounds of pressure was smashing into his body. He snapped his attention back to the creature to see water spraying to the sides of his white-hot shield, which had dimmed to a bluish-orange color and shrunk to half of the size it was a second before.

He hadn't been prepared for the shield to feel as if it were an extension of his body, he hadn't prepared for feeling every bit of the frigid pain that cold water crashing into the shield of flames would cause him. Steam poured over his shield and into his face and arms. Derrick was surprised that his skin was not boiling, and he mustered up all of his strength to focus on the shield.

The shield began to slowly grow back as the creature lunged a couple of lightning fast snaps at Derricks head but it would instantly retract when it got less than an inch from Derricks fire shield, but that did not lessen the effectiveness of the eardrum crushing sound of its monstrous jaws slamming shut. Derrick's shield had grown back to be just shy of its original size and it became white-hot once again.

Superheated steam filled the single-level home and the creature's stream of water was beginning to slow considerably. The steam was circulating back inward to the monster's hands and condensing back into water but at a much-slowed rate. A surge of excitement filled Derrick as he realized he could win this battle. He was stronger than this thing, even though his shield had diminished in size; it was still becoming apparent that he was winning.

Derrick then saw that not all of the steam was going back to the creature as more than half of the steam was bypassing the monster and trailing off behind it, absorbing into Elise's hands like a supercharged vacuum sucking the moisture from the air and from the creature. Her face glowed brightly as the creature began to collapse to its knees. Elise turned quickly and sent the water that she had compiled in her willpower jetting through a nearby window and out of the creatures range of absorption. She turned back to the creature as it was spitting at another one of Derrick's fire balls, but it was too weakened to leap back and it was immediately scorched by steam and flames, leaving black suet on its face and neck while its body smoldered with small flames continued to engulf it.

Elise continued to drain the moisture from the creature's body until it finally fell flat onto the floor dislodging its boney neck completely from its body. Derrick was amazed to see that there was merely a half of a foot bone that was imbedded into the creature's body. Elise continued to suck all of the moisture from the creature's body until there was not an ounce left. Somewhat exhausted, Derrick extinguished his shield and moved painfully toward the gruesome body lying on the floor. He and Elise arrived at the body at the same time and they both saw movement inside of the charred body. They quickly looked at one another and took a step back while looking back at the creature. It slowly became apparent that the movement was one lump moving upward towards the spot where the bone head and neck had detached from.

As it got to the shoulder blade area its impression against the charred skin showed a human face that looked strangely familiar to Derrick. Elise and Derrick moved to the top of the creature's body and witness the emergence of the top of a head like the crowning of a baby's during birth. The head was scorched as well and some skin peeled from it as it surfaced, leaving pink flesh exposed in some areas and other areas scrapped down to the bone. The face was easy for Derrick to make out now, especially since he had just seen him yesterday.

"It's GutTer" Derrick said while filling with confusion as he stood there looking at a creature from the darkest corner of a nightmare laying on its stomach and now the head of his most hated enemy, attached and facing up. GutTer was dazed and barely clinging to life. When he saw Derrick he tried to speak, but his mouth had melted shut. The lips pulled apart slowly and painfully, the skin stretching like melted cheese before the lower lip won and the upper lip separated just under the nose, exposing his entire upper row of teeth and gums.

"I ... hate ... you ... I, kill y—" he gurgled, barely discernable without the use his lips, which were now dripping down his chin, exposing his lower gums and continuing to melt down past his chin as the rest of the face followed toward the floor. "Yhhh ..." his voice rolled into a death rattle as his head hit the carpeted floor in a muffled thump that seemed to be far too anticlimactic of an ending to Derrick. He was hoping for an explosion or something.

"That's the guy you'd mistaken for me?" Elise asked incredulously.

"Yeah, that's GutTer. I can't say that I'm sorry he's dead; he's wanted me dead for a long time now," Derrick said emotionlessly. Derrick looked directly at Elise and asked her in a perplexed voice "There's no way that was a costume, right?"

"Absolutely NO WAY!" she said adamantly.

They were both confused but elated to have won their first real battle. Tina, Chris, and Lashey were outside and at their wits' end as Derrick and Elise got them packed and into the car. They tried to explain as much as they could on their drive to the hotel. Tina was uncommonly attentive to what they were saying; she didn't interrupt or even raise her voice once on the entire ride.

CHAPTER

Bad Neighborhood

Caleb's eyes darted around trying to see something in the room, but he could only see the skies in his dream, nothing more. He closed his eyes to concentrate on what he was feeling and hearing in the hotel room. He wished so hard he could just wake up, but that didn't feel possible as he lumbered in that place of paralyzed limbs, when the mind knows it's sleeping, dreaming, but is unable to wake up from it. Consciously hearing and feeling what was happening in the room but helpless to do anything about it no matter how hard he struggled, as that epic battle with himself raged to step over the thinnest of invisible lines in the war of asleep and awake.

Caleb's eyes flung open in dreamland and he immediately looked down to his chest to see a slit appear as if a surgeon was in the process of opening him up. Aubrey leaped forward, covering the wound with both hands, and she closed her eyes and looked up toward the sky.

Caleb felt the pain from the slice begin to ease and then completely dissipate. Aubrey removed her hands to reveal that the cut was now gone. Caleb closed his eyes once again to concentrate, and he began to frown. "They're laughing! They're—"

Caleb clinched his teeth together in pain as a *B* was carved into his chest, followed by an *L* and two *O*s. Aubrey immediately began healing the wounds. Caleb's anger and pain quickly shifted the scales in the battle to awaken. His eyes flung open, awake from his dream, and he saw a hand holding the knife that was carving into his skin. Caleb swiftly brought up his own hand and caught the wrist of the assailant with a powerful grip.

The masked faces looked into Caleb's angry eyes and their eyes sprang wide as if they were looking at a ghost. The one carving into Caleb's chest dropped the knife instantly, backing away from Caleb's grasp on his wrist, but he couldn't break free. He tugged three times to free himself before Caleb released his grip on the man's wrist.

The criminal stumbled backward into his accomplice and they both crashed to the floor, dropping the bag of medications they had pilfered from Caleb's room; they had even taken the IV drips that Elise had set up. They sprang to their feet and scrambled straight for the exit door. Moments later one of the drug addicts stumbled back into the room, grabbed the bag full of meds, and ran back out of the hotel room while bumping into everything possible like a pinball before finding the exit.

Blood was flowing from Caleb's chest; he reached for the nightstand and pulled out a handful of gauze to press against his new wounds. He was quickly becoming aware that the pain medication was starting to fade. His remaining charred muscle, nerves, and flesh began to flare until he was in all-out excruciating pain. He wondered where Elise and Derrick could be and prayed that they were safe—and he prayed for God to ease his pain. He prayed this over and over again until he finally passed out from the pain or God's mercy; whichever came first was okay by him.

Caleb opened his eyes to see Aubrey working frantically. She was working her way up his right leg now. He shifted his eyes to his left leg to see that it had been finished. He opened his mouth to speak but instead felt a surge of excruciating pain from the last of his burns to be healed, on his lower back—or was it his entire back now?

The pain was relentless. He could not even identify the point of where it began or where it ended. If only it weren't so horribly consistent, Caleb thought. If only every nerve didn't feel like it was on fire. He was trying to determine if his whole body was burning. Maybe Derrick had changed his mind and dropped out of the group, because this pain was indiscernible, all-encompassing. *Is that why Aubrey's working so hard? Am I burning all over again?* he wondered.

Dear Lord, please ... he pleaded in his head, and he opened his eyes to see a thin black woman bustling around getting ice packs and dispersing them as fast as she could to the open wounds on his lower back. He focused on his legs but did not see any new burns on them, yet he still felt the pain as if they were burning—at least he thought he did. He threw his head back in anguish as the pain coursed through his whole body like he was burning alive.

His vision darkened while looking toward the door to see two figures that resembled Derrick and Elise. Derrick turned quickly and hurried out of room toward the front door. Caleb continued to phase incoherently between timeless pitch blackness, and the hotel room, and the dreamland where Aubrey seemed to be fading in and out. Her not being with him in dreamland seemed to cause a pain even worse in the pit of his gut, an emotional black hole leaving him hopeless and with no will to continue.

CHAPTER

Derrick's Recovery

Derrick intentionally slammed the hotel door behind him as he exited room number 23, hoping someone would act suspiciously, which would give him a place to start. Almost everyone loitering in the area turned to look but only one person took off running, leaving two more people standing nervously in front of room number 46.

Derrick walked straight toward the two that were still standing there. One was a short black man around 23 years old, maybe 5'4" with a very skinny build and the other was a black man also, not much taller at about 5'7" but rounder and wearing a pair of sunglasses. They watched Derrick coming towards them and his body language made it absolutely clear that he was ready to deal with the problem. The one wearing glasses finally became too jumpy when he realized that Derrick was heading directly to them, he frantically looked between Derrick and his accomplice, then took off in a full sprint running away. The skinny one unknowingly backed into the closed door to room 46 and was startled by it, as if the door were someone else waiting in ambush.

Derrick laughed and stopped in front of the short, skinny black man standing with his back pressed against the door so hard that it seemed as if he were trying to back through it. "What up?" Derrick said bluntly.

The guy's eyes were wide and hopping all around as Derrick smiled devilishly at him, knowing that the mental game of this confrontation was already won, since this guy was stoned out of his mind. Derrick leaned in toward him and brought a flash of his fiery will into his eyes, causing them to glow a deep yellowish-red color.

The junkie's eyes grew even wider than they had been which amused Derrick with the thought of them popping out of his skull. He fought back his urge to laugh as the junkie ran off, stumbling and tripping over everything in his path to get away.

Derrick tried the knob but it was locked. He directed the heat to his hand and squeezed tightly as the knob and all of its gearing melted down on both sides of the door. He pushed it open to see two more guys frozen with fear staring at the melting knob. One man was in his late twenties and was white as the other was black and seemed to be around the same age. They had been shoving Caleb's drugs along with many other kinds of loot into bags. As Derrick approached the white one on the left, the junkie started throwing up on the bed and all over his bag of drugs. Derrick stopped in his tracks and changed direction toward the black man on the right. He snatched the bag from the petrified user's hands and dumped its contents onto the bed, away from the puke. Derrick rolled his eyes at the sight of everything that fell out of bag. Packets of cocaine and weed, containers of pharmaceutical pills, and several containers with all sorts of different pills mixed together.

The white junkie who threw up started running toward the door, but Derrick raised a wall of fire in front of the exit. The guy fell backward away from the door. Derrick felt a surge of confidence from looking at the wall, but then the fire suddenly faltered, leaving only a couple of thin lines of flame in front of the door. Derrick focused hard on his creation, but the remaining tendrils of flame only flickered twice and then faded completely.

Derrick turned back to the black junkie and picked up a used syringe between his thumb and forefinger, frowning when he realized that he had lost his Band-Aid and the white tip of his finger was exposed. He chose to wait until this encounter was over before putting another Band-Aid on to cover it, and he thought to himself that he would work on that wall of flames later, too. Then he swiftly ignited the syringe while looking at both of the junkies. "This is definitely one way to die," he said suggestively. Then he cast the syringe across the room and it landed in the bathroom sink, smoldering.

He picked up a prescription bottle and three vials of Caleb's liquid pain medication. He retrieved two other meds that had Caleb's name on them as well. He was going to go through the other bags but figured he didn't want to waste his time rummaging through all of their stolen shit that was covered in puke, Caleb was almost completely healed by Aubrey and Derrick had already found the strong meds for Caleb's instant relief.

To make his point clear, Derrick held Caleb's meds up to their faces. "These belong to us and you'll be dead if you even walk past our door again!" He exited the room but then turned back to send a small fireball onto the drugs that he had dumped on the bed. They went up in a quick flame, and the two junkies scurried around to put the fire out and save as many of the drugs as they could.

Outside of room number 23 Derrick stopped and pulled out a new bandage, put it around his finger, and then walked into their hotel room to see Elise sitting at the couch nearest to the entrance door. She was slouched down almost flat with her arms crossed, thumbs digging deep into her wounds, ripping and scraping away whatever scabs had tried to form throughout this crazy day.

"Can you get these in Caleb quick?" Derrick asked her.

"Yeah, fine," she said flatly. "He's healing up just fine; Aubrey's touching him and healing him, and that's all he could ever want. Everything's just fine."

Derrick could sense some pain in her voice as she kept saying *just fine*, which he was beginning to understand meant not, but Elise wasn't nearly as bad off as he thought she'd be when she found out that Caleb and Aubrey were a pair.

Derrick looked to the other couch, where his family sat watching TV. His mother's eyes met his with a heavyhearted gaze, and Derrick assumed that his mom must have some type of female awareness sort of thing which instinctively knows the faint trials of a comrades fallen heart and then he wondered if all women had such a thing.

Elise got up with the meds and took them into Caleb's room, and moments later it was almost as if everyone could sense the relief of Caleb's pain in the air. Everyone became more relaxed ... except for Elise, who went straight into the bathroom.

"So where to, Mom? Aunt Laura in Chicago, Aunt Eva in Florida, or Colorado with Aunt Georgia?" Derrick asked knowingly, because he knew his mother had always preferred the rare trips to Colorado because the mountains made her feel safe, as if they were her defenders. Derrick hesitated for a moment when he heard the sounds of the showerhead turning on, but then he resumed working out the details with his family.

CHAPTER

Finishing the Healing Process

Caleb opened his eyes to see Aubrey's beautiful face in front of him. He was calm now, pain free, but questioning his sanity because it was as if she was even more beautiful than before, and that couldn't be, because very soon her beauty alone would captivate his entire existence.

His mind recalled the pain and he grimaced at the thought, but not from the burns—it was when he recalled the pain he'd felt when she was gone. Had that actually happened? Had she left his side even for a minute? How could she stand it? How could she leave and not feel every ounce of the solitude he'd felt tugging at her soul as well? How could she sustain that empty-pitted feeling? It was like a severe, constant hunger pain ripping at his abdomen that could only be quenched by her presence.

Did she feel the same; was there a chance this effect was just on him? For sure there was some effect happening. Love is an effect, isn't it? But is it supposed to be physically crippling? That kind of pain was not something the world could keep a secret. Caleb simply had to find out.

"Were you gone?" Caleb asked Aubrey softly.

"Yes I was," Aubrey said pensively. "I felt like something was wrong out there … but I couldn't stay away," she said vaguely before continuing, "I can't describe it … it was painful to be away, an aching … replaced by utopia now that we're together again." Her face flushed instantly, and Caleb refused to let a breath of air pass by before diving to her rescue—or maybe his?

"I know exactly what you're saying, what you were feeling, because I felt it too, when you were gone." His smile was met by her warm lips pressing against his, and then floating was all he could think of, being weightless and floating, anchored to the earth merely by the gentle touch of her soft lips, the effortless movements of their mouths in complete unison as they explored insights of their passions with a most tender kiss.

"We're leaving," Caleb said out of the blue, his mind still foggy from the kiss.

"Yes, leaving," Aubrey managed to say before continuing to kiss him. Moments later they released their embrace and Aubrey found the strength to talk again. "Where are we going?" she asked.

Caleb, still amazed by the effects of a simple kiss, was barely able to clear his mind and answer her. "Oh … no … I mean after you heal my lower back, we over here—Derrick, Elise, and I—are getting directly on a plane to come and get you." Caleb rolled over quickly, and Aubrey had her hands on his lower back healing the area before Caleb even got flat.

****

Derrick had just hung his cell phone up and continued talking to his family when Elise emerged from the bathroom with a somewhat brighter demeanor. Derrick looked up at her and then went back to speaking with his mother. "It's going to be $4,000 for a flight to Colorado that takes off tomorrow morning at eleven." He looked expectantly at Elise for a moment.

"We ain't got that, Derrick," Tina said with a blank expression on her face.

"Don't you worry about the money, Ma. I'll—we have that and plenty more for you three to live for quite a while on, and I will be sending more later, too," he said confidently.

CHAPTER

Insights

Aubrey and Caleb lay on a bed that was ten feet long, ten feet wide, and three feet thick. The mattress was a white satin encasement of down feathers and the pillows, blankets, and sheets were all harmonious to one another. The frame was made of four trees, one at each corner of the mattress. Each tree stood three feet tall and was composed of six branches that were naturally woven to extend from the trunk of the tree in two directions, three woven branches reaching out to support the foot or head of the bed and the other three branches reaching out to support the sides of the bed. In all four directions the branches from each tree intertwined with those of the two adjacent trees. Underneath and at the center of the bed stood a tree very similar to the other four, but this tree had twelve branches that reached out to the four corners and fused into the other trees' trunks.

They were still at the top of the tall hill, full of wildflowers, and at the base of the hill a beach stretched out wide. Volcanic rock and cliff shelves were being bashed by the ocean to the left and uniquely beautiful trees and other vegetation ran off the right.

The sky was now like a mirror of the ocean's soft blue tint, unmarred by clouds, not a single blemish as far as the eye could see. The sun had begun to peek over the horizon, and it was impossible to determine if the sky was being lost in the ocean or the ocean in the sky, as the two seamlessly merged so faintly that even the reflections of the rising sun made it appear whole.

Both Caleb and Aubrey found themselves touching one another every time they looked at the scene in front of them, partially in disbelief that a scene could be so aesthetically perfect but mostly to remind themselves to breathe, as it truly took their breath away.

"Do you believe?" Caleb inquired.

"Yes I do. Just look at that sky, sun, water ... how couldn't you?" she responded, and Caleb exhaled a tiny sigh of relief and embraced her tighter. "Do you really believe this is all something ordained by God?" she asked.

"Yes, I believe that Jesus has us on this path for the greater good of God," Caleb said with internal strength.

Aubrey pulled away from Caleb slowly and lay on her back, nestled the blankets around her as she looked into the blue skies above with a solemn expression. "I'm Jewish, Caleb. I don't believe that Jesus is our savior, just a prophet," she said sadly.

Caleb looked at the sun, which looked like a perfect circle of light, exactly halved by the ocean, but the thinnest of lines between its reflection on the ocean's surface and the actual sun was impossible to distinguish.

"Belief is what I call tolerance, Aubrey. The belief in 'God' is to be tolerant of life itself." He turned his head to Aubrey. "I believe that before Jesus was born, good people still went to heaven after death," he said as Aubrey nodded slightly. "Do you believe that?" he asked her directly, now looking into her eyes.

"Yes, definitely. There are many in the Bible that are talked about for their good deeds before Jesus was born," she replied while contemplating all of the biblical stories she had read and heard.

"I agree too; I believe that God has given us many paths to heaven. I believe that they range from Jesus to Muhammad, to Buddha and all between, all the way to good karma; I see the belief in 'God' or the 'higher power' as a tolerance, and those who have an intolerance to tolerance—to what I call God—are not following God at all but are only following an institution. Doesn't matter if they blame it on misguided religious beliefs or man's misinterpreted words that lead to fanatical crusades or holy wars." Caleb took her hands gently while looking desperately into her eyes, his own nearly welling up with uncertainty and fears of how devastating to their relationship it could be if they disagreed.

"We believe, and that's all that matters, Aubrey. Please, I beg you, don't be intolerant to that," he said with his head lowered, praying to himself that she agreed.

Aubrey dove into Caleb with the most emphatic embrace, that embrace of whole strength, where one squeezes as tightly as one's muscles can to express that feeling—that this is everything I have to give, that I am so in love with us, that I spare nothing, not an ounce of me is reserved outside of love.

"I want to sleep my life away," Aubrey said silently into his ear and Caleb held her even tighter. "I … I can't breathe …" she gasped, and Caleb instantly released his stout grasp of her apologetically.

"I'm sorry, I just … I'm sorry, Aubrey, I didn't mean—"

"It's okay, Caleb. Believe me, it's okay. If I ever had a choice of how I wanted to die, that would be the exact way I'd want to go … smothered by your love," she said while looking deeply into his ocean-blue eyes. "But before then it sounds like we have a lot to do," she said with an inspirational smile that filled Caleb with purpose.

They both sat up and moved to the edge of the bed, feet dangling as they watched the rising sun. The comforting rays against their naked bodies washed away all modesty and sealed the gaps of individualism to make them like one being. Aubrey nestled closer into Caleb, deep in thought, and then she continued to speak.

"If you believe in God or a higher power, than you are tolerant … and any intolerance about another's tolerance is *not* good." She looked to him thoughtfully during a slight pause. "It's almost too simple to believe anything else but 'it'—in regard to God's intention, that is," she said slowly with resolution before injecting some candor. "I wonder what they would think about that in the Middle East … or here, for that matter."

Aubrey's eyes suddenly shifted focus but not position as she continued to look into Caleb's eyes. He waited patiently, assuming that she must be getting up for school; after all, it was Monday morning out there. She focused back onto Caleb's eyes. "One last test," she said, and Caleb gave into the reality of it, thinking of all the things he had to do also, starting with informing Elise and Derrick about where they were going next, including setting up plane tickets and such.

"I guess you have to leave now then?" Caleb said sadly.

Aubrey grinned slightly. "Do you think I've been lying in bed asleep for the last two days out there?" she gave a teasing smile. "I've actually been going through all of the motions out there, like on autopilot. She goes—I go through the day doing virtually everything I would have done. Actually studying and mingling with my friends."

Caleb remembered something she had mentioned, which was why she had gone from his dreamland for a while. "Something's wrong though, right? Last night you were talking about something bothering you and that's why you were gone."

She looked down at her hands and started fidgeting with them. "Concerned, yes, because I have one more final today and I'm not sure how the me out there in the real world will do on the test." It seemed to Caleb like there was more to it than just that, but Aubrey wasn't saying.

"You could go check on the real world you" he said but then reflected on the pain of being away from her, and he quickly made the assumption that that was what she was not saying: that she was afraid to leave here without him. She was silent, just looking at her hands trying to muster up the courage to go.

"What if I could come with you?"

Her eyes sparkled with excitement at the idea. "That would be great!" she exclaimed. "But how?"

"I'm not sure—how do you do it?" he asked.

Aubrey looked deflated at the thought. "I don't know, Caleb, I just feel where I'm at, like a connection that's already there," she said. "Whose dream is this again?" she asked with a nervous chuckle.

Caleb's laugh was no more convincing than hers, and he thought to himself that he had basically approached leaving the dream the same way as she had just said when the thugs were in the room carving him up. "Where are you right now?" he asked.

"Getting ready for school," she said flatly.

"Okay, let me try this," Caleb said as he closed his eyes and concentrated hard on the outside world. All he was able to receive at first was himself in the hotel room, but with some effort he could extend his vision from there and see all throughout the hotel. He found it odd because he remembered it being a pretty full hotel with people all around outside and hanging around cars, but now there were only a few people in a couple of rooms. The rest of the complex was vacant, with only one car in the parking lot other than Derrick's car and his Uncle Seth's rental. At the other car there were three men, and he guessed that they were gangsters.

One of the gangsters was shorter with a dark complexion and wearing parochial school clothes. *Strange, that's for sure*, Caleb thought, but inspecting these guys was not getting him any closer to leaving dreamland to be with Aubrey. He opened his eyes, looking dejected. "Nothing." He lowered his head in thought and then raised it with excitement once again. "What if you go back there, to your reality, and I'm sure I'll be able to follow you," he said brightly.

Once again concern clouded Aubrey's eyes, and Caleb guessed it was fear of the pain. "I'll be right behind you, and if I'm not you can come back immediately," he assured her. She accepted his terms, closed her eyes, and raised her head to the sky. In a flash of white light she was gone. In a heartbeat Caleb felt a longing pull in the pit of his gut. It quickly shifted to gnawing hunger that was ripping at the lining of his stomach.

He closed his eyes quickly, looked to the sky, felt the connection to Aubrey, and let go of himself. He opened his eyes and was in the bathroom with Aubrey in a flash, which sent the pains away immediately. Caleb hadn't noticed it but both Aubrey's' were in the bathroom. The real world Aubrey was taking her morning shower as the dreamscape Aubrey was hunched over with one knee on the beautiful burgundy-tiled bathroom floor, one open palm on the cool tile floor and one arm at her stomach. Caleb assumed that the pain had just left her too. He hurried over to help her to her feet. Their faces showed relief, but he couldn't help but fear waking up and being without her.

"How am I supposed to survive that kind of pain while you travel from LA all the way here to Florida?" Aubrey asked with a shaky voice.

Caleb was contemplating the question when he realized that the shower water was running. He looked to the beveled glass shower, which stood alone, perfectly sequenced with the whole bathroom, and he wondered how much a bathroom like this would cost. But he lost that thought at the sight of Aubrey's bare silhouette in the shower. "Hey, I'm over here" dreamscape Aubrey said while guiding Caleb's gawking face back to hers by his chin. "I mean, I'm over here, too," she finished.

Caleb really looked at her and for the first time since they had jumped out of their dream space atop the wild flower hill and into wherever he was now and realized that she had clothes on now. He was surprised that he hadn't noticed the lovely white spring dress adorned with several medium-sized flowers of yellow, blue, red, and green. It hung from her mature body perfectly. "You look beautiful," he said sincerely.

She blushed. "You look quite dashing yourself," she teased.

Caleb looked down to see his rather preppy attire of khakis and a blue oxford button-up shirt with loafers to match. He promptly focused on his body and how irritating these clothes would feel against his wounds and realized that there was none of the irritation or pain that he had become so accustomed to over the past few days, and he smiled at Aubrey. "I can't thank you enough for all that you've done for me," he said, and she blushed again. His expression became one of deep thought for a moment, and then he turned his head to the Aubrey in the shower again and then back to her in front of him. Elated, he said, "We don't have to worry about being apart when we're awake."

Aubrey was clearly confused. "How would you know that?" she asked.

"You and I felt the pain of being apart, you see? You and me, in dreamland." He gestured to the Aubrey in the shower. "She clearly felt no pain, in the real world."

Aubrey looked thoughtfully to the shower and then back at him. "You're right, I would have known if she—if I were having anything painful happening to me."

Caleb replied in a supportive tone, "I would have too, just like how when that thug was carving into me, I felt every bit of it—and thank you once again for saving my life on that one, too," he said gratefully.

CHAPTER

Schools Out

They toured the mansion that Aubrey called home as the real-world Aubrey got prepared for school. Her father was a forward-thinking man who was the benefactor of very large amounts of land that his family had owned for years. He wisely kept some for sentimental reasons and sold large amounts of urban lands for developing city projects along with rural areas where he had anticipated growth spurts. By the time he was forty years old he was officially a real estate mogul, buying and selling properties in several countries with his insights and a Midas-like touch.

By the time they had finished touring the house, the real-world Aubrey was already at school taking her first test. In a closed-eyes flash they were there looking over her shoulder at her answers, which were all correct to the best of the dreamland Caleb and Aubrey's knowledge. Aubrey was a detailed worrier so she remained standing there supervising the test as Caleb strolled around the room investigating the other students' tests and occasionally touching through students, which allowed him to see the past few days of that person's life as well as their thoughts, including thoughts of their futures.

That was how he had been able to see Markus's plans regarding the prodigies and his cult-like followers, the foot soldiers. Or were they employees? He wondered how things were going with that situation between Derrick and Markus and he also thought of Elise for the first time in a while. He was unsure if he should harbor any guilt if her feelings would be hurt, even though he really had done nothing to lead her on, but nonetheless the guilt was there because he had also done nothing to discourage her.

He continued examining the female students thoughts and overall was pretty pleased that most thought fondly of Aubrey. They admired her beauty and kindness, with the exception of a couple of very jealous girls who couldn't wait to graduate so they would never have to see her again. Caleb didn't know much about Aubrey's past, regarding her personal life, so he tried to steer clear of touching any boys and finding out something she hadn't felt like sharing just yet, if ever, and he was okay with that.

Aubrey kept looking at him strangely, trying to figure out what he was doing, because she was unaware of this particular talent that Caleb possessed.

He stared at Aubrey standing there looking back and forth between him and her real-world Aubrey. He could only admire her beauty and couldn't help but to think how lucky he was. It was then that he noticed that he wasn't the only one staring at her. In the row behind and to the right of the real-world Aubrey was a redheaded boy, pale with blemished skin, staring at the real-world Aubrey with a disturbing look in his eyes.

Caleb definitely was second-guessing his decision not to peer into boys' thoughts and made an amendment for this one guy to find out what was behind his look, what it was in his and Aubrey's past that could justify such an evil stare. The guys in her past were really none of Caleb's business, but this temptation was far too great for him to resist. As he passed Aubrey, she looked up at him, smiling, but Caleb was not looking at her as he walked directly toward the boy, focused completely on him.

She looked at Caleb's eyes to see where he was headed and saw the boy he was headed directly toward. She stiffened up and her face quickly shifted into a fearfully intense expression that grew more frightened with every step he took toward the boy. The closer Caleb got to him the more he wanted to stop himself, but the untold story in the boy's eyes dragged Caleb closer and closer. When Caleb reached out to touch the boy's hand, he saw that his own hand was shaking as it entered into the boy's space.

Shock consumed Caleb's face as he snapped his head toward Aubrey while simultaneously jerking his hand back from the boy's space. Aubrey was now staring at Caleb with a blank expression; Caleb continued to stare back into her eyes as he now lowered his whole body into the boy's space, sitting there at his desk. Dreamland Aubrey took a step toward them, and she could see the outline of Caleb's body quivering inside of the larger body of the red-haired boy. She stepped nearer and saw the red-haired boy's body beginning to quiver slightly and then shake until the shaking turned into violent convulsions and the boy's hands gripped the desk, causing it to rattle and squeak loudly, as if it were being torn to pieces from the boy's strength and jarring movements. Everyone in the room turned to watch with fear in their eyes.

Then with one last ripping convulsion, the boy tore the arm-desk portion completely apart from its hinges while hopping up high straight out of the chair. He gripped the desk part of the seat so tightly in his right hand that small amounts of blood seeped from underneath his nails. The rest of the chair flew into the air from the force of the boy jumping out of it and crashed into the wall, breaking into pieces. Caleb fell to the floor and now lay there holding his rib cage, mouth gaping open trying to catch a breath of air. The boy was looking down, trying to shake his head clear—and then with one incredibly fast yank of his head he was staring maliciously into real-world Aubrey's eyes. She shrunk into her desk from the horrific glare, and then the boy bolted out of the classroom. Caleb jumped to his feet and stared into dreamland Aubrey's eyes with a fear so deep it was as if the blood had been sucked from his whole body, and he now stood there as white as a sheet, trembling.

Caleb's senses rapidly came back to him and he darted for the door, grabbing Aubrey's hand on his way. "We have to follow him!" he shouted as they exited the classroom, her expression stunned as she tried to keep up with Caleb's pursuit of the boy.

They exited the building in time to see him get into his car and speed away. "Do you know where he lives; that's where he's going ... do you know where it is?" Caleb said urgently.

"Yes I know where he lives ... what's going on, Caleb? I'm scared!" Aubrey's voice was shaky.

"We have to get there now!" Caleb demanded. Aubrey closed her eyes, raised her head to the sky, and in a flash was gone; Caleb did the same and instantly followed.

They appeared outside of a half-story bungalow-style house with a veranda. The pillars on both sides of the porch were made of brick that had been marred by time, an occasional brick missing brick and virtually all of the rest cracked or chipping away. At the top where the half-story pitch stood were four tiny windows in a small row across, and Caleb wondered if there was more dirt and residue on the outside of the glass or the inside. The siding on the house was the original one-inch wood slabs all around, but needless to say, the lack of upkeep on had left them tattered and in desperate need of repair.

Caleb looked around the neighborhood and noticed that this one house stuck out like a sore thumb, as the others were all well-kept, remodeled, and in some cases even extended. One in particular that was a larger colonial home was very well kept and landscaped. Aubrey pointed to that house. "My best friend since grade school lives there," she said distinctively, and Caleb acknowledged her but then turned back to the broken-down house.

"What's going on, Caleb, talk to me," Aubrey pleaded.

Still facing the house, he looked at Aubrey from the corner of his eye and asked, "Who is this guy?" Then he began to walk toward the house and before Aubrey could give an answer Caleb continued to speak. "You stay here and let me know right when he gets here, okay?"

He hurried into the house by simply phasing effortlessly through the doors and navigated through it as if he had been there before. He headed straight for the basement of the house and down into it. It was dark and musty. The floor was either made of dirt or a former concrete floor had been pulled up, and small amounts of dust would stir into the air with each step that he took. He saw six easels around the space, each with a painting, and Caleb believed they were done by the boy, but there was some particular paintings that Caleb needed to find, ones he had seen when reading the boys thoughts.

Giving credit where it was due, Caleb was pretty impressed by this boy's artistic ability. They were mostly landscapes of faraway imaginative places which contained light strokes, fantastic shading, and carefully transcending hues so slight that they dared the viewer to touch them just to confirm that they were painted. They were all very tranquil settings with occasional passionate strokes in them, which bordered on anger. Caleb caught himself wasting time thinking about the paintings; shaking himself and thinking that he was no art critic, he focused on his investigative skills. He noticed that the room felt smaller than the upper level, but there were no doors that he could see.

"My dream," he said to himself, and the room slowly lit up from no apparent light source. Caleb felt all around—walls, rafters, anything he thought might be a release for a hidden room. He focused on the north wall because that was the direction in which the room seemed drastically shortened according to the layout of the house, and the base of that wall seemed not as worn by time.

The wall appeared to be constructed on top of a smooth cement block. He knew it was concealing something and he wondered why he was letting himself be constrained by these objects. He simply walked straight through the wall and into a ten-by-fifteen-foot room that had shelves attached to the north wall stuffed full with art supplies and other knickknacks. A workbench stood against the wall to the west of the shelves with a stool at its side.

Several easels were there with canvases on them facing the north wall, and several more were stacked against the side of the workbench. He saw two stacks of photos on the edge of the bench. Caleb walked directly to them, picked them up and started shuffling through them quickly. The first stack seemed to be pictures of infant baby girls, and Caleb shuddered as his thoughts shot to the dirt floor in this basement, or tomb, whatever it was.

He couldn't tell how many different infant girls there were because he had never been too good at differentiating babies, and besides, he was there looking for one particular picture right now. He had already begun thumbing through the second stack of pictures when the hard, cold reality rose up into his throat like a dry lump of clay, leaving a small aching and the inability to swallow for a moment. He picked up the first stack of pictures again, but this time one by one he flipped each of them around to see the back sides. *One-month Aubrey*; he tossed it aside and grabbed the next one: *Aubrey-two months old*, and on and on until he got to the second stack. *Aubrey, age thirteen*.

He turned slowly to see the paintings that he had past when going to the photos first. The first painting that caught his eye was the one he had seen in the vision while being in the boy's space. A picture of the boy lying lifeless with his arm comfortably placed around Aubrey, who lay beside him, also lifeless. There is a small-caliber bullet hole in his forehead and a trickle of blood falling from it. Her neck has red marks of strangulation, her eyes are closed, and there is a smile on her face. The smile looks strange, unlike any smile he had seen on Aubrey's face before. They are both wearing graduation caps and gowns.

The pose was meticulously arranged to match another painting beside it of an older couple and the man seemed to bear a striking resemblance to this boy. The pose was exactly the same, but there was a black thread attached from the corners of this woman's mouth to her upper cheeks and pulled tight to give the impression that she was smiling.

Her eyes were not closed; instead they retained that deadened, glossed-over cataracts look—but not in a dull, partially opened, lifeless manor. No, her eyes were extremely widened, to the point that almost three-quarters of her entire eyeballs were visible. Blood vessels were bulging, and she was looking downward.

Caleb had seen enough and had to find out what Aubrey knew. He also felt an uncontrollable urge to get to Florida as soon as heavenly possible!

He looked back to the desk and focused on a spool of fishing line already threaded through a surgical needle, and his stomach turned as it dawned on him why there wasn't a trace of black thread on Aubrey's face in the painting.

He quickly met up with Aubrey who was still outside waiting for the boy to arrive. "What do you know about this guy?" Caleb asked politely, trying to hide the dread coursing through his veins.

"We became friends when I was nine or ten years old," she explained. "I was here to play with my friend Elizabeth quite a bit and he was always around, shyly watching us. One day we asked him if he wanted to play too, and for a long time after that it was mainly us three playing together, nothing weird. All three of us would hold hands, until one day when he just wanted to hold mine; Elizabeth and I both had crushes on him and it felt strange with him holding just my hand, but I liked him and Elizabeth wasn't mad, so."

"A crush in grade school doesn't explain this," Caleb thought out loud. He asked her, "Is there anything more?"

"Yes there is," she said while nodding and looking at the ground. "His parents died … murder, suicide; it was all over the papers and everyone knew about it. I think I was the only one he would talk to after that; he wouldn't even talk to Beth. And honestly, Caleb, I never knew what to say to him, and that would upset him and he would say some terrible things to me. I was scared and I told my parents."

Caleb began to realize that it was the boy's parents in the painting beside the one of Aubrey and him.

"What did they do?" he asked, and her frown of disapproval said it all.

"They restricted me from any contact with him at all and they informed the police about it. The police were accusing him of misconduct, and it all got blown way out of proportion." She began fiddling with her hands. "He was almost sent to an institution because of everything, but his older brother was able to get him and the house … I've never talked to him since then—well, until the other night, I guess," she said reluctantly.

"The other night?" Caleb asked.

"Yeah, when I was with you. Or more like, when I wasn't with you," she said.

Caleb again remembered her saying something about feeling that something had been wrong, but before he had assumed it was her fear of the pain of their separation.

"I guess my mom needed me to get something from the store. The real-world me bumped into him at the store and I—she was talking to him as if nothing had ever happened. I wasn't aware that she was even talking to him until I felt the real-world me starting to feel threatened," Aubrey explained.

"Threatened how, Aubrey?" Caleb tried to say as calmly as he could, but too many pictures of bad things were running through his head, and it came out more panicked than calm.

"I'm not sure what they were talking about, but when I got there ..." She paused. "He was saying how he was looking forward to graduation night ... and it was the disturbing way he said it that scared the hell out of me! I didn't say anything to him at all after I took over the real-world me. I just got out of there as fast as I could," she said with tears rolling down her cheek.

Caleb wanted to know more about this boy; something told him that every detail counted. "Aubrey, where did his parents die?" he asked quietly.

"The basement."

Caleb turned to look at the house. "1449. And what street is this?" he urged.

"Collins Point," Aubrey said curiously.

"What's his name?"

"John," she responded, and Caleb tilted his head slightly as a gesture for her to continue. "Owens, John Owens is his name," she said.

Caleb nervously looked up the street in both directions. "How far is the school from here?" he asked.

"Like five minutes at the most," she said while looking expectantly toward the street.

"He must have changed his mind about coming home or else something's happened along the way. We don't have time to waste standing here, though." Caleb focused all of his attention on Aubrey. "I *need* you to stay away from him, understand?"

"He's going to be at graduation tonight; I can't miss that because my parents have a big celebration for me immediately after," Aubrey said.

Caleb pursed his lips and ran many thoughts through his mind but ended up reluctantly agreeing with her. She should be safe at the graduation party; there would be people around her at all times during and after the graduation. But he was confused about something. "How can you have finals today and graduation tonight?"

"Oh, that was because a teacher had an accident on her way into the school one morning and so she pushed the taking of that test back. It was optional but could raise your grade if you took it today, and I have a B+ in that class now, so I elected to take it for the A," Aubrey said, sounding almost monotone. Caleb could see that all of this was starting to wear on her, and he needed her be alert and on her toes until he could get to Florida.

"We're needed in the real world now, and you know what to do. I also need you to call the police and tell them about this," Caleb said.

"And tell them what Caleb? I still don't know what's happening," she expressed earnestly.

"Baby, please just stay away from John; he wants to kill you. Don't go near him, and I don't know … tell the police there's a weapon of mass destruction in John Owens's basement if you have to, sweetie—tell them anything, just get them there."

Caleb took a step closer to try and comfort her by gently grasping her hands, peering deeply into her eyes. "I love you with all that I am and with everything that I ever will be. I will not let anyone or anything take that away from me, ever." He wiped the tears from her eyes and pressed his lips softly against hers. Their mouths, partially open, slowly and gently slid closed with a longing for more as he pulled back, releasing her lower lip. He then looked up to the sky with closed eyes and in a flash he was gone.

CHAPTER

No Time to Waste

Caleb hurried out of bed and for the first time in what seemed like forever to him, there was no pain and he was completely rejuvenated. He grabbed a pair of pants from the closet, and unconsciously glanced at the full-length mirror on the wall as he passed. He stopped, immediately frozen in his tracks as what he just saw registered. He took three steps back to see himself fully clothed in the same uniform that he had seen his entire life.

There he stood, in the reflection, with the same clothes that the people in the blue cast wore—the same cord dangling, but from above both of his elbows and down into apparatuses around his forearms. He had never seen that before, always just one elbow, and the thing that ripped at his entire being was that the image in the mirror was cast in the same bluish-turquoise hue. He looked himself up and down noting that every movement in the mirror was mocked as a show of cruelty—or was it a true reflection?

Unable to determine his sanity, he stepped out of sight of the mirror's reflection. All he could think was that his mother was gone. That this was a sign of his death—or was any of this real at all? It doesn't make sense, you live and you die and then go to heaven, or hell, or purgatory, which is where? Here on earth? He thought to himself, but some say this is hell that we're living now and others say it will be hell here on earth after the reckoning. The thoughts were going through his head so fast that he had to try and stop them completely before he ends up babbling to himself in a corner.

He knew there was no time or need for him to start doubting himself or his faith. He knew one thing for sure and that was that he stands strong for God and that his is not to question why but his is to do or die. Which meant…?

He stepped back to the mirror to see his mother as clear as day in the reflection, no distortions in the least. He stood so still it would make a statue envious. Time must have passed, he thought as he fixated on his mother's presence for countless moments before he felt his first blink as a reference to time. It was as if she stood before him, no glass or interpretation of space that would dispute it.

He raised his hand timidly as confirmation, to touch her, just to know she was real, but the movement of her lips quickly distracted him. "Be Careful Caleb," he saw her mouth. But he couldn't understand her facial expression; both happiness and sadness tugged up at the corners of her mouth as if an effort to express her joy. "I'm so proud of you," he saw her say before realizing that it was now just him standing in front of the mirror, hand stretched out with the tip of his finger barely touching the glass. Just him standing there longing for his mother from the very core of his existence.

He attempted to gather himself while getting dressed and bursting into the other room to see who was there. Elise lay on the loveseat asleep, and Derrick was sleeping on the sofa. Caleb looked at the clock that rested on an end table and saw that it read 7:55 a.m.

It took him a few moments to realize that time difference was three hours between California and Florida, and he felt that time wasn't completely against him—or was it? "We have to leave now!" he said with an enormous sense of urgency.

Elise and Derrick jumped to their feet to see Caleb waving his arms in an effort to rush them up. Derrick dashed to the window and looked through a small opening in the drapes, assuming that they were being attacked.

Elise rushed to Caleb while rubbing the sleepiness from her eyes and asked, "What is it?"

"It's Aubrey, she's being stalked, and he's very close!" Caleb said, and Elise looked at Caleb for a moment before she relaxed a bit and stood upright from her readied position. She looked at Derrick, who was still looking out of the window and being very careful not to disturb the curtains.

"We have to leave now! We need to call the airport; where's my phone?" Caleb said while rifling in and out of both rooms, frantically searching.

"My family's next door Caleb, I need to get them to a safe place… No, you two need to get them safely to the airport and put them on that plane, I can handle the situation outside and then meet up with you at the airport" Derrick said and then returned his attention outside of the window.

Elise reached under just one of her arms to press against her wound and, she hoped, to clear her obvious tension from the chaotic situation.

"What are you talking about Derrick?" Caleb demanded.

Elise's mind cleared pretty fast after the shooting pain washed away the remaining fog like a slap across the face. "They're here, aren't they?" Her words came out rapidly.

"Yeah, but only one car with two soldiers and a prodigy-Curtis," Derrick answered with mixed feelings about Curtis being there. This gang shit is not much different than what's depicted in the mafia movies; learn to trust no one and it's the ones closest to you that usually ends up taking you out Derrick thought to himself. He glanced back to Elise.

"You Caleb and my family need to take the Camry" Derrick said.

"Of course," Elise responded, grabbing her duffle bag and hurrying behind Derrick, ready at the door.

"Please protect them for me Elise-without them I have nothing," Derrick said quietly but it spoke in volumes to Elise.

As Derrick began to open the door, Caleb called to both of them, "Wait, wait, what's going on?"

Derrick turned to him. "Marcus knows we're here, and he's got some of his boys outside waiting for us. I need to get their undivided attention so you guys can escape unharmed. I don't know if it's just these guys or if there's more hiding out there," Derrick said in a low voice.

"I just saw the whole area in my dream, and it was just those three out there," Caleb said. Derrick and Elise looked at him strangely and then shifted their attention back to the situation outside. Derrick cracked the door open slightly to confirm that there was only three cars outside and to prepare to dash.

"Wait a minute," Caleb demanded. "We're not leaving anyone behind!"

Derrick closed the slight crack in the door and turned to Caleb as Elise took a step back, but remained in a readied position.

"What do you propose?" Derrick said urgently.

"Same plan works for me but we're not leaving this parking lot without you… You handle these guys Derrick and then get in the car and we'll all go to the airport together," Caleb said encouragingly.

"Fine, but if it gets too hairy you get my family away safely and then you can come back after that. Agreed?" Derrick said

"Agreed" Caleb answered while grabbing his bags and keys "I'll get the car Elise, get Derrick's family in quickly" He said while going into line behind Elise, taking her duffle bag from her as he passed. She shot him a quick glance as he took position behind her.

"Thanks," she whispered to him.

Derrick opened the door and headed straight across the parking lot toward the thugs waiting for him. He held his hands high in the air so they wouldn't get jumpy. They began shuffling their feet nervously as they watched Elise come out right after Derrick and head to the room next door with a key in her hand. Caleb followed her out and headed straight to the trunk of the Camry which was parked right next to Derrick's car.

One gangster pulled out a sawed-off shotgun and the other an AK-47, and they aimed the guns at Derrick but then the gangster with the AK-47 began to raise his gun in Caleb's direction. Derrick recognized the confusion on their faces and started waving his hands to get them to aim at him. "Hey, hey, I'm the one you're lookin' for—don't mess with them, they don't mean shit to you!" he said loudly to keep their attention on him.

When he got to them, they ordered him to his knees, and Derrick promptly complied. "What the fuck are you doing, Derrick?" Curtis bellowed. "Who the hell are they—?" Curtis stopped abruptly when he saw Derrick's mom, brother, and sister come out of the second hotel room with Elise and approach the car that was now running with Caleb inside. Derrick looked over his shoulder to see what was happening and felt relieved to see them getting safely into the car. Curtis watched and seemed to immediately accept what was happening when he saw it was Derrick's family seemably trying to leave town to escape Markus' wrath. He shifted his attention back towards Derrick who was now looking very stern at Curtis.

"Markus sent us with instruction to pick you up, not your family, yet… Smart move getting them out of town, but you know he'll make you tell where they've gone before he… we are done with you," Curtis said reluctantly.

"If I go back with you, you know exactly what he's going to do to me, Curtis."

The gangster with the AK-47 took a step closer to Derrick and placed the muzzle of the gun against Derrick's temple and for the first time Derrick felt like he no longer had control of the situation. He had spent too much attention on his family and now the gangsters had gotten too close—they had the drop on him, and he was not coming up with a way out. He figured his only chance was if the one with the gun against his head would remove it for even just a second, then he could have a fighting chance.

The thug with the shotgun gave a head motion that sent Curtis to the rear car door to open it. That same gangster motioned with his shotgun for Derrick to get up and head for the car.

Caleb looked at Elise and thoughts of her shot through his head—thoughts of her confused life due to a masochist fuck that was so wrapped up in his momentary satisfaction that he would put all innocents in jeopardy! Ruination that Caleb would not accept. He looked back at Derrick's family, people who were only trying to survive this environment. He thought of Derrick, who stood against it all at this moment to protect his family from harm, and Caleb decided.

If he were destined to be blue then this was the time! He realized that both of his feet had pressed hard against the gas and the brake simultaneously while he'd shifted the car into reverse. He released the brake and the car shot back toward Derrick and the thugs.

Derrick was shifting his gaze between each of the thugs with guns; the muzzle of the AK-47 still against his temple. He had heard tires squeal as Caleb began the long brake torque, and Derrick knew the very moment Caleb had released his foot from the brake and rocketed in their direction, because the thugs both raised their guns toward the oncoming car. At a moment's notice he was there, and the driver's side door of the car swung open as the car screeched to a stop. Caleb leaped out of the car, heading toward Derrick, empty-handed but screaming at the top of his lungs.

But his help was too late. Derrick had already grabbed both barrels and sent a massive surge of heat down through each of their chambers. Both guns exploded simultaneously, the wave of heat pushing the ignitions straight back into the gangsters. Their bodies flew lifelessly backward and bounced off of their parked vehicle.

Curtis was shocked, leaning against the now-bloody car. He looked down at his dead partners and quickly raised his hands to surrender. Derrick approached him, grabbed him by the collar, and walked him away from the car. "I can't believe you were going to deliver me to him," he said.

"I-I was just doing what I was told, Derrick; you know this shit ain't personal," Curtis pleaded.

"Nice, you seem to be grasping the power of slang all of the sudden, but pretend I'm your Markus now so *English* mutha fucka, English!" Derrick insisted

Caleb had gotten back into the car and drove up to the two of them to urge Derrick to hop into the car so they could leave.

"Don't worry, friend," Derrick patronized, "I need you to tell Markus something … I'll be back for him! What he's trying to do is wrong and I'm shutting it down! I'd advise you to get out while you still can, *friend*," he concluded with malice in his tone.

He shoved Curtis onto the pavement then turned to the car that he and the thugs had come in, a hundred feet across the lot. He sent an arching flame from his hand to the car, which went up in flames, then Derrick snapped back to his old classmate, "Don't be a part of this gang shit when I get back, Curtis! And you better not be at a college feeding that shit to innocent people either! I'll track your ass down, believe that!" His tone left no uncertainty.

He turned to the burning car again and sent a solid blue flame at it, causing it to explode instantly. He looked back down at Curtis with flames burning in his eyeballs and winked. Derrick got into his car, and they sped away toward the airport.

After putting Derrick's family on the plane to Colorado, Caleb, Elise, and Derrick booked last-minute passage on a flight headed to Florida. They had convinced passengers to swap seats so that all three of them were seated together. Elise took the window seat and quietly urged Derrick to sit beside her, because she still was not quite over or accepted the whole Caleb being with Aubrey thing.

The three were pretty quiet as they each reflected on the last few days—how different their lives were now and the unknowing of what was next.

Derrick was wrestling with himself about talking to Caleb about a few issues, and he figured no better time than the present. He leaned toward Caleb and whispered, "Did you notice that brown circle on your left bicep?" Caleb just nodded while looking at Derrick. "Well, as you were being healed I touched you and …" Derrick brought his right hand up and removed his Band-Aid.

Caleb stared at him emotionlessly until an edge of disgust started to wash across his face, which was quickly followed by a huge smile and a shoulder nudge. "Had you going there, didn't I?" he said while laughing at the surprised-looking Derrick, then he put his hand up for a soul shake and held on to Derrick's hand after. "Mi casa, su casa. Welcome, my body, heart and soul brother," Caleb said very sincerely and then released Derrick's hand.

Derrick felt a strange feeling of kinship with Caleb and thought to himself about how right he was about becoming good friends with him. "Ummm, I have one more question …" he said. "You said that you see what a person's plans are now, right—in your dreams, I mean?"

Caleb nodded while looking into Derrick's eyes, anticipating the question he was building up to.

"What was I gonna do … I mean … could you see if I went through with it or …?"

Caleb took a few moments sitting there motionlessly staring at Derrick. "All that matters is you're here with us now. The Lord works in mysterious ways, Derrick," Caleb whispered.

Derrick rolled his eyes at Caleb's reference to religion but not so adamantly this time. "The other day I told myself that if 'God' could show me a selfless act that I would consider his existence," he said while adjusting himself closer to Caleb. "You've done that, Caleb, and I like to consider myself a man of his word … you've done your part; the rest is up to him," he said as though it were a challenge directly to God.

Caleb simply laid his head back against the headrest and closed his eyes.

Two hours later he woke up in a puddle of sweat and screaming.

"You're okay, you're just dreaming!" Derrick said as he held Caleb's forearm firmly, though he immediately reconsidered what he had just said, given who he had just said it to. "Okay, let me rephrase that—what did you see, Caleb?"

Caleb, shaking and visibly disturbed, tried to answer. "All I could see was both of them, John and Aubrey … dead!" Caleb stuttered out "It wasn't a painting … I tried to sense her, but I couldn't feel her anywhere," he paused unable to speak, "only the pain of her not being with me." Caleb dropped his face to his hands with disgust at not being able to save his soul mate and what it would mean to the rest of his life. Suddenly he began to welcome the thought of becoming one of the bluish ones. Derrick put his arm around him.

"It really could have just been a bad dream, right?" Elise said, leaning forward to speak.

"I don't know. If it was just a dream then why couldn't I sense her?" Caleb asked. "We have to get there now! We need to be there already!" he said despondently.

"We're landing now, Caleb," Derrick consoled. "You'll see; everything will be fine. Have some faith, my brother."

CHAPTER

Aubrey's Fate

A dream? Why so dark? It had to be a dream which meant that Caleb was here. My heart leaped with excitement; the thought of looking into his gorgeous eyes—so sad, so sincere, and his handsome face that I could stare at for days without blinking once.

"Caleb?" I called out hesitantly against the dark while rising to my feet, but I instantly felt the restraints at my wrists and ankles holding me down. The fear dried my throat so quickly that it hurt. I tried to bring my hands up in order to feel my neck for injuries, but I couldn't break them free.

Swallowing was painful, but I managed to do it a couple of times, and I realized that the pain was on my neck as well—an irritation of my skin as if it had been rubbed way too hard, or ...

"Caleb, please say something, you're scaring me."

I could feel someone near and I prayed it was Caleb, but other possibilities began to enter my mind. I refused to think of the one most frightening possibility, though; I still have hours before graduation, and Caleb assured me that everything would be fine. He assured me that he would be here and that he wouldn't let anything happen to me. I believe you, Caleb, please be here.

How long had I been in this chair ... where was I? Fear began to slither around me as I sensed whoever was here with me shifting around, now standing behind me. I could feel the heat from his or her breath on the back of my neck, the stench of that breath like the polar opposite of my Caleb's sweet breath. This person was so close now that I could also smell the musty body odor coming from him; it couldn't be a woman because I have never smelled a female with that husky of an odor. I leaned away from the smells which caused whoever it was to back away from me. I instantly envisioned the thing from my nightmare and my body became rigid with fear.

I battled against the fog in my head to recall my last memory. I remembered being in dreamland with Caleb. He said he loved me; I couldn't stop thinking about that for a moment but then regained my composure and continued my process of recall. Caleb had emphasized that I stay far away from John Owens. I remembered driving home, parking in the garage, closing the garage ... door, I think ...

My thoughts became clearer, and the sheer terror of my realization pushed the word out of my mouth.

"John?" I gasped as the fogginess in my head was replaced by the horror of my situation.

"Only three tries," John's deeply baritone voice broke through the darkness with a rumble. I'd never known his voice to be so frightening, and I heard him make his way to the other side of the room through the dark.

He flicked on the light and leaned against the wall with his arms crossed, a smug, emotionless expression on his face. I instinctively pulled against the ropes to get away as the fear flushed all of the color from my body and caused the room to feel even colder.

I'd never seen so much hate in someone's eyes before; they stared through me as if he'd already killed me, and now there was just the simple task of depriving me of air to conclude the act. I instantly knew why my neck and throat were sore; he had strangled me before, but why had he stopped? Why was I still alive? I turned away from his look that told me I was going to die now and started thinking beyond this situation that had me trembling so hard I was shocked the knots in the ropes hadn't untied from the vibrations of my body.

"Did you know you were being followed?" he asked in that deep tone. He looked at the painting of him and me, and then he peered at me from the corner of his eye with childish grin. "You deserve that ... you ruined my life and you deserve exactly that." His tone stayed the same as he spoke, no elevation, no emotion. "You had me put away for trying to be your friend, and ever since that day I've had this night in mind for you and me!"

"But I didn't, John ..." I exclaimed, and he seemed genuinely surprised that I'd spoken. He quickly silenced me with the raise of a hand, but I wasn't sure if it was that I had said or that I was pleading that startled him.

He closed his eyes and nodded as he recounted his speech to see where he had been interrupted. I wondered how many times he had run this scene through his head, and it was clear to me that my speaking was not a part of it.

"You had me put away for trying to be your friend and every day ever since that day I've had this night in mind for you and me. This would be a date you could never refuse; I shouldn't have stopped choking the life out of you in your garage today!" He managed to transform his perplexed look back into that dark expression of his that dug holes into me.

I attempted to calm myself by thinking of my parents' kindness and how all they wanted for me was to be a happy, God-fearing person and how passionately my mother wanted grandchildren. My parents would always ask me what I wanted to be when I grew up, and there was only one correct answer—happy!—and I hoped to God that they knew that because of them, I was. I thought about my friends and how they would react when they heard about this. I began to see why the death of a young person touched so many people: because we have not even really started to live. No marriage, children, mortgages, no real life to speak of except for thoughts of what we could have been.

"I thought that maybe you'd feel bad for me and beg me to be your friend after that," John continued, "but instead you ran from me—but you could never run from this, you—"

I burst into his monologue, hoping that keeping him off track could help me somehow. "John, it's not too late, we can go out, just you and me. We can date, John; I won't say no, I swear," I said in a desperate voice that shook along with my body.

His eye took focus on my face for a long moment before glassing back over with defeat. "It doesn't matter anymore. It knows you're here and it's close," he said, and I felt sorrow in his voice.

"Whose close, John? Who's following me?" I begged.

"I don't know what it is, but it hates you more than I ever could. I think … thought that you deserved what I planned for you, but …" He squared his back against the wall and averted his eyes to the floor. "No one deserves what it plans to do to you. Not even you." The fear now in his voice frightened me to a new level of terror, an incomplete thought, frantic terror.

"Help me, John, please?" I blathered out quickly, unsure if I was even speaking, as the fear rang in my ears so loudly that I felt deaf. "Let me go, get me out of here, please, John!"

I saw it in his face the very instant he decided to help me and he sprang to action, sliding to his knees in front of me, feverishly ripping at the knots of the ropes around my ankles, when he suddenly snapped his head up to look at me and the dread on his face acknowledged the fact that we were too late.

His body soared backward through the air until he crashed against the wall he had been leaning against before. His feet dangled above the ground as if an invisible force was holding him against the wall.

I screamed as I saw his head getting closer to the ceiling and as the pain stretched across his face, followed by his tortured cry. I looked to his feet, which were now stomping against the floor in pain. I looked down in anguish, my eyes pressed closed tightly, wishing I could cover my ears, wishing I wasn't here, wishing I wasn't hearing the ripping of clothes and the sound of skin being torn asunder.

I grudgingly raised my head, faced forward with my eyes still shut tightly. Fighting against the paralyzing fear, the sounds of cracking bones and splatters of what I could only assume were parts of John falling to the floor. But the worst of it all now was that he was still moaning in a painful agony that does not express itself by volume, but by quivers of air seeping through new blood-filled holes not there by God's design.

I slowly peeked to the left from the corner of my eye and saw that his body was still in one piece and was surging as if he were going to throw up, but instead of regurgitating, with each lurch his body seemed to take on new form. I turned my head directly to him, disbelieving what I thought I was seeing.

His body was now twice its original size, with rolls of fat like whale blubber hanging from his distorted frame. Torn skin exposed and even released small portions of intestines that were still attached had but sagged, fallen to the floor. Its head and neck were now crammed against the open rafters of the ceiling so hard that a couple of the rafters had snapped under the pressure of the creature's growing body.

I looked at the former boy's now-bulbous face hoping to recognize John a little, hoping that he was still in there, that I could speak to him, try to stop this. As I began to speak I had to fight back the urge to throw up when the left side of its face began to melt, the blending of blood and flesh marbling downward, leaving his left eye settled halfway down his cheek but still attached by the vessels that disappeared into the darkness of the empty eye socket.

It moaned loudly, exposing its bloody mouth; its human teeth were each being pushed out from their roots by blackened, jagged teeth that looked like volcanic rock, thick and abrasive at hundreds of spots along the way down to their razor-sharp edges. The black, coarse, monstrous teeth were spotted with dangling pink fleshy remains of the human gums they had shredded to pieces as they grew.

"Speak to me, John! John?" I screamed.

The creature's left eye shifted to me in the chair, and I could see it trying to focus on me as the right eye was looking all around the room, seemingly to assess its situation.

"John, is that you?" I asked while looking at the fallen left eye.

The creature attempted to brace itself with its left arm against the wall, but the wall just toppled over against the creature's weight, revealing that we were in a hidden room of what seemed to be a basement with a dirt floor. The creature jostled to regain its balance while the right eye frantically looked around the room for something to brace it.

"Run, Aubrey," a twisted, multi-pitched voice cried out from the creature as it reached to a rafter for bracing. "Get up, Aubrey, run; I'm trying to fight it …" The right eye's gaze landed on me and the eye widened wildly. "Run …" a tortured voice rang out again, followed by a splatter of blood as if a blood vessel had exploded inside of the left eye, which proceeded to fill with the deep-crimson color. The creature easily removed the blood-filled eyeball with one tug and flung it into the side wall, where it splattered, spuming out much more blood than could ever be contained by a single eyeball no matter what its size.

"Pathetic, both you and that lackey over there!" the creature said with an angelic voice. "He would have never killed you, the fool! All of his time and efforts for what? How do you derisory things call it? A date, mating … love?" The creature's laugh rang through the air like wind chimes.

The irony of its voice was so distracting that it was almost impossible to discern its ridicule. A strange sense of calm entered me as my fears washed away, and it was suddenly as if I were just having a simple conversation with my parents or Caleb and not some hideous creature across from me.

"Who are you?" I asked inquisitively.

"I am from the beginning and will be past the end of time. All of you were born to be like my kind, yet some of you still cling to your insipid God with some hope of salvation from yourselves—fools you are, but we'll not relinquish until all hope of their so called God is gone and we are all that remains!" it said while edging closer to me. I felt no fear, just a nagging voice in my head.

"Did that answer your question ... *honey?*" It seemed to hesitate on that last word, as if it pained the creature to say it, and the nagging voice in my head began to grow a little louder.

"What... is your, name?" I asked, unsure why I was trying to stall—at least I think I was trying to stall.

"*Il n'importe pas que vous m'appelez*; just know that I have always existed for this moment. My one purpose was simply to bring you two home before it was too late. Don't you see, child? I am your salvation, but make no mistake—with or without your souls I will conclude my *raison d'être*," it said gently, but the words began to seep through the cracks made by the nagging voice in my head, which was now shattering the creature's foggy veil of deception.

It was coming nearer as the voices in my head became clear; everyone that I had ever loved seemed to be in my head screaming for me to wake up—not to give my soul to it. And above all was Caleb's voice begging me to hang on, reassuring me with his love and begging me for more time.

"You're no salvation!" I shrieked out, and instantly my fear came flooding back in on me relentlessly.

The creature stopped for a moment and narrowed its eye at me while speaking in a rattling, demonic tone. "I really wanted your soul, too ... *n'importe*—your lives will do!"

It began to close the distance quickly with the support of the rafters to maintain its balance. I looked at one of the rafters, wishing in the back of my mind, and suddenly it cracked and then completely broke due to the creature's weight against it. I shifted my attention to the next rafter, the one its other hand was on, and this time the rafter exploded into fragments and also brought a little of the upstairs floor down on the wallowing creature's head.

I looked to the ground still wishing—no, praying, as vines grew from the dirt floor and wrapped around the creature's arms. It pulled against the vines and they began to snap, but for every vine that the creature would break, two to three thicker ones were there to replace it, and they even started impaling themselves through the creature's arms before diving back into the earth as if they were awaiting my next command.

I chose to ignore a crashing sound that came from upstairs, concentrating only on this chunk of demonic justice in front of me, and if more were to come crashing in, I would deal with that then. The creature struggled against the vines trying to pull him down. With its palms flat to the ground it had quickly turned into a battle of strength, and mine was failing fast. I looked to the ground under its chin and willed a sharp spear-like branch to grow from the ground, hoping that it would be easier to bring the thick stick up than it had been trying to bring the creature down.

Vines were now snapping more rapidly than they were being replaced as further evidence that I was losing this fight, and fear again began to creep in at the edges of my mind.

"Aubrey, Aubrey, where are you?" I heard Caleb's voice call out feverishly.

"Here, Caleb, in the basement!" I shouted as loud as I could, and I instantly feared that it could be just another trick this thing was using to distract me. I looked at it to see a devilish grin spread across its face. The life flushed from my own face as the monstrosity ripped its right arm free from my vines. I sat there exhausted and expressionless while I watched the creature reach to its left arm to tear those vines to shreds.

From nowhere something dropped from the partial hole above the creature, and through my weary eyes it looked like the creature's reinforcements had arrived. I tried to gather what strength remained within me to sit up straight and raised my head high, looking down the bridge of my nose at the creature, trying not to imagine all of the foul things that would come next but to simply face them head on and not to give this thing my soul—no matter what came!

But instead of rallying, the creature stopped tearing at the vines holding its left arm down and frantically started trying to reach its back with its right arm. When reaching back failed, it bucked forward in an attempt to fling whatever it was off of its back. At that moment a guy and a girl came flying down the first flight of stairs to the basement and stood on the landing and stared at the creature's back in amazement for a second. Then the boy's hands started to glow with blue balls of flame in them.

I looked back to the creature, which was just narrowly missing the sharp stake I had summoned in front of it earlier as it flopped around try to … wait, I saw a face—it wasn't another monster on the creature's back … it was a person! His hand wielded a kitchen knife, being plunged into the back of the creature so fast that I had been missing it before. My mouth fell open as I realized whose face it was that I'd seen in that split second.

"Caleb!" I shouted, elated and frightened to death for his safety. I looked back to the stairs to see that the two who must be Derrick and Elise had already come down the last flight, and Derrick was firing a thin line of flames almost like lasers into the creature's stomach and the left side of its face. Elise was touching the ground, causing water to come from all directions into the ground to soften it up.

I looked back to the creature and saw that Caleb was beginning to lose his hold on the creature's back. As my fear for him grew, so did my sense of pace, along with a massive surge of energy that easily pivoted the thick, sharp stick in the now-muddy ground below it. My timing would have to be just perfect as the creature lurched forward—that split second when Caleb was still going back … "Now!" I thought while sending the stick up into the creature's lower chest area and out through the back of its neck. The stick grew in diameter as it kept rising through the house above.

Caleb smacked into the rising stick and flew off the creature's back, coming to a stop only a foot away from me. After catching his breath from the blows he hurried to his knees and held me with a passion so deep that it made me feel like nothing could ever break this bond, and all I could think of was how safe I felt at that moment. Whether in the midst of mayhem and madness or while floating on a cloud in dreamland, my life lived and died at Caleb's side. Within moments I was untied and we were driving away in what I assumed was a rental car.

CHAPTER

A Fist

I was very happy to finally be with Caleb in person, but the images of everything that just taken place in that basement continued to haunt me, and judging from the somber mood of the other three, I thought it was safe to say we had all been moved by the way this whole thing had such a grasp on our lives. But the worst was that things seemed to just get darker and more dangerous with no obvious reason for why we should continue.

From my position behind Derrick in the driver's seat, I looked to Caleb beside me as he stared blankly at the back of the passenger seat. I touched his hand, which caused him to flinch, then I looked down to our hands, which rushed out the thoughts racing through his head and washed away the concerned look on his face, which now donned a heartfelt expression of the realization that we'd done it. We were together at last, and more importantly, alive. We instantly embraced and it felt so familiar, so natural to bend it simultaneously into a deep, blood-pumping kiss.

"Really?" Elise commanded.

I couldn't be sure how long we were locked in that kiss before her voice snapped us back from our blissful union. We both looked up, startled, embarrassed to see Elise's face scornfully glaring at us before she turned back to the front, arms crossed tightly across her chest, and then slowly she looked out the passenger window in silence.

Caleb and I held each other as Derrick pulled up to an oceanfront parking place and turned the car off. We sat there for a while, Derrick occasionally looking over at Elise, who never stopped staring out of her window, and I wondered if these people were always this quiet. This felt like a very unnatural silence, and I was beginning to think that Caleb and Elise had a relationship that I was not aware of. Caleb would never do such a thing, would he? But I couldn't start doubting him now, and besides that, I just knew I'd be dead one way or another without him. I just had to stay calm.

"Would you like to stretch your legs?" Caleb whispered to me. I nodded quickly while opening my door and hopped out of the car, shutting the door swiftly behind me. Caleb slid out of his door, and we met at the front of the car, but Caleb was careful to keep a small distance between us until we were out of the car's sight. He reached down and took my hand, but I gently pulled it away and turned to face him.

"Why didn't you tell me that you and Elise were in a relationship, Caleb?" I said firmly but calmly.

"No, it's not like that at all. There's nothing between us; we almost kissed once, but I did nothing," he said with assurance.

I believed him, or at least I wanted to, so I guess that WAS that. But if that was all then why so much tension? "Awkward." Oops, I hadn't meant for that to slip out, so I tried to breeze by it. "Are you guys always so quiet?" I asked to change Caleb's thoughts away from how cold that uncomfortable response could have been taken.

"No, not like that, but I know that Elise likes me differently than I do her, and apparently Derrick is aware of it too." He looked perplexed but continued. "I don't know what to do and obviously Derrick doesn't either, or he would be doing whatever needed to be done … I guess."

His frustration about the situation was clearly getting to him, and it amused me a little to see how well he'd been handling all of these terrible situations, but put a girl's hurt feelings into the mix and he started speaking gibberish.

"You're a girl—I mean, woman. Is there anything we can do to, you know … make things different than this—how it is …? You know what I'm saying; why are you torturing me like this?" he said, flustered. I held back my urge to laugh at how much he just seemed like a stammering little boy.

"I'm sorry, Caleb, that was mean of me. You're just so cute when you babble on like that." I took his hand and we walked through the sand to the edge of the water. "I believe I can talk to her. You know, let her know how this is no ordinary connection. I'll let her know how we suffer physically when we're apart and other facts so she doesn't feel rejected."

"Yeah, that sounds like it might work, but you two should be alone when you talk about it and nowhere near water," Caleb said, but only half-jokingly, which didn't settle too well with me. He backed us up from the edge of the water and we sat in the sand.

"There's something else I have to ask you, okay?" he said, and I felt a little nervous because I thought he knew we could talk about anything, that we had nothing to hide—or could this be something even worse than what had just happened in the basement?

"Sure," I said pensively.

"Will you come with us to wherever it is we're going?" he asked with much gravity.

I was taken aback slightly; I had assumed he already knew that I would follow him to the ends of the Earth. "Wherever you go I want to be with you, Caleb," I said to him with complete certainty, and then I put my fingers in the sand between us and I could feel the tips of them tingling as I wished, or willed, a gesture of my love for him. I raised my hand, and beneath my palm a stem had already come out of the sand. It grew so gracefully, as if it were a ballerina dancing for us. The sunlight reflected off of it like it was made of diamonds.

As it grew, gracefully spinning to display all of its beauty, I wondered what it would be ... I mean, I knew it was a flower, but what kind? My heart was racing with excitement. I looked up at Caleb, wanting a moment of eye contact and acknowledgment that he was seeing what I was, but he was so mesmerized by the flower that he didn't even notice me looking at him. The expression on his face as he watched so intently warmed my heart and soul; it was precious to me to know how special this very moment was for him. Who was I kidding? This moment was equally just as special to me. I found myself literally torn between which of these, the two most beautiful things in the world, to watch.

I chose to watch Caleb, but it really wasn't a choice at all, because I could not bear to look away from the light playing off his face, bending with his angelic features and dancing in his deeply soulful eyes. He finally looked up into my eyes with the most sincere look on his face and a single tear trickling down his cheek. I tried to just steal a quick glance at the flower, but when I looked, its magnificence froze me.

The stem of the flower had turned into a diamond with lovely shades of gold and green. It had such wonderful details, such intricately blended colors flowing through it, giving it the appearance of being alive ... Or was it actually alive? At the top of it sat a splendid rose with crimson-red color flowing inside of the diamond petals—strong, but no thicker than an actual rose petal. It was utterly amazing, and to make it even more spectacular the light tints of the red pigments followed toward the moonlight as if it were glowing or reaching out to it.

I handed it to Caleb, who gently took it, marveling over its beauty. He looked at me and then to the moon just beyond the ocean's horizon.

"What a perfect end to a very long day," he said, and I hated so much to end his ideal ending to this disastrous day, but there was still one more detail to discuss—and it would be worse than John's basement, but in different a way.

"We still have to talk to my parents," I said, trying to make the words sound as soft as I could, but I was sure he heard my anxiety between each word.

CHAPTER

Meeting Aubrey's Parents

Elise sat unmoving, numb to her environment, eyes simply focused just outside of the car window on a heaped pile of sand that looked like a ruined sand castle. She tried to debate how long ago the sand castle was built and if the elements had brought it down, or had someone destroyed it, but the thought was hard to hang onto with the image of Caleb kissing Aubrey in her head.

When she thought of that she would squeeze hard against her now-healed wounds, wishing she had a scalpel and a bathroom with a lock on the door. She wondered why she felt this way when she and Caleb hadn't even talked of them being a couple—and that angered her more, the thought that she had been so stupid as to not have expressed her feelings to him when she'd had the chance.

Adding to her bafflement, she had never had a need for a boy before, not even a desire until now. *And look where that's got me*, she thought as the anger began to turn outward with thoughts of Chester and the idea that she'd deserved it, that she'd somehow invited it to happen. Like there was a sickness inside her that any good man would see and never be interested in, so her life had been relegated to despicable men like Chester or … to women. She felt a slight enlightenment knowing that even if she was destined to never meet a decent man, if such a thing even existed, there was at least possibly a more meaningful bond that could be built with another woman, a much greater one than one built with a man.

"Are you going to get past this or wallow in self-pity this entire time?" Derrick said casually.

Elise barely noticed that he had spoken, and if it weren't for the masculine tone to his voice, which grated her sense of growing calm, she wouldn't have heard anything at all. She wondered, had she always felt irritation at the sound of a man's voice? She knew that she had always fought harder against her male opponents, especially when they were talking shit, but that didn't make her something that she wasn't, she thought.

"It's none of your business!" Elise snapped.

Derrick looked away from her and toward the ocean in front of him. "I know it's none of my business—and believe me, I'm not trying to make it my business, either … It's just, look at them, they're obviously meant to be together or—"

"What do you mean-meant to be together?" Elise asked quickly but unable to remove the angry edge to her voice like she had wanted to while asking that question.

"It's clear to see that there's something special between them, like they've been together forever or something—like they're on some damn lifelong honeymoon. Its kinda coo', almost makes you feel encouraged," he scoffed aloud before finishing, "and jealous at the same time."

Elise rolled her eyes while still looking at that mound of sand and started to think that now everyone was against her on this.

"I'm just saying that if you opened your eyes to what's going on and not what you think you lost you just might figure out what it's really supposed to be about," Derrick said with a slight edge.

"Fuck off," Elise stated as a conclusion to the conversation.

Derrick opened the driver's door, got out, and slammed it behind him before going to sit on the hood; He was quite content until the thought of his family and their welfare came to mind, and then he wished that this whole thing was over so he could be with them, protecting them.

Derrick saw Aubrey and Caleb coming into sight as they returned to the car. Instead of waiting for them there, he figured he would stretch his legs and meet them halfway. When they met up, Caleb immediately stepped forward.

"I was so rude earlier, and I'm really sorry, man," Caleb said while reaching out to shake Derrick's hand. He pivoted toward Aubrey and delicately gestured in her direction. "Derrick, this beautiful young lady is Aubrey—Aubrey, this is Derrick." Aubrey and Derrick shook hands.

"It's a pleasure to meet you. Caleb has told me so much about you and Elise," Aubrey said in a soft, affectionate tone.

"Ditto. And it's great to *finally* meet you too; I thought Caleb may have been exaggerating when he said how lovely you are, but I should have known better than to think Caleb would exaggerate or lie about anything," Derrick said. "Nice flower," he added. "Where'd you get it?"

Caleb simply gestured kindly to Aubrey. Derrick looked at the closed stores that surrounded the beach and back to the flower and thought that something as delicately crafted as that flower couldn't have come from one of these stores anyway, after all. He wasn't even sure that the finest of jewelers could craft such a thing, but here it is, and then it clicked in his mind.

"Yes, I get it, Mother Earth, right? Very well done, but I think it's gonna have to explode or something to really help our situation," Derrick joked, and they all laughed at the irony. They walked back to the car and Caleb informed Derrick of their next task, which involved them speaking to Aubrey's parents.

The ride to Aubrey's house was quiet and full of mixed emotions until they pulled up to the house. Derrick and Elise were amazed at the house's size and the meticulous attention to detail surrounding it, from the yard to the architecture of the home. Derrick wondered if insects even dared to approach this home and secretly kept his eye out for even a trace of a cobweb.

Elise felt better after seeing Aubrey's house because she, too, had been brought up in the biggest house possible in Devils Lake, North Dakota, and look at the things that had happened there. She landed on the thought that Aubrey had a nice set of skeletons too—skeletons that Elise would bring out into the light for Caleb to judge, and then he would see that she was best for him, not Aubrey.

Elise was the one who had rejected the big house and being lavished in the lifestyle—she would have never thought of having her friends (if she'd had any) over to her Devils Lake mansion. She considered herself obviously the stronger of the two girls now present and she was determined for Caleb to see that too.

Aubrey had already given Caleb a tour of the house, but he was now marveling at how accurate his dreams were to the real thing, and he felt an even stronger sense of absolution with their mission and that it was ordained by God, Jesus, and the Holy Spirit.

Aubrey felt a sudden sense of panic when she realized that somehow she had forgotten to consider the situation of her guests. It was usually the very first and last thing that she thought about. As she'd grown up, she always tried to take friends' situations into account and not include activities that involved friends coming to her house if she felt it would cause a rift in their friendship, because she had lost several friends because of their inability to relate with her anymore after visiting her home. She was appalled with herself for being so stupid, and embarrassment flushed bright red in her cheeks as she tried to figure out how she could have done such a thoughtless thing.

Just then Caleb's hand lightly rubbed the top of hers and instantly her beet-red face began to lighten into a rosy blush, and when their eyes met she was reminded of why such a thing could have happened and how unimportant someone's thoughts of her home and other material things actually were. It was as if all of the little issues that she had trouble getting over didn't matter anymore; they were now like tiny molehills, impossible to view from atop the highest mountain, where she and Caleb resided.

"Pretentious much?" Elise mumbled to herself just loud enough for all to hear while walking to the front door. Derrick gave a sidelong glare to Elise while Caleb and Aubrey remained hand in hand, shoulder and arm rubbing against one another as if they were communicating with each other by the touching of their arms, eliminating all unnecessary space between them.

Before they could reach the door it swung wide open and Aubrey's mom gushed out and embraced her. Aubrey's free hand embraced her mother in return, followed by the reluctant release of Caleb's hand; their fingertips were the last to separate and then simultaneously they each slowly shut that hand in a manner that was as if they were still holding something vital. Aubrey now held her mother with both arms but with one hand still clinched as she reassuringly glanced back at Caleb.

Aubrey's father was focused on her, eyeing her up and down, and while Derrick and Caleb assumed that he was looking for any visual injuries, Elise had different thoughts altogether. Her father certainly couldn't have helped but see that Caleb had been holding her hand and that now they must be hiding something in their clinched fists. He lifted his shoulders slightly in an imposing manner and focused on Caleb and Aubrey's hands.

"Where have you been?" her mother snapped, but then she reeled it back in to a loving mother's voice of concern. "You missed your whole graduation, and we had to turn everyone away from your party because we were so worried about you."

"It's a long story," Aubrey said quietly. "John was invol—"

"Owens?" her father said quickly with a hint of concern embedded in a sea of anger. Caleb felt a small amount of relief to know that they were both on the same page with that one. "I'll have that matter dealt with once and for all!" her father concluded before shifting his eyes accusingly between Caleb's eyes and his still-clinched hand.

Caleb was trying to uphold a strong physical stance, but not so strong as to be a threat to her father's alpha-dog attitude. He realized that her father was looking at him strangely, which confused Caleb for a moment, until he looked down to see that his hand was unconsciously clinched, eagerly waiting for Aubrey's hand to return to it. He slowly opened his hand palm toward the ground and, clearly to the father's surprise, nothing fell to the ground.

He looked back to Aubrey, whose hand was still clinched, so he gently reached out toward Aubrey's fist and she opened it to grasp his hand. Her father was trying to think hard and fast to figure out the situation in front of him as he pulled his daughter to his side while measuring up the three strangers. He put his arm around his wife's shoulder and pulled her to him too. Aubrey looked at Caleb and the others with a confused expression on her face, and then as tears started to well up in her eyes she pulled away from her father and walked to Caleb's side. Their self-assured covenant strengthened visibly as she took Caleb's hand again.

"Mom, Dad, this is Caleb, Derrick, and Elise," Aubrey said, looking at Derrick for a moment and then locking eyes with Elise and continuing to speak. "They are all very special friends to me." She focused her attention back to her father with an air of defiance.

"If that's the case then they should come in and make themselves at home," her father replied with a not-so-convinced tone.

"Yes, by all means you have to come in. I'm Maggie and this is Kevin," her mother rang in cheerfully. "You all look hungry; have you kids eaten today? Let me fix you something to eat," she said while eagerly entering the house to prepare something.

"Excuse me," said Elise. "May I use your bathroom to wash up?"

"Of course you can, darling, follow me," Aubrey's mom said.

"I have to get some stuff from the car first, so please, you go in. Aubrey can show me the way," Elise said quickly.

"Oh, okay, Aubrey if you could that would be great. I have some things to put together," Aubrey's mom said in an excited voice, and Caleb started to ascertain just how rarely she got to entertain people here.

"Come in, boys, it seems we have a lot to talk about, wouldn't you say?" Kevin said. He took visible note of how Caleb and Aubrey released hands in the same painfully longing way. Derrick noticed that this irritated him from the way his jaw muscles articulated each grind of his teeth. Derrick glanced to the couple to see that they were still in their love-filled trances.

"Yes sir, we believe we have quite a bit to talk about," Derrick replied, and Kevin seemed surprised for some reason, looking at Derrick.

"Oh, so you do talk. See if you can get his attention so we can go inside."

Derrick gave Caleb a firm nudge, which got his attention. Caleb noted that Kevin continuously glared at him while holding the door open for them to walk through. Caleb was beginning to realize that perhaps Kevin was not so keen on his little girl going from high school to house wife in a day, so Caleb vowed to himself to try and restrain his attachment to Aubrey while they were there and maybe whenever Elise was around too.

Aubrey appeared at Elise's side just as Elise had managed to pull her duffle bag from under several other full bags. "Can I help?" Aubrey asked politely.

"No, just the one bag," Elise answered abruptly.

"Elise, I was actually hoping that we would get some time alone, you know, so we could talk about things," Aubrey said with a small amount of fear or desperation, she really couldn't decide which.

"Yeah, we can talk. You can tell me where the bathroom is and I can grunt at you as I pass by," Elise said quickly. She recognized that her defensiveness was on high alert because even though it was the last thing on Earth she would ever admit, what she was seeing between Caleb and Aubrey looked more than real; it actually seemed more surreal that they appeared as they did, like some long-lost lovers who needed one another to breathe or something. Elise thought about how Derrick was saying that it encourages you and makes you envious at the same time, but Derrick couldn't really appreciate her pain because in her mind Aubrey had taken her place with Caleb ... the fact that it should have been her that Caleb needed to exist.

Aubrey felt a little hurt by Elise's rejection and completely exasperated by her own determination to make things better without an ounce of effort from Elise. "Yeah, well, guess what? I told my mother I would take you to the bathroom so that's what I'm going to do! And you might try to think about the rest of us because this is not all about you; it's about all of us.

And it's about how we obviously need each other to survive. That's, if you ever open your eyes and see what's going down," Aubrey retorted, and she immediately felt a little better at having confronted her. First enduring the fight in the basement and now here with Elise—it was amazing how much her self-image and strength had changed since meeting Caleb, she thought. Elise felt the sting of the words, mostly because they made sense, and once again she would never admit it but she almost felt a slight twinge of admiration that Aubrey had stuck up for herself.

"This situation doesn't need you giving my parents any extra concern, is all I'm saying ... it's going to be hard enough already," Aubrey finished, then she turned and led Elise swiftly to the bathroom before joining Caleb, Derrick and Kevin, who still stood in the foyer. Kevin had a portable house phone in his hand, which was ringing from the speaker when he pulled it down from his ear.

"Okay, she's here now. Is it okay to go to the den now?" he asked while looking at Caleb.

"Why are you still standing?" Aubrey was saying before being cut off again by her father.

"He thought that it would be best if we waited for you before proceeding, so ..." He trailed off as an attempt to belittle Caleb for such a silly request before he continued, "you guys go into the den; I have this call to make and then I'll meet you in there."

"Dad, no, please don't call the police! I mean, I'm quite sure they're already there," Aubrey said in a panic.

Caleb put his hand on Aubrey's arm and turned to say something to her but Kevin shifted his hand up to silence Caleb before he could get a word out.

"She can still speak for herself ... Caleb," Kevin said, and the meaning slashed deeply at Caleb. Then he asked his daughter directly, "What do you mean, Aubrey?" but at that moment a calm, deep voice answered on the other end of the phone.

"Yeah Kevin what's up?" the voice said, Kevin brought the phone back to his ear and attempted to speak secretly into the receiver, "I'll call you back," then he hit the end on the phone. "Aubrey," her Kevin insisted.

"It was loud and the house was clearly destroyed, so I think the only thing calling the police at this time would do is tell them that we were there," she said feeling a little sleazy as she heard the words coming out of her mouth.

"And John?" Kevin asked, which pierced her soul like an ice pick. She hadn't put all the pieces together until this very moment. Tears streamed from her eyes and her mouth moved inaudibly, crushing Caleb's heart, and he quickly held her to his chest to calm her and shield her from her father's interrogation.

Caleb attempted to gather himself but was too awestruck by Aubrey's pain to speak, and now it seemed as if they were comforting one another. They both trembled, and Caleb slowly lifted his chin up high and looked Kevin in the eyes. Derrick put a comforting hand on Caleb's shoulder and then one on Aubrey's as he approached Kevin and stopped just inches in front of him.

Derrick was three inches taller than Kevin and just a little bulkier than him as well, but Kevin had lean muscle tone, as if his workouts consisted of running and boxing training. He tried to look around Derrick to his daughter and Caleb but Derrick moved his head so it was between them again. "John's dead," Derrick said plainly.

As the words sunk in, Kevin squared up to Derrick's unnerved expression, reading him to judge if he was telling the truth. Shortly, he seemingly determined that he was.

"Let's have a seat," he said while extending his hand to Derrick. "It appears I owe you and your friends a debt of gratitude," he said as they walked to the den.

Minutes later Caleb and Aubrey entered the den arm in arm, Aubrey holding the rose she had made for Caleb in her free hand. Its faint glow pulled back toward them as if they were the sun. They sat in a loveseat directly across from Kevin, and when they did Caleb released his arm from around Aubrey. As he did a visible blanket of despair covered her up again, and the glow in the flower shifted to the left as if reaching out to Caleb.

Caleb noticed this and felt comfort knowing that this was some sort of emotion-sharing effect. He felt so much sorrow for John Owens and the tiny details of fun Aubrey shared with him, sympathies for his life being as it was and many other things that Caleb himself could never have felt because he hadn't known John Owens personally.

Now that he had stopped touching Aubrey, he was immediately able to clear his head and address the matter at hand. He looked at Derrick appreciatively for his ability to handle the situation, because it could have gone south quickly.

Caleb slid his hand to hold Aubrey's and instantly felt a wash of emotions as Aubrey's sorrow lessened, and Caleb fought against it affecting him. It worked, and he was able to maintain a clear head and help Aubrey at the same time, but he made certain that the only contact they would have was hand-holding until she had calmed.

Kevin had missed most of the subtle emotional exchange that had just taken place because he was enamored with the flower's beauty. Caleb observed that Kevin's attention was on the flower, and knowing what it felt like to look at it, Caleb spoke quietly so as to not disturb the feeling of calm. "Beautiful, isn't it?"

Kevin brought his head up gingerly to meet Caleb's eyes. "Yes ... quite beautiful," Kevin said completely before looking back to the flower.

"Your daughter made it for me," Caleb said a little louder.

Kevin's expression gradually became curious, and he looked up at Caleb, baffled. "How could that be?" he asked incredulously.

Caleb wrestled with himself on how to answer that question, then he looked at Derrick, who guessed exactly what Caleb was thinking and gave an encouraging head gesture. Caleb turned to Kevin with his chin high and back straight.

"Your daughter is what we call an earth elemental, sir," Caleb stated in a factual manner before gesturing to Derrick. "Derrick is a fire elemental," Caleb added.

The room was silent for a moment as Kevin fought back the urge to roll his eyes, but that battle was obviously not easily won, and sure enough he rolled his eyes before speaking. "After all of this buildup you've put me through I actually forgot for a moment that you're just a bunch immature kids!" he said as if he was hurt by some attempt to fool him.

Derrick's head fell into his hands from the exhaustion of this long day, and he was exasperated by the thought of the challenge ahead of them: getting Kevin from his current mind-set to the mind-set of letting them leave with his daughter—and without having them all arrested, either. With his head still resting in his left hand, Derrick extended his right hand and ignited a blue flame that hovered just above his hand. Then Derrick looked directly into Kevin's eyes before lowering the small flame into his own palm, engulfing the entire hand in the blue fire. Kevin cautiously extended a finger toward Derrick's flaming hand, slowing but not stopping his movement when he felt the heat radiating from it.

"It's an extraordinarily hot fire, sir," Derrick said, to be interrupted when he heard Aubrey's mother, Maggie's voice.

"Food's ready, everyone," Maggie called out while turning the corner into the den. Needless to say, the expression on her face was priceless when she saw Derrick's hand on fire and her husband reaching out to it. Everyone looked to Maggie awkwardly, except for Kevin, who quickly ran the tip of his finger across the top of the flame. Such a gesture wouldn't have hurt if it were just a normal flame, but …

"Fuck!" Kevin screamed out, immediately squeezing hard against the pain in his hand, as if that would help.

"Maggie, do you have a large plastic bag that can be filled with ice and a roll of duct tape?" Derrick asked quickly, his tone igniting urgency in Maggie, who turned and ran into the kitchen to retrieve the items without asking any questions.

Just then the door on the room's south wall opened and Elise walked in calmly and went to the only seat available, toward the rear of the room, all the while watching the situation unfold. Maggie ran directly to Derrick and handed him the bag of ice and the tape. He slammed Kevin's hand into it then instantly wrapped several rotations of the duct tape around the man's bare wrist.

"You should see a doctor about that … there'll be nerve damage," Derrick said plainly.

CHAPTER

Internal Battle

Caleb and Derrick were in a room together on the lower level across the hall from Elise's room. Aubrey's room was on the top level near her parents' room.

After a couple of hours asleep, Derrick heard an agonizing moan coming from Caleb. He rushed to the wall and flipped on the lights to see Caleb lying in the center of the bed, very still. There was a ring of blood around the top of his left forearm. In his sleep he lifted his left arm and it slid apart at the blood ring, leaving the forearm lying on the bed as blood began to spray from his arm. He quickly grasped onto his elbow with his right hand and the blood spray slowed. Unlike moments before, now he was shifting around in violent motions, and additional wounds and bruises began appearing.

Derrick ran across the hall to wake up Elise since she had been the one bandaging and medicating Caleb all of the time before Aubrey arrived. After assessing the situation for a moment, she knew that the only one who could help was Aubrey. She ran upstairs but when she got there was unable to tell which room was Aubrey's. Wasting no time, she picked the one on the left to burst into.

"Aubrey get up, Caleb needs you now!" Elise screamed. "What? What's this about?" Kevin asked in a panic.

"Shit!" Elise whispered loudly, then she turned and ran into the next room.

"Aubrey, Caleb needs you!" Elise rang out, shocked to see Aubrey already walking to the door while putting on her robe.

Elise grabbed her hand and they both hurried toward the lower level. "What's going on, Elise?" Aubrey asked.

"He's sleeping and something's happening in there that's going very badly for him!" Elise rattled off.

"What's this all about?" Kevin shouted to them, but they didn't stop to respond.

"I couldn't fall asleep in my room, and I'm definitely not going to be able to sleep now, Elise! What am I—?" Aubrey was saying when Elise cut her off.

"I've got your ride for that—the problem is that we don't know what you're up against, so get ready for anything, Aubrey!" Elise finished as they raced into Caleb and Derrick's room.

Elise ran to Caleb's luggage and started sifting through it looking for the vial of general anesthetic. Aubrey leaped onto the bed and started healing the bruises and lacerations as they were appearing, but another would come as soon as she had healed one.

Kevin and Maggie rushed into the room to see Aubrey touching Caleb's injuries and to see them disappear. They watched in fear as Elise hurried toward them with a syringe, naturally assuming it was for Caleb.

"This is not working, Aubrey; he needs you in there, not out here!" Derrick said urgently.

"I got this, Derrick—move!" Elise shouted as she pushed past Derrick. Aubrey barely flinched when Elise jabbed the needle into her shoulder, though her parents became livid at the sight.

"Wait—why did you do that?" Kevin screamed as he moved in quickly, but it was too late as Elise pulled the empty needle out. "What did you give her?" Kevin demanded while grabbing Elise by the shoulders tightly with both hands, the bag of ice on his left hand not hampering him much from shaking her roughly.

Before Derrick could react to assist her, Elise had grabbed Kevin's left wrist where the duct tape was and in one motion twisted the wrist downward. Then at the speed of light she twisted it back behind him while spinning to his rear to put Kevin in a chokehold. She did not wrench on the left arm or tighten the chokehold as she said rapidly, "I'm going to let you go now if you calm down. Okay? Are you calm?"

Kevin simply raised his right hand open and above his head. Elise released him and he stepped to his daughter, who now was lying beside Caleb, asleep.

After a long moment of silence Kevin turned to Elise with a dark look on his face. "What is this?" he seethed at her. Derrick stepped forward and prepared to beat Elise to the punch this time if he should attack again.

"You saw it; Aubrey has the gift of being able to heal others, and she's single-handedly saved Caleb's life several times already." Elise paused for a moment thinking of what she had just said. She had a sudden realization: things are as they're supposed to be for all of their sakes. Caleb would certainly be dead by now if Aubrey hadn't come along when she did.

But then she got back on track and continued instructing. "When they sleep they share a … hell, I don't know, a conscious space. When they're both asleep and not together he has told us that the pain is unbearable. They love each other and they'll take care of each other in there no matter what. So for now, you two just pray or whatever you do, just don't distract us."

When Aubrey entered into the dream world everything appeared normal: the wood-woven bed on top of the wildflower-filled hill, beautiful skies above, sounds of the ocean crashing against the rocks below. But then she heard different crashing sounds—of rocks smashing against one another—and from the sonic-like sound waves from each collision they must be very big rocks.

Aubrey ran to the area just over the hill where the sounds were coming from to see two different Caleb's fighting one another. One Caleb stood over the other reaching one arm into the air, and just above that hand a boulder about three feet around appeared out of thin air. As she watched he willed it to hurtle at the Caleb below at a remarkable rate of speed.

The boulder broke into tiny rocks and dust against the massive stone shield the other Caleb had formed, kneeling and bracing himself against it. He was struggling to hold the heavy shield in place, and with each boulder that struck, the shielded Caleb's knees would slam into the ground, leaving huge indentations that he would try to use for footing while attempting to push his shield back up into protective position before the next rock hit.

Just then Aubrey saw that the Caleb below with the shield had a severed arm, exactly as her Caleb, lying in bed. Panic set in, and she ran as fast as she could down the hill to him, sliding the last several feet so she would be able to stop just behind him. She immediately began healing the lacerations and bruises on his back and legs.

She couldn't be sure, but as she was running down the hill she thought that she had seen someone else off to their left. While healing the wounds, she looked back to that spot fifty feet away from them, and there stood a pale boy dressed in casual clothes just watching everything taking place. She presumed that he was with the other Caleb; he seemed harmless for now, but she was determined to keep an eye on him to prevent any surprise attacks.

Caleb looked down to Aubrey with relief on his face. "Grab my waist," he said in a loud whisper.

Aubrey clutched his waist and her hands absorbed into him, fusing them together at Aubrey's wrists. She knew that she should have freaked out about no longer being able to feel her hands; it was as if they had just disappeared, and now her wrists were where she ended and Caleb began. She thought about the very thin lines separating her reality from dreams, fantasies from nightmares, and felt comfort with how natural it felt to be this way, as one with Caleb.

With Aubrey's help the shield rose with ease as she and Caleb stood strong against the oncoming rocks, sending the crashing fragments directly back into the other Caleb's face now. The real Caleb whipped the shield away, sending it sailing into the other Caleb's chest unmolested, as the doppelganger's hands were in the air conjuring more boulders. The shield slammed him to the ground, screaming like a wild animal being mauled, a sound that abruptly cut to silence when his last two hovering boulders plummeted onto to him from above.

They stood there, Caleb watching the pile of rubble for any movement and Aubrey glancing between that and the other boy, who was now standing less than twenty five feet from them. She tried to recall if they had moved in his direction during the fight, but she didn't think they had. When she looked back toward the boy again he was just standing there still but noticeably closer, maybe just fifteen feet away. "Caleb," she peeped.

Caleb looked back in the boy's direction and instantly she knew he had been aware of the boy's presence the entire time. Caleb swiftly pivoted so he was facing the approaching boy, Aubrey still attached to his waist, peeking around from behind to watch the boy intently.

"Stop there!" Caleb commanded, but the boy was already standing very still, just five feet from them now but not once did either of them actually see the boy moving which created an eerie feeling with them. The boys hands were open with his palms out as if he were surrendering or declaring that he comes in peace. "Why are you here?" Caleb asked directly.

"Don't know," the boy said bluntly while looking over Caleb's shoulder at Aubrey. "Where is here?" he continued, turning his attention to Caleb.

"This is a very private place," Caleb answered. "No one's ever been here except for us."

"That doesn't tell me where I'm at or how you got me out—" The boy stopped midsentence, his eyes wide open while walking backwards.

Caleb pivoted again back to the rocks to see that the other Caleb had gotten up and was charging him. The other Caleb had converted his hands into two long blades that he lucidly wanted to impale the real Caleb and Aubrey with.

At the last second, the real Caleb raised his arms and in the blink of an eye a four-foot-wide, ten-foot-high, leafless tree rose from the ground. The real Caleb fell backward, arching hard to get away as quickly as possible from the blades piercing through the tree. He narrowly escaped the full brunt of the icy sharpness, one edge cutting through his shirt and lightly slicing his chest as he landed on top of Aubrey behind him.

Caleb and Aubrey shuffled to their feet as quickly as they could while the other Caleb started to pull his blade hands back out of the tree to continue his fierce attack. The real Caleb lurched to put his hands on the tree as if it were home base. When his hands touched, the tree started to swell and shift into a darker color. The tree's swelling pressed against the blades such that no matter how hard the other Caleb pulled, they remained stuck.

Caleb clutched his clone's forearm, and the texture of wood grew down through the blades and continued until the other Caleb's shoulders were also a part of the mighty tree. He struggled to break free, but the tree stood as steady as a rock.

"What are you?" Caleb demanded, and the other Caleb simply made some animalistic growling sound before locking his glare onto the real Caleb.

When finally he spoke, it was in a voice as if he had severed vocal cords, each word more distracting and demented than the next. "You are what I are, I, you, me ... we hurt us with tree! Please no tree," he said while swaying his head like a serpent without diverting his attention from Caleb's eyes in the slightest.

Caleb and Aubrey were both disturbed by the creature's voice, which reminded Aubrey of John's voice when she was trapped in his basement. The tones in both voices spoke in a range of pitches in unison, from that of an infant, a child, a boy and a girl, and finally one other: a demonic tone that neither Caleb nor Aubrey believed a human's vocal cords could even produce.

"You look like me, you're not me, you filthy thing!" Caleb said, and Aubrey could feel the stress and uncertainty flowing through him. Aubrey's connection allowed her to feel his every emotion, and this creature frightened him more than anything he could imagine.

"You, we—tell us how what feels. Us do those things do make it real …" the twin hissed out with a cackling undertone.

Caleb's hatred for this thing spilled over, and he stepped forward to hit the creature with his severed arm. As his upper arm came down toward the creature, his forearm simultaneously grew back, except with a heavy rock in place of his fist.

The Caleb look-alike saw the rock out of the corner of his eye and leaned away from the oncoming blow. In that split second as the rock crashed into the side of the creature's head, its color took on the exact shade of the rock. A thunderous sound cracked throughout the area from the enormous collision as Caleb's rock hand shattered, and both he and Aubrey stumbled backward.

They moved back toward the other Caleb to see that the right side of his face was now a hard, polished stone. The creature now spoke from just the left side of his drooling mouth, which made him even more difficult to understand. "We, us, more strong than thought," he said while looking over Caleb's shoulder at Aubrey. "No fair … one 'gainst two, make fair, me add somethin' new," he said while casting a gaze to the pale boy. The boy was within hearing distance but quickly shuffled back farther when he heard what the other Caleb had said. The clone snarled at the boy and then turned his attention to the sky.

The wonderful blue aura of Caleb's and Aubrey's love was now being pushed out by blackened clouds that began to float across the sky like a cancer, their ominous shapes only revealed by frequent lightning strikes. Caleb stepped back, a strange look spreading across his face as he watched his sky transform before his eyes. He looked back to the creature's half-stone face and saw it smooth out and turn into his mother's face, followed by the rest of the creature's body transforming into the form of his mother.

She stepped back from the tree fully intact. She looked to Caleb with sad eyes, and Aubrey couldn't believe how even more beautiful she was without the blue cast against her skin. Caleb fell to his knees, pulling Aubrey down with him.

"You could have tried harder, Caleb … you could have searched for cures, you could have tried to find a substitute drug or put me in a cryogenic chamber until you developed a cure," the form of his mother said to Caleb, who dropped his head in remorse for the things he hadn't tried. Aubrey sensed that these were futile thoughts had indeed raced through Caleb's mind after finding out about his mother's condition, and even more after her death. These were things that could never be expected for anyone to do, especially in such a short period of time.

Aubrey listened closely as she—no, not she. Aubrey listened closely as *it* spoke and realized that she was hearing two voices speaking. "You killed me, and now you're killing your father, letting him lie there alone to die, as you did me."

Aubrey whispered to Caleb, "That's not your mom, Caleb; listen, it still speaks with more than one voice. And your mother would never say these things, you know that! Snap out of it, Caleb; it's playing on your guilt!" Her whisper had grown to a demanding voice because she could feel Caleb's emotions clouding his thoughts, feel him giving up. She shouted, "For God's sake, Caleb, she's not even in the blue light!"

"You can make everything up to me and your father, Caleb; everything can be good again and we can paint, swing, and talk forever if you just do this one thing," it said while holding a dagger out to Caleb with its left hand and holding its right hand behind its back.

Caleb looked down in defeat. Aubrey tugged at him, begging him not to take the blade. He reached for it with his handless left arm while a hand grew outward from his wrist. His open hand waited for the creature to give him the blade. At the same moment the creature brought a broadsword up from behind its back and started to swing it downward toward Caleb's bowed head.

The moment the dagger touched Caleb's left hand he whipped his right arm up directly toward the creature, willing the dagger to rocket through the air and into the creature's chest. The blade's impact was so fierce that it knocked the creature back three feet and onto the ground, the broadsword flying out of the shape-shifter's right hand.

Caleb scrambled to his feet, dragging Aubrey behind as he closed the distance to the creature. Caleb summoned a great stone mallet and rapidly brought down a crushing blow onto the creature's body before it could transform its body into stone for defense. By the time Caleb was bringing a second blow down, the creature had changed its body to stone, but at the last moment before impact Caleb changed his mallet into a heavier, stronger steel one, which crushed his enemy's entire right arm into stone rubble.

The massacring hit stopped the creature's stone transformation immediately, before it could cover its neck and head in the protective granite. The pain writhed through its face and fear was evident. Its face instantly changed from the image of Caleb's Mother into a demented version of Caleb with dark rings around it's black colored eyes. Its mouth and teeth mangled and twisted in agony as Caleb brought down another blow, directed at its body. Caleb felt a rush as he realized the creature was vulnerable at its head; a blow there would finish this instantly—but it was too late to adjust his swing, which creamed onto the creature's left side. That hit decimated the creature's left arm and shoulder, down through the chest and rib cage on its left side. As Caleb raised his weapon for the final blow, Aubrey quickly turned her head so she didn't have to see what that mallet would do to soft tissue; despite knowing that this was something evil, like a demon, it did still look like a her Caleb.

Caleb stopped the oversized mallet above his head with a mixture of emotions when he saw the pale boy's hands suddenly clasping the creature's head. "What are you doing? Move!" Caleb shouted.

At that instant the creature just jerked as if it had just been hit by a freight train that knocked all air from its body. Its mouth opened wide and its nostrils flared, trying to capture a breath of air from anywhere possible, but to no avail. Life rapidly faded from the creature until its dead eyes displayed that blank stillness that no living thing could duplicate.

"Yeah, so this is just a dream you say," the pale boy said disbelievingly.

"Yes, a dream, but like no other—and you are the last piece of our puzzle, air elemental," Caleb said confidently before asking his name.

The boy was obviously confused but determined to understand. "Shane," he answered before firing a question of his own. "Why do you call me air elemental, and what is this puzzle?"

Caleb told Shane everything he knew about what had taken place and what he believed. Shane listened intently and had many questions. Shane also informed Caleb that a small misunderstanding in school—and maybe a lack of good judgment on his part—had landed him innocently in a mental hospital.

Caleb and Aubrey felt his sincerity and eagerness was genuine and informed him that they would be on their way to Seattle to meet him in the morning. Caleb and Aubrey woke out of dreamland together.

Aubrey's father reluctantly agreed to let his daughter go, but only if his associate Rocco accompanied them and that Rocco would be the decision maker of the group. Rocco had joined them in the morning to fly to Seattle with them. He was 5'11 older man in his forties with salt and pepper hair and mustache. His build was sturdy with a slight roundness to his stomach, but Rocco definitely looked like he could hold his own and then some. His facial features were very stern and non-emotional as you could tell that through his years he rarely smiled because it looked like a smile would actually crack his stone cold poker face. He had a strong Italian accent and immediate mob connections came to mind when anyone met him.

Out of the group Aubrey was most disturbed by Rocco's presence but mostly because she had never heard of this associate of her fathers and the fact that he was polar opposites of anyone she had met or heard of involving her father's business. He definitely came suddenly and veiled in a shroud of mystery or was it secrecy? Nonetheless she was determined to find out the whole story during this excursion.

CHAPTER

A Loony in the Bin

I grabbed the first chair I saw after entering the commons and dragged it loudly past three more sets of round tables with four chairs neatly placed around each, purposefully banging into and catching hold of a couple of them on my way to the windows at the far wall, leaving the chairs behind me in disarray. I slid my chair in front of the far corner window and sat, looking out of the window.

All of the obstructions these windows had blocking the view of the parking lot aggravated me, vertical bars on the outside to keep us crazies from jumping to our deaths that I'd come to resent, considering it was my life to end if I wanted. The windows also had metal framing and screens to keep bugs out when they were open. Irony, bugs wanting in and me just wanting to be squashed like one on the pavement below.

My thoughts fluttered to some of the people I'd want to push out of the window before I jumped. I knew I wanted to focus on that dream, but I had to be careful not to lose track of my thoughts. It was so easy to lose my thoughts when they forced a red pill down my throat. Didn't matter though, because no matter how hard they tried, they could never take my names from me. I assured myself of that daily as I repeated the names over and over in my head all twenty-one, over and over and over …

It would all be over now if Henry didn't tell that fucking janitor about what I had planned. Granted, it wasn't inventive at all—just follow the plan of those who'd gone before me. Shoot every person on my list then finish with me and school's out before noon, easy enough if the only person I knew didn't rat me out!

Henry was number two on the list now, and the janitor, Fred, was at three. Nick was and would always be number one; Craig number four; Tiffany, five; Shawna, six; Jake, seven; Ben, eight; Becky, nine; Carl, ten; Ben Henderson, eleven; Sarah, twelve; Matt, thirteen; Chris J., fourteen; Christopher, fifteen; Charles, sixteen; Diane, seventeen; Chris A., eighteen; Jenny, nineteen; Greg, twenty; and Pete, number twenty-one.

The list was easy to remember since most of them had been in their positions for well over two years. Henry and janitor Fred were the latest to be added.

I found myself fluttering back to that dream again … was that real? It had to be … it *has* to be. I would never get out of here unless it was. I couldn't do the list from here, not before some died of old age, and I wasn't having that.

I wouldn't have to put up with this miserable planet of idiots and I wouldn't leave this list behind; not a single one was to escape me—I wished I could remember exactly what that dream was about. "This fucking pill!" I screamed. I shifted my eyes around the room to see who had heard me but not really knowing why, since I could give a shit about what anyone thought of me. Only orderly Sam and … who was that? Sam was working with someone I had never seen in here before, someone with his head down while drawing or whatever he was doing. Several papers sat in front of him with various drawings and writings on them, it appeared.

His hair was just like … I tried to see the name written on the top of his drawing but couldn't quite make it out, but his hair. His hair was just like Nick's hair, and his frame looked a lot like Nick's. "Fucking Nick!" I screamed at him, and he looked up, shocked to see me.

This was the fuck that was jealous that his prom queen girlfriend liked me, but when it came down to it the bitch was too scared to hurt the jock's feelings by going to prom with me. He'd made her laugh at me, I know he had, but that didn't matter because they'd both pay, starting with Nick, right now!

"I'll kill you!" I yelled out at him while standing from my chair. "I'm guessing you're sorry for taking that picture of me in the shower, right, Nick?" His eyes grew large with fear. "I bet that you're sorry for posting it on Facebook too, right, Nick?" I screamed at the top of my lungs while running in his direction. I could give a shit that he was six feet of muscle head jock; my rage would cut him down to my five-foot-four frame and much shorter! I would leave nothing! I grabbed a chair as I charged toward him and I saw the fear in his eyes.

"Number one, Nick," I said as I threw the chair, sending it hurtling straight toward his head.

Sam used his forearm to deflect the chair away from Nick's head, and I eyed Sam with hatred for what he'd just done. Sam was already close to being on the list and that just clinched it—Sam was on my death list!

Nick seemed to just now notice that he was being attacked and he jumped out of the chair to cower away from me. Sam-bo raced around their table, which I was starting to climb over, and he grabbed me from behind just as I was preparing to launch into Nick's chest.

"What are you doing, Shane? That's Benny—snap out of it now; it's Benny you're attacking!" Sam grunted while holding me from behind. I struggled with everything I had but couldn't break his grip. My anger was raging so violently in Nick's direction when suddenly the papers on the table in front of him flew up and through the air; Nick even stumbled backward from the force of the wind.

The dream was true! I could feel them getting closer, my powers becoming stronger, and this changed everything, with the single thought of being all-powerful. Why would I want to leave this tormenting planet when I now could be the source of all torment?

I reached my hands up to touch Sam's arms, and his hold weakened, then he completely dropped to his side. I turned to look at him while still keeping hold of one of his arms. It was just like what I had done in the dream, touched him and concentrated on sending all the air from his body. It was as if I could hear his lungs collapse when the last of the air exited his body and he fell to his knees.

I was not sure why, but I felt several different urges course through my veins. One was to completely finish this useless person, but I also felt this nagging urge to release him, because being in jail or something would only delay my escape into a new world of endless possibilities.

I fought my desire, my instinct to kill him and released his arm. I watched as he struggled to take in air and to not fall to that dark side called death. He had broken blood vessels in both of his eyes, which I thought looked funny against his dark skin. I turned to determine what I would do with Nick, knowing deep down inside that I would not be able to resist killing him.

When I saw him hiding on the other side of the table I realized that his hair was different, and his shape had changed, too ... He looked like Benny, not Nick; was Sam-bo right about him being Benny and not Nick? I narrowed my eyes at him, inspecting his every feature until I was certain that this was not Nick.

Sam's gasping for air drew my attention back to him as he staggered to get back up on his feet with the aid of a chair, which didn't look too stable under his shaky weight. I looked back to confirm that the other guy wasn't Nick once again before closing the gap between me and Sam. He tried to back away from me but ended up just falling to the floor again. I kneeled down to whisper darkly into his ear,

"You're right, that's Benny," and then I quickly grabbed his forearm. Air began to escape from his body again. He began to kick and move his arms all around as he stared at me with wild eyes, but no matter how hard he flailed he never stopped staring at my eyes. As his struggle slowed I knew the exact moment he died because he stopped staring as his busted blood vessel eyes rolled up into the back of his head, leaving only the whites of his eyes showing. I felt more emotions in that brief moment than I have ever felt. Honestly I felt like I was born again and nothing will ever be the same from now on.

I strutted back to my room wondering if it would feel like that every time and assuring myself that since no one else witnessed it they just might blame it on the deaf, dumb Benny. I closed the door for privacy as I plotted this new lease on life. That goody-two-shoes Caleb was the only one standing in my way at this point. He didn't even have power outside of his dreams. I felt great as all of the details of that dream flushed back into me.

He'd said that once I committed to this group he didn't dream of that person anymore. I knew I couldn't have him in my head again or he would see my intentions, so I agreed immediately to join their group—hell, why wouldn't I? It was my only chance of getting out of here.

He had no power, and I bet he couldn't hold his breath for longer than two minutes ... two minutes were all I needed with him alone, and then I would be the leader of this group. Under my leadership we wouldn't be looking to do a damn thing that was good, and my list would be our first task to complete!

I laughed to myself at the thought of what was happening, then I began running my list through my head once more, two names added. Caleb was now priority number one; sorry, Nick, you're number two. Three was Henry; Sam-bo was number four, I laughed to myself just thinking about how easy this will all be and then I continued on with my precious list; Fred the janitor, five; Craig, six; Tiffany, seven; Shawna…

To Be Continued

ABOUT THE AUTHOR

Gregory Morrison attended college at the University of Northern Iowa and moved to Minnesota, where he has lived for the past twenty-five years. He has three children. This is Morrison's debut novel.

CPSIA information can be obtained at www.ICGtesting.com
Printed in the USA
BVOW030847181111

276434BV00005B/21/P